GW00858044

ANGIE FRANCOMBE

RUPERT STAR

TWELVE DAYS
TO TWELVE

Copyright

Copyright © 2017 by Angie F. Francombe

All rights reserved. This includes the right to reproduce any portion of this book in any form without the prior permission of the author.

First printing: 2017
ISBN-13: 978-1981245116
ISBN-10: 1981245111

For

Mike,

Graham, Jonny, Will,

Family, and friends,

and for my lovely dog Porsche,

for being the best companion a writer could have.

Chapter One

THE ESCAPE

Twelve years ago

Vincent Star tiptoed the short distance from his bed to the door, following a small ray of moonlight filtering in his small, dark, and cold shed.

His heart thumping heavily against his chest, he listened intently as he thought he heard footsteps. A deep feeling of emptiness invaded his heart whilst listening intently, but the sound of silence brought back his peace and he went back to lay in his bed, thinking that he was most likely having a bad dream, but within seconds, the same noise came out of the dark, clearer and louder making him jump out of his bed. He could hear the footsteps in the distance as they crunched their way through the snow towards the shed, where he and his family had lived for the last three months, in the middle of nowhere and over the highest mountain of the Swiss-Alps.

Vincent's searching eyes struggled in the dark to find the wooden crib beside his bed. His search stopped. A tiny body moved, safe, in a deep sleep. Vincent had been made sure that neither evil nor good could have found him and Serena and their three months and three-day-old baby, named Rupert. It was the most secure hiding place to fulfill their dream, as they had planned to see him grow big and strong until he reached his most dangerous and wanted age.

Vincent stood in front of the door peering through a small hole – his heart stopped when he realized that the dark figures getting closer were of a human being and his companion. The putrid stench of a decomposed animal revealed his companion-beast's identity, he knew just too well. Vincent's only wish had been to never see them again. His blurry vision struggled to focus, although his mind and body were fully awake. He had grown a full beard and moustache since they had moved to their new home. His sapphire blue eyes, which usually shone brightly, had dimmed and were now underlined with dark smudges.

"Serena," Vincent whispered, as he approached his wife and gently shook her shoulder. She moved fast as if an alarm has gone off.

"Has he found us?" Serena asked and sprang out of bed. Serena quickly got dressed, tied her scarf around her neck and pulled her beanie over her ears. She stumbled whilst fitting her feet in her snow boots.

"Keep calm, if Rupert starts to cry we won't have a chance to save him," Vincent warned, "get him ready to go," he said.

"Are you sure it's him? Could that be that mysterious friend of yours? Are you going to tell me who this person is now?" Serena pleaded.

Vincent turned his head away and walked towards a small window in the front of the shed.

"It's Alan isn't it?" she demanded. "He's the one you want me to trust. He's the wrong person. Since Rupert's birth, he hasn't even bothered to come and see him. He may have changed in these last three months."

Vincent remained quiet and continued to stare out the window.

"Daltom's not alone, that beast is with him," he said, "I can smell him."

Serena covered her face with her hands and slowly swept them back through her hair.

Vincent could clearly see baby Rupert gazing up at his mother as she dressed him as quickly as she could. Serena finished wrapping Rupert in his blanket, and looked inside the wooden crib, her hand searched in between the blankets and the mattress, looking for something. She gave a sigh of relief as she pulled out Rupert's only soft toy, as if she had found a gold treasure. She looked at the toy in her hand, closed her eyes as she pressed the toy in her chest then placed it gently inside Rupert's bag.

"He doesn't need a toy," Vincent shook his head slowly.

Vincent leant down, kissed Rupert on his forehead and gave Serena a strong, warm hug and slowly let go of her, pointing at the back door, turning his head away, to hide the fear in his eyes.

"They're getting closer. You've got to go now." Vincent said.

The man outside stood wearing a black hooded robe, looking menacing and powerful. The moonlight exposed his long pointy face and high cheekbones. His eyes, buried under a pair of thick eyebrows covered in snow, probed into the shed. His name was Daltom.

A sudden blast of cold wind coming from behind, made Vincent turn around. Serena had left the back door of the shed half open. He raced over to the door, closed it and pulled the wall hanging over.

Vincent kept his eyes fixed on Daltom, who had now stopped pacing in front of the shed. Daltom suddenly looked up at the sky and threw his arms in the air as if pleading. The clouds had lifted so that the moonlight reflected off the snow, lighting up the forest almost as if it were daylight. Vincent could not hear Daltom's words. But then, as if by command, the grey clouds blocked out the moonlight. The gentle breeze that had been blowing, picked up and moved the dark clouds sprinkling a fresh dusting of snow over the mountain, disguising both, the sound of their footsteps and their prints in the snow.

The beast bounded along the track stopping in front of Daltom. This was Begnon, Daltom's creation. Begnon had a cat-like face with piercing black eyes and bright red pupils. Standing upright on its back legs almost reaching Daltom's waist. His broken tail dragged on the floor and his grey and wrinkly skin was covered in hard, spiky hair, like elephant's skin. At the end of its hands and feet were long claws, filthy and needle sharp. A rotten stench of skunk emanated from its body.

Daltom and Begnon seemed to be arguing. Daltom grabbed Begnon by the scruff of his neck, when release, Begnon cowered down at Daltom's feet.

"Hiding in a rock hole, just like the rat you are, I see," yelled Daltom. His voice cracked as it echoed in the air. "With all that intelligence you claim to have and you couldn't do any better than this?"

Vincent picked up an orange ball, which wriggled by his feet.

"Don't intervene," he said, holding the box in front of him. "We must stick to the plan." He dropped the orange ball back on the floor. It stopped wriggling.

"Come and get me, if you're brave enough," Vincent replied as he closed his eyes for a moment.

"Give me the baby and I'll spare your life," yelled Daltom.

"Never, he'll never be in your hands," replied Vincent.

A loud crash beside Vincent made him jump. He turned quickly, just in time to see that Begnon had smashed in the front door beside him. The source of the putrid smell that had invaded the shed was now right in front of him. Begnon had made his entrance. He was standing on all fours pulling his claws from the wooden door. Daltom stood behind his beast. His black hooded cape swung around his legs with the breeze as he pushed past Begnon and over the shattered door.

"Where is he?" Daltom demanded, pushing everything out of his way and stopping in front of the empty wooden crib. Daltom took off his winter gloves and rubbed his fingers over the headboard where Vincent had carved Rupert's name.

"So, Rupert is his name," Daltom reached inside, inspecting the blankets. He picked up Rupert's pyjamas and held them close to his face.

"They're still warm," he said as he threw the pyjamas on the floor and turned to Begnon. "Look around and see how they got out!"

Daltom walked slowly towards Vincent and stood only few millimetres away from Vincent's face.

"Where are they? Tell me, or I'll kill you right here and now." The veins in his shaky hands were like long, blue worms writhing inside his paper-thin skin. His face had turned red as he yelled at the top of his voice.

"Kill me? You wouldn't dare. Your desire to control this world will keep me alive." Vincent provoked. Daltom punched him in the face but Vincent put up no resistance. Daltom hit Vincent again knocking him of his feet and made him collapsed to the ground.

"You thought I wasn't going to figure out the puzzle you wrote," Daltom shouted, "I don't need you,"

"We made a deal, you must keep your word," Vincent yelled.

"Master, you don't need him. Kill'im, kill'im—" Begnon croaky voice made a sudden stop as he pulled aside the wall hanging that had been covering the back door.

"Over here," it shouted, "this door, look, that's how they escaped. The woman took the baby this way. I can get them,"

"I want the boy," Daltom shouted.

Vincent stood up and ran in front of the back door, blocking the way. Begnon grabbed him by his legs and threw him across the room. Vincent landed face down on a wooden table, the impact breaking its legs. As Vincent tried to stand up he could see Begnon striding slowly towards him. Begnon pounced and landed on Vincent's back. He could see Begnon's reflection in a small mirror in front of him and squeezed his eyes closed when he saw the creature pull out its oversize claws. He felt the claws slide down the length of his back, as they cut open his skin like a razor blade. Daltom walked over and kicked Vincent's legs. Begnon's face had turned red, his eyes scheming and his claws up in the air ready to strike again.

Daltom raised his hand. Begnon turned his face away and sniffed the air. It hid his claws slowly, walked around Vincent and stood beside Daltom by the back door.

"She couldn't have gone far, I can smell new flesh, they went that way," said Begnon, pointing in the direction Serena had gone.

"Die Vincent!" Daltom yelled. His grave voice sounded like thunder and echoing through the forest outside.

Vincent lifted his head a little and opened his eyes slowly. He could only see the orange box in front of him and hear Daltom's coursing words far, far away mixed with the sound from a flock of birds flying away. Vincent closed his eyes in defeat. His broken body lay on the ground. He was left to die inside the shed.

***

Serena had picked her way through the thick forest undergrowth which bordered the near by ski-pitch. Rupert was on her back, tucked inside his baby pack. She sped down the mountain track, stumbling on the icy surface. Rupert's legs and arms bounced in tandem with each other as his mother ran over the bumps in the path. Her breathing laboured and her legs struggled to support her weight.

Serena tripped, and as she stumbled trying to regain her balance. Her left foot collapsed down a deep marmot hole. A cracking noise came from her ankle, and she let out a cry of pain. She fell to the ground, landing heavily on her side, upsetting Rupert. He began to cry.

Serena scrambled to get the baby pack off her back. She held Rupert close to her and rocked him to calm him down. Unable to go any further, she looked around then rose slowly, dragging herself to rest against the nearest pine tree. Rupert lay on her lap, staring at every movement she made. Her tears streamed down her cheeks as she played peekaboo with him.

"I'm sorry, I failed you," she cried.

As if Rupert was able to understand her words, he kicked his little legs in the air and twisted his arms, holding on tightly to Serena's pinkie finger.

"I love you," she said, holding him on her lap. Rupert responded in his best baby talk, by blowing bubbles all over his chubby face, causing him to blink one of his eyes quickly as if he was winking at her. Serena's tears of pain and anguish soon turned to laughter.

Chapter Two

HEADS OR TAILS

The sun rose in a hurry, as if sent for a rescue. Instead, it could only be a witness of the events, which were about to unfold today.

"Ah, so there you are..." Came a thunderous voice from the forest. Serena opened her eyes wide and turned to see the huge figure emerging from the darkness of the woods.

"Alan! I knew it was you," she grimaced.

Alan stood over two metres tall. His huge winter jacket just managed to cover his frame. His long, thick dreadlocks, which were dyed yellow at the ends, threaded with green, yellow and red beads at the tip hanging down to his lower back, gave him a frightening appearance. Alan has an angular face, broad nose, wide mouth and lips. His eyes were brown, matching his brown velvet skin.

Alan hurried over and leant down to help Serena to her feet, but her left foot was still twisted and unable to move.

"Daltom... ha... has found us! Vincent's st... stayed in the shed, waiting for them," she said with trembling lips.

"Please, take him and don't stop until he's safe. Daltom... will find me soon," she said slowly.

"I can't leave you like this, you're hurt." Alan examined her foot concluding from the purple-green bruise that had already formed that Serena was not going any further without help.

"You were supposed to come with me. The baby needs you, not me – I'll carry you," he said.

"No, our priority is to save Rupert. If we don't get him away from Daltom, then everything we've been working for will be lost. I'll just slow you down, and Daltom will be able to follow us, he can sense where we are, but this way, he'll have no trace to you. You must go, just as you and Vincent had planned."

"Daltom will kill you," Alan said, staring at Serena as he felt her eyes penetrating his soul in her plea.

"This isn't how Vincent planned it, I don't like babies. I can't be responsible, for him, look at me, what do I know about babies?" He said as he dropped his arms to his side.

"You delivered him," Serena said.

There was a moment of silence between them.

"Besides, I can tell you don't trust me," Alan said.

"No, it isn't that," Serena put her head down as if agreeing with Alan then she looked up at the mountain and back at Alan.

Alan noticed Serena's hazel eyes losing brightness. He understood that he had no time left, nor any choice. He reached down, slipped his giant hands into Serena's hands and gently took Rupert from her arms. Serena's eyes followed the movement of Alan's hands as he carried away the most precious thing in her whole world.

He held the baby against his chest with one arm and reached down with the other to pick up the baby bag.

Alan cradled Rupert with his left arm and strode down through the snow with the baby bag over his right shoulder, leaving Serena alone and scared in the snow.

You don't abandon a wounded woman in the middle of nowhere, with her enemy chasing her. Said a voice in his head, which sounded just like his Grandfather. Guilt descended on Alan's heart like a heavy cloud. He stopped and squeezed his eyes.

You can't go back, you must take that baby to safety. Said a more authoritarian voice in his head, which sounded just like his

Grandmother. The first voice knew better than to argue back. Alan shook his head realising his Grand Parents would never change – not even with them in heaven. He continued walking, looking back from time to time. The outline of Serena was getting smaller and smaller until she finally disappeared in the distance. Alan arrived at the bottom of the mountain where he had parked his vehicle. A black Mini awaited on the side of the road, it was covered in white dust as if kissed by the snow. It was Alan's best companion. He was emotionally attached to it and treated like an old friend. After wiping the snow from its windows Alan gently put Rupert in the baby seat and drove away.

"Here we go little man, consider yourself free." He said.

The spectacular view of the mountain chain in his rear view mirror guarded his back for a long time, but no matter which angle he looked at it, he did not appear to be putting any distance between him and the mountains.

Rupert travelled safely next to Alan's personal belongings, the sound of reggae music, played nice and low, softening the road noise, so that Rupert could travel in peace.

It was almost an hour after Alan had left Serena behind that he began to relax and think clearly about the magnitude of the task in front of him.

Find a car park, Alan, drive-in. Alan heard another voice in his head, it did not sound like either of his Grandparents this time, it was Serena's voice.

Drive in, drive in, the voice repeated. Alan immediately thought of the ghost stories his Grandmother would tell him and his cousins when they were kids, but this voice sounded real it felt too close, as if Serena was sitting in the passenger seat.

He shook his head again to scare the idea away. He then remembered he had felt a strange connection with Serena when she pleaded for him to take Rupert. It was something he had never experienced before. With an urgent need for a break Alan exited the motorway. He drove into the park and stopped at the side of the road. He felt uncomfortable hearing Serena's voice. It was simply not possible.

"Am I going mad, oh no, she must be dead now, and her ghost is chasing me," he thought.

The bag, the bag, he heard.

"Okay, okay, whatever it is, please stop, you're freaking me out."

Alan stared at the bag propped up in the front seat – it was as if the bag was talking to him. He made up his mind to open the baby bag. In it, he found some bottles of milk, a blanket, and a weird soft toy.

"What are you?" He tossed the toy next to Rupert, dug his hand into the bag one more time and felt a few envelopes. His hand came out holding three envelopes, each addressed to a different person. The first envelope had his name on it, the second one, was for the Swiss Bank Manager, and the last one, to the Godparents, and in small writing read Mr and Mrs Curdy.

Alan scratched his head, gently inserting his fingers between his dreadlocks, his head was not itchy, but his mind was. He had the feeling that he was going to regret opening the envelope with his name written across the front. As he removed the letter, he quietly wished to himself that there would be some instructions on what to do next. As if on cue, Rupert began to cry.

"Shh baby, be quiet please," Alan tapped his head with the envelope, not quite knowing what to do or say. He reached into the baby bag and grabbed one of the bottles of milk. Remembering from his time feeding goats during his childhood in Jamaica, Alan placed the bottle in Rupert's mouth. Rupert stopped crying as quickly as he had started and drank greedily from the bottle.

"That's a good boy," Alan said slowly, as he smiled and caressed Rupert under his chin. Soon enough Rupert was fast asleep again in the back of the car. Alan reached down, to read his letter.

Dear Alan,

If you're reading this letter, you must be running from Daltom with our son. Thank you, my friend. After our last confrontation with Daltom, we knew that he was going to come back for Rupert. The only way to keep him safe is to send him away from us. We want you to take him to a family we have selected. Apologies for what I am about to say, but as you looked into Serena's eyes, you were hypnotised so that she could communicate with you through telepathy.

"I knew it," Alan said to himself and continued to read.

Serena will be able to guide you, but the hypnosis will last only for twelve hours, so, my friend, do your best to follow her instructions today. I know it isn't what we'd initially planned, but we had to ensure that if Daltom captured you, you wouldn't be able to pass on any information to him of our plans. Serena will guide you to a couple living in Geneva. You are to give them the envelopes marked

Godparents and Swiss Bank and wait for them to read them. This couple will be asked to be Rupert's godparents, and we want to ask you to please stay close to him until we are able to be with him again. I know it's an imposition for us to ask, but we trust you with our lives and that of our only child. We will be with you and Rupert again on his twelfth birthday. Keeping Rupert alive is the only way we can stop Daltom.

Our hearts are full of gratitude towards you,

Vincent.

"Hypnotised! Twelve years!" Alan growled.

He stared incredulously at baby Rupert.

"Who are you?" He asked. Baby Rupert did not move.

After a few hours, Alan found himself driving beside the lake. The view of the mountains was now on his side. He looked back at Rupert in his rear-view mirror and felt relieved to see Rupert fast asleep.

"You are in for a big surprise when you wake up little fella – listen, you're adorable but the truth is, I'm stuck with you. I haven't been able to take a nap or have anything to eat – I've got to look after you every minute, that's not cool, nope, that's not cool at all. Are you listening? No, of course not, you are sleep."

"Okay, so what do I do next?" He asked. "This can't be right – the day is going fast, I've got to get Rupert to safety, and I'm waiting for voices in my head to tell me what to do."

Alan, Alan, wake up, the voice echoed in his mind. Alan jumped.

"I'm awake," he said.

The people we've selected to be Rupert's godparents live in Geneva. It's two o'clock now, and in two hours you're to meet with them, she said.

"Any names?" He Asked.

You'll need to go to the Botanical Gardens, which are on the corner of Chemin de l'Impératice, go in through the main entrance, take the path up to the conservatory. Sit on the third bench you come to, and at 4:15 a couple will walk in front of you with a strange looking dog. It will be getting dark, so be alert, you're to get their attention and give them the letters. It'll all be fine, just trust me, and thank you again. Serena's voice said.

"Okay, clear, but how will I recognise them?" Alan asked.

Search, was the only word Alan heard.

"Okay, I will, but what for?" There was no response.

At last, Alan knew where he was going, but he still did not know who he would be meeting. His stomach started to rumble so he decided to set off immediately.

"Two more hours to drive, little fella," he mumbled. The heavy snow had covered the road markings, but he could see clearly the safety-sticks on the side of the road. He drove towards the city thinking about Serena's last message. It had been strange and had left him feeling unsettled. What would happen if I don't get to the Botanical Garden in time? He asked himself.

Alan had been on the road long enough with just the one break. He decided to stop at the next village to stretch his legs and to get something to eat. He knew that he was getting closer to his destination and the thought of passing the baby to someone else was somehow reassuring to him.

I'll drop baby Rupert with his new Godparents and then I'll have a well deserve rest, he thought. After having a nice hot bath. He had always liked the idea of a hot bath, but they were usually too small for him. He hoped that Rupert's Godparents would have the perfect bath for his size. His stomach made louder noises, forcing him to abandon the idea of the bath. His face light up once he spotted a petrol shop.

Alan drove slowly looking for a parking place for his Mini. He smiled when he spotted the last place on the road at that time of day, on Route de Lausanne, even for his mini.

"How convenient," he said.

It was a blue parking zone, so he took out his blue parking disc and displayed it on the dashboard of his car. The front tyres were just outside the blue zone by ten centimetres. He stood there, looking at his front tires covering the blue lane, holding his chin in one hand. It should be ok, he said to himself. A car drove by, the driver staring at Alan. Alan smiled with pride. The driver did not smile back.

"Two cups of hot chocolate please," he ordered over the counter whilst passing his shopping basket with food for the rest of his day to the shop attendant at the till. The woman looked up at him and stared at the bundle in his left arm.

"Careful, the chocolate is boiling," she said, "how old is he?"

"About three months old," Alan replied.

He put all the food inside the baby bag with special care and went to the nursing room in the back. It was the first time he had to change Rupert's nappy, but he managed to do so without too much of an ordeal. With Rupert in a dry nappy and a bag full of food, Alan set himself to continue his journey. He smiled at the shop attendant at the till staring at him.

"Are you running away from the police?" She stared at the bundle in his arm. Alan looked outside through the window and saw two police officers clamping his back tyres.

"They gave me this note. I said I didn't see the driver." She showed Alan the penalty ticket.

"What?" Alan cried.

'Parked outside the blue line, Restricted Area, wheel clamp at this time of the day.'

"You have to be kidding," he said.

"You parked outside the blue line," the lady said.

"By ten centimetres," complained Alan, *Swiss* – he mumbled.

"No madam, I'm not running away from the police, but my car is all I have." Alan felt robbed. He stared at his Mini, then pulled baby Rupert tight to his chest and closed his eyes. He knew that he had to let his old friend go. That was the hardest but also fastest decision he had ever done.

"You can still go and stop them. You're a big man." Said the lady, holding the door with one hand and the other behind her back.

Alan looked at Rupert, took a deep breath and closed his eyes when he exhaled.

"Are you Mr Bodden, the Martial Arts teacher?" Asked the lady. Alan lifted his head slowly. He stared at the lady and said nothing.

"I knew you were familiar to me, you taught my grandson. You probably won't remember him. But, I'm afraid you still have some explaining for me, before you walk out of this shop with a baby that is clearly not yours as you have no idea exactly how old he is." She took her hand out from her back and put down a bottle of pepper spray. Alan widened his eyes and looked back at the lady. She shrugged her shoulders.

Alan continued the rest of his journey, as a passenger. The lady from the shop gave him a ride in her old white Mercedes. She dropped him at the Botanical Garden at ten past four.

It was mid-winter, and there were only a few people in the gardens at this time. He found the benches, which had been described in the letter, straight away. The first and second seats were covered in snow, the third one, the one protected from the snow by a tree with thick supporting branches, was occupied by a young couple. He paced up and down in front of them uneasily checking his watch.

"4:13! You two have two minutes to leave this bench," Alan said silently gritting his teeth, but there was no sign of any movement by the couple. He wished he could also communicate telepathically – they would then soon be gone. Deciding there was no alternative, Alan stood in front of the couple sitting on the bench and in his most intimidating voice, demanded.

"I need this seat… now!"

The young couple gaped in disbelief. Alan knew they were on edge already from his pacing up and down. Quickly they gathered their things together and shuffled off into the cold early evening, without complaining – or at least not within earshot of Alan. He sat to wait. He looked down at Rupert, who was wrapped warmly in his blanket.

"Well, here we are, I guess we just have to wait and see who turns up." He said, tickling Rupert under his chin.

Alan looked up and almost immediately, a man appeared, running with his dog. "Where's the woman?" He asked, tapping his foot impatiently on the ground. A few seconds later, a couple appeared along the path. They were walking slowly, dragging their feet on the pavement, shoulders down and eyes focused on their phones, but there was no sign of a dog.

This isn't working, it's 4.15, and there's no one here. He said to himself.

Just then, a weak, barking noise came from beside him. Alan looked down to see a tiny dog beside his bench. The dog had a big head, and eyes as if they were popping out of its face. Its collar was attached to a long leash held by the couple he had seen coming up the path towards him. Alan saw that there was a fixed water bowl beside the bench. The dog timidly growled at Alan and started to lick the block of ice inside the bowl, as if it was part of his walk routine.

"Quiet, Cerch, be a good dog," said the man.

Alan looked at the couple and repeated in his mind the last word Serena had said.

"Search! That's it," Alan said, "excuse me,"

The couple looked up in astonishment as Alan stood up and towered over them, their heads bent backwards, as if staring at the sky.

"Is this your dog Cerch?" He asked.

They looked at each other and then at Alan simultaneously eyes wide open nodding their heads.

"Well, yes it is, we're sorry if… our dog… Cerch… disturbed you," said the man, trying to swallow the knot on his throat and looking for his wife, who was now cringing behind him and holding the dog tightly, not daring to look Alan in the eye.

"No problem," said Alan politely. He was amused at the impact his appearance had had on the couple.

"You don't know me, but I have something that belongs to you," He said, scratching his head once again.

The couple did not move. Their eyes scanned him up and down, their mouths half open.

"I'm afraid you are confusing us with someone else." The man said. He turned aside to continue his walk.

Alan examined the couple in front of him, trying to find a reason why Vincent would have chosen them. The man's head barely reached Alan's chest. He had a wide body with a thick neck. His hair was dark and frizzy, and he wore a beanie that looked too small for his head. His deep, dark eyes, were staring at Alan as if he was in a trance. His wife was slightly shorter than him and shaped like a pear with legs. She had long, straight, blond hair, a large nose and sleepy blue eyes. The man folded and unfolded his arms repeatedly. Eventually he settled by pushing his hands deep inside his pockets. The woman kept on passing the dog from side to side in her arms.

Alan broke into a smile and handed them the two envelopes.

"Allow me to show you, see, this are your names, aren't they?" Alan pointed at the small print on the envelope. Mr and Mrs Curdy.

"Yes, that's correct," the man replied.

Mr Curdy took the envelopes with trembling hands and examined both sides. He passed them both unopened, to his wife. She quickly chose the letter with 'Godparents' marked on it, slid her nail under the leaf and opened it. She took out the letter and held it up seemingly in front of her husband for them both to read.

Their eyes widen as they read through the letter. Mr Curdy looked up at Alan in disbelief.

"A stranger wants us to be the Godparents of that baby, what's this, a joke?" He swallowed.

"It's not a joke, and here's the baby, his name is Rupert. I suggest you read the other letter, it may help you to make a decision," Alan said.

The second envelope was addressed to the Swiss Bank where Mr Curdy worked. His wife slid her nail one more time under the leaf and opened the letter. She stood frozen. Her eyes looked as if they would pop out of her head, much the same as her dog Cerch.

"But we can't, we won't, this is just impossible, we…"

Mrs Curdy put the letter in front of her husband's face, cutting him off.

"Shhh, look at the numbers, honey!" She said.

"We can't just become parents overnight – we've no idea how to look after a baby," he said.

Mrs Curdy grabbed her husband's arm and pulled him aside, turning away from Alan.

"Look at those numbers!" she said. "If this is all true, we don't need to know how to be parents. We can pay someone to do it for us, and besides, how hard can it be? Everybody seems to be able to do it, and it's not forever. And after all, we've done a pretty good job with Cerch,"

"Oh come on, Cerch is just a dog," said her husband, raising his voice.

"That's how most people start a family, with a lovely dog," she raised her voice back.

Alan could hear every word they were saying, he stood rooted to the floor. Eyes wide open, staring at the couple in front of him.

The man began to look for something in his pockets. He pulled out a coin and threw it up high in the air. A dim light from the afternoon sunset caught the coin as it spun up in the air, landing on the palm of the man's right hand. He quickly covered the coin and looked back at his wife.

"Heads or Tails?" he asked.

"Heads," she quickly chose. Mr Curdy held out his covered hand and revealed the winning side of the coin.

"I won!" she shouted.

They both strolled towards Alan. He turned away, one hand covering his mouth. Alan could not believe what he had just witnessed. Mr Curdy's action was colder than the air he was breathing, how could he. He thought.

Mrs Curdy had a beaming smile on her face. She walked, stroking her little dog's big head. Her husband still had his hands deep in his pockets, looking down at his shoes as he slowly arrived at where Alan was standing.

"Sorry. We didn't introduce ourselves. Although, I assume you already know who we are. Nevertheless, this is my wife Stephanie, and I'm Gilbert, Gilbert Curdy." The man offered Alan, his hand.

Alan took hold of the man's hand and shook it firmly.

"It's my pleasure, Mr Curdy. Madam, I'm Alan, and this seems to be your new Godson, Rupert."

Mrs Curdy stretched out her arms and took Rupert from Alan. Briefly, she held the baby in the air for one second and then passed him back to Alan.

"The letter says that you'll be close to the child, is that correct?" Mrs Curdy asked while typing something on her phone.

"Correct. I hope that's fine with you," Alan said.

"Absolutely. Done, it's all on my calendar – you'll be his nanny," she said, looking up at Alan in the eye with a closed lip smile on her face.

A heavy silence fell over the meeting. Lost for words, Alan stared at Mrs Curdy. She turned and proceeded to walk off down the path. The title of nanny did not appeal to Alan at all. It certainly was not anything he had planned. He stood bolt upright, pushed his chest out and put on the fiercest face he could muster, to show that he was not going to be a nanny, but Mrs Curdy was already halfway down the path.

Mr Curdy turned back from watching his wife disappear down the path.

Alan did not like how things had developed – Even worse, the thought of him being a nanny, but he had promised Vincent, and besides, he did not have any other plans for the next twelve years.

Alan and Mr Curdy caught up with Mrs Curdy at the gates. The couple led the way out of the Botanical Garden, followed by Alan, holding Rupert fast asleep in his baby blanket.

Mrs Curdy cuddled Cerch while he looked over her shoulder, the dog barked and growled at the package Alan held in his arms.

They all arrived at a small apartment, a sofa for two, a table for two, and two small bedrooms. The apartment was the size of the bath Alan had hoped for. Mr Curdy showed him to the guest room, which he was to share with Rupert.

Alan sat with Mr and Mrs Curdy in front of the television holding Rupert on his lap. At 8pm Alan excused himself and went to his bedroom.

"Please make yourself comfortable – just one thing, make sure the baby doesn't cry too much," said Mr Curdy.

"Don't worry, he'll be a good boy," Alan replied.

Alan set himself about preparing Rupert's meal. He checked the baby bag and found there were no bottles left, only three small plastic containers with formula milk inside it. Add warm water, said a yellow Post-it note on one of the containers. Alan took the containers to the kitchen and in doing so he passed the lounge where Mr and Mrs Curdy were talking.

"What was the baby's name again?" Mr Curdy asked.

"Rupert, not my choice, but an interesting name, I guess," said his wife.

"Not as interesting as his wealth," Mr Curdy said and smiling at Alan. He then pointed Alan towards the microwave oven.

Alan fed Rupert, checked the bed and noticed that there were two mattresses, one on top of the other, he took one and put it on the floor. He put Rupert on the bed and with a pillow and quilt he made a safe and comfortable spot, and gently placed Rupert in the centre.

Alan was half sleep, he took his shoes off and lay down on his mattress, his body was aching, and his mind needed to be switched off.

What a day, he grinned to himself. Saving Rupert was certainly the proudest moment of his life. As he slowly drifted off to sleep, he checked on Rupert one more time.

"This seems like a mistake to me little fella, your future was determined by the toss of a coin. Scary all very scary, night-night."

Chapter Three

A WALK ON THE BRIGHT SIDE

Tuesday, 10th November

Away from the mountains, in the prestigious city of Geneva, sits a splendid manor house with an unobstructed view of the Alps, the peak of Mont Blanc and the splendour of Lake Geneva. It belongs to Mr and Mrs Curdy and it is house number eight.

Despite the less than enthusiastic start to Rupert's stay under the roof of Mr and Mrs Curdy, in an affectionless environment, the first years of his life passed relatively normal, and without incident. His new godparents had decided they would spend the first few years traveling the world, before settling down.

As it happened, Switzerland was the ideal location for Mr and Mrs Curdy to begin their new life. It had been almost five years since they had left on their world travels, coming back with some family additions of their own. A daughter, named Miana, and Cerch's replacement, Jeeves, Miana's new pedigree dog. During their time away, the Curdys had deliberately not kept in contact with any of their friends, to minimise the risk of any uncomfortable questions about Rupert's surprise appearance, as well as their own newfound wealth.

Rupert was now eleven years old, eleven years, eleven months and eighteen-days-old to be precise. He was tall for his age and had grown into a handsome young man. His head was covered with thick wavy, brown hair. Long dark lashes, framed his intelligent hazel eyes. His nose was straight, although slightly too large for his face, and his lips were well defined, outlining a friendly smile.

Rupert's appearance was in stark contrast to Miana, who at seven years-ten months and five days old was small for her age. She had inherited her father's dark eyes as well as his frizzy hair, which her mother had managed to find a way to straighten permanently. Miana had just lost her front teeth, but this had still not stopped her from chatting more than anyone in the entire house.

The Curdys had decided to ignore Vincent's letter that they were to be only his godparents and had raised Rupert as their own son, so he had no reason to think otherwise. But, like most children of his age,

Rupert did wonder sometimes whether he was actually related to anyone in his family.

"Eeaaaoo … you stink – Someone needs to take a shower around here," Miana said, the minute Rupert walked into the kitchen.

"Hmm, first for breakfast again. Where's everybody? Fine, I'll eat alone," Rupert said, tempting Miana to complain.

"You're not funny, how can you miss the best kid in the family," Miana said, as she poked her tongue out at Rupert, and quickly checked the table to make sure everything was in place, "pink plate, pink glass, pink knife, pink fork, pink napkin, pancakes, and syrup – perfect." She said.

"Oh, there you are. Didn't see you there, could you pass me the pink, oops, I mean drink," Rupert said.

"Very funny, you're just stupid. You stupid, stupid boy, Mummy! Rupert is annoying me again," Miana shouted.

Just as Miana screamed for her mother, Alan entered the kitchen. The butler brought Alan a cup of black coffee.

"Thanks, Eugene," Alan said. He placed his phone and keys on the kitchen table, as usual, to have his morning coffee.

"Morning, Alan," said Mr Curdy. He kissed Miana on top of her head. Mr Curdy wore a navy cashmere dressing gown and a pair of purple suede slippers, with his initials embroidered on the top. His eyes fixed on the newspaper.

"Good morning, Mr Curdy," Alan replied.

"Rupert," Mr Curdy said when he looked at Rupert.

"Morning Dad," Rupert replied.

"Morning, Alan," said Mrs Curdy walking behind her husband while tapping her face gently with her fingertips, feeling her cucumber mask. Mrs Curdy wore a gown matching her husbands with white rabbit skin slippers. She blew a kiss to Miana.

"Good Morning, Mrs Curdy," Alan said.

"I heard you were annoying your sister already, you must stop this, or else..." she said, looking directly at Rupert.

Rupert gave a heavy sigh.

Both Mr and Mrs Curdy placed their mobile phones next to Alan's on the kitchen table.

Eugene moved the phones creating space for the breadbasket.

"Oh…oh, someone's going to get confused here, those phones are all identical." He mumbled as he walked away with the basket.

Rupert was wondering what was going on. Everybody was in the kitchen, and he would much prefer being on his own, or just him and Alan as usual. Somehow seeing his parents and Miana first thing in the morning seemed like a bad omen.

A muffled wooden sound came from the three phones on the table as they began to vibrate, all at the same time. Alan was first to reach for his phone, but it would not unlock. Mr Curdy seemed to have forgotten his password. They had mixed up the phones as they rushed to turn their alarms off.

"Why's everyone's phone ringing at the same time?" Miana asked.

"It's only a reminder, honey," Mrs Curdy said.

"A reminder to everybody?" She asked.

Rupert saw when Mr and Mrs Curdy exchanged phones and glared at each other. Mr Curdy ran his hand jerkily through his hair while Mrs Curdy's eyes flitted around the room.

"Can we go?" Rupert asked Alan.

Alan jumped. He seemed lost in his thoughts. He pushed away his coffee with shaky hands spilling a quarter of it on the table and grabbed his keys.

"Are you all right?" Rupert asked.

"Couldn't be better," he replied.

Both Mr and Mrs Curdy were sitting at the kitchen table. Neither of them had even so much as sipped their tea. Rupert saw Mrs Curdy putting six spoons of sugar into her tea. Mr Curdy kept on vacantly stirring at his tea, which he had just poured from the teapot, even though it had no sugar or milk. Miana paid attention to every movement her parents were making. Rupert followed her gaze each time.

"What on earth was happening to them? He thought.

"Just a minute, Rupert," called Mrs Curdy.

Rupert turned around while putting his sports bag over his head and adjusting the strap. He looked up at Mrs Curdy. What have I done this time? He thought to himself.

"We received your school report yesterday. You have a really bad start this year. Why can't you try to do better? I heard Esteban Lambert is top of the class again this year." She gave him a stern look.

Rupert closed his eyes, shrugged his shoulders with resignation and just listened. It wasn't worth saying anything. He had heard it all before.

"This is an embarrassingly weak report – even for you," she said.

"Thanks," he mumbled.

"This can't continue this way. I've organised tutoring classes to help you out. Your first tutor will be waiting for you at home after school today, Alan make sure he is back here on time."

Rupert imagined himself sitting behind a desk for the rest of his life, taking infinite extra lessons.

"I don't want any tutoring," he said.

"I wasn't asking you. I was telling you," Mrs Curdy said, "your violin teacher tells me you're not participating and–"

"I hate violin," Rupert interrupted.

"And your Mandarin is appalling. You changed from German because it was boring, so now you're the only student at 'College du Romandie' who can barely speak one language, do you understand? One language! Esteban can speak four, play the violin, the cello and is top of his class. You're to come home straight after school, no playing around with your friends. Esteban's mother tells me that he takes after school lessons in every single subject, so why can't you?"

Rupert listened to his mother while she rubbed the success of Esteban in his face. She did not know what Esteban was like at school and that he cheated in every test. He waited a few minutes to be sure his mother had finished her lecture and to swallow the giant knot in his throat.

"Can I go now?" he asked.

Mrs Curdy did not reply. She turned her back on him and held her magazine in front of her face. Rupert stayed silent for a moment, shoulders down after being defeated on a battle he had not fought. Rupert could feel unsettled emotions he was certain he never felt before.

He turned around and walked out of the kitchen, his mind playing his mother's words over and over and the familiar look on the faces of everyone, who had just witnessed yet another instalment of needless criticism. The knot in his throat blocked his breath. He needed to get some fresh air. He started to run as soon as he stepped out of the door to get in front of Alan, so that Alan would not see the tears in his eyes. It seemed that today was his mother's turn to have a go at him, they took it in turns, but her words were sharper and hurt deeper than his father's.

"I can't, I can't grrr," Rupert growled as he took off his sports bag and threw it on the floor. He turned around and with long, firm strides walked back to the house. Alan ran back and stood in front of the door, blocking Rupert's way back into the house, arms open wide like a gigantic bear to stop Rupert from entering.

"Calm down, young man, don't let your emotions ruin your life,"

"I don't have a life. I hate everything I do, everything I wear, this house, the club, the stupid violin, they're all part of the package I don't want to belong to any longer," his tears ran down his cheeks.

"Come with me. It'll all be okay. We can go somewhere else,"

"No, Mum will just find out, and you'll get into trouble too."

"Leave it to me, I'll sort it out for you," Alan said.

Rupert dropped his head and shoulders, closed his eyes and saved his anger for another moment. They were coming more often these days.

"I don't want it to change for just a day – I need it to change forever – help me to get out of here, please," he said.

"Look, you're only eleven, there's not much you can do for now, except be patient. All children have parents who tell them what to do. That's what parents do, believe me, you're not the only one."

"Mum would rather have stupid Esteban as her son, so she could show him off to her friends and be the envy of everyone at the club, can't you see that?" Rupert said.

Morris, the driver, rushed around the car and opened the back door. Rupert sat quietly in the back. Morris stayed silent there was more information in the silence and lack of eye contact than any words Rupert could say.

"Morris will take you today, school is only half day and I have a few urgent things to do, Alan said.

The morning incident had set Rupert off. At school, he distanced himself from everyone. The memory of his mother's criticism was still fresh in his mind. He could hear her words echoing in his ears. Rupert learnt nothing new that morning at school.

He finished school ten minutes earlier and Alan was not there, so Rupert decided to go somewhere else on his own.

He walked slowly down to the boat moorings at Port Choiseul in Versoix, a town just out of Geneva town. It was only a ten-minute walk from his school. This had been Rupert's favourite place since he was a toddler. A place, were he could throw as many stones as he wanted and nothing would get broken. Rupert remembered running up and down, picking up pebbles and sticking them in his mouth, knowing that Alan was going to make a scary face for him to spit it out instantly. But today Rupert was not running, he was not happy, he was not a toddler any longer. He got close to the water. The tiny waves ebbed and flowed, the water kissing his shoes, inviting him to play. Rupert refused. He bent down to pick up a hand full of pebbles. The icy water was cold, almost painful on his knuckles. One by one, he skipped the stones across the water, he watched them disappear, wishing he were one of those stones so that he would be gone from his house once and for all.

Rupert saw Alan coming to meet him. On the way back, Alan tried to make conversation with Rupert, but he would only grunt in response to his questions. Rupert stared out his window, the same sports cars, parked on the side of the road. At the next traffic lights, it was the entrance to his street. A big iron gate opened slowly for the car to drive up and around a water fountain. It stopped in front of the entry to the house, and Rupert rushed out, wishing he was invisible, but he knew he was in everyone's eyes, no matter where he was.

"Master Rupert!"

Rupert looked at Eugene.

"Yes, Eugene?"

"Your mother wants me to give you this letter," said the butler.

"Who's it from?' Rupert took the envelope, opened it and read it in front of Eugene and the three maids, who were setting the table for dinner.

Dear Master Curdy,

Congratulations, you have been awarded singing lessons from one of our qualified teachers at Boni Pueri. Rupert read the remaining of the letter in silence.

Mr Korviatello will be delighted to have you as his private student, he will contact you to arrange a meeting this week. We hope to see you soon.

"What's this? Where's Mum?" Rupert demanded from Eugene as he squashed the letter in his hand, crushing it so small that it almost disappeared.

"She's not home yet. She'll be back for dinner," Eugene looked guilty, having to give bad news to Rupert. Would you like something to drink?" Eugene asked.

"No," Rupert replied.

Rupert ran upstairs, throwing the crumpled letter across his room so that it rolled under his desk. He paced back and forth in his room while holding his head in his hands, his mind unable to find a solution to his problems. He picked up a small, yellow book with a worn out cover resting on his desk, his eyes spotted the calendar with a big red circle on the twenty-first, and made him realise that his twelfth birthday was only twelve days away and then it dawned on him what he would do.

"Things can't carry on like this. I have to do something about it, I know I can do it," he said out loud.

"Whom are you talking to?" Miana asked. Her high-pitched voice echoed in Rupert's ears, he turned around and saw a small head with pink hairpins poking around the corner of his door.

"No one," Rupert shouted, "why are you spying on me – you little pink monster."

Rupert heard greeting noises coming from downstairs. Miana pointed her finger and wriggled her little body from side to side, her chin up in the air as a sign of victory, she knew that her mother had arrived.

"Mum, guess what –" Miana shouted as she ran downstairs to tell on Rupert. A few seconds later came the inevitable summons.

"Rupert–" Mrs Curdy shouted.

"It's not true, I said sister," Rupert shouted back.

"Little brat," he mumbled under his breath.

"Rupert–" shouted his mother again. Rupert jumped. He had not noticed that his mum was standing right by his door, where Miana had been a minute ago. Her phone alarm went on again. She rushed to turn it off so that the phone almost dropped on the floor. It was the same sound as from this morning.

"Rupert, honey, don't call your sister names," she said, and that book, it looks filthy – lip-reading? Don't waste your time reading stupid old books."

Honey? Rupert repeated in his head, he had never been called by that name before. He put his hand behind his back to hide the old book. Mrs Curdy started to press all the buttons on her phone. Her phone slipped from her hands, but she caught it in the air. Rupert stared at her shaky hands.

"Okay, let's have supper," she said.

Aren't you going to tell me off? He asked mentally.

Mrs Curdy turned around and went down the corridor. Miana skipped along the corridor to join her mother. They walked down the stairs towards the dining room. Rupert followed them, keeping his distance. He hated having to listen to Miana's stories, they all started and ended the same way, I want, I want, I want.

"Mummy, I want you to buy a book on child sipology like Tina's mummy did," Miana covered one side of her face, meaning it was a secret but anyone close by could perfectly hear every word.

Rupert rolled his eyes. Here we go,

Miana continued.

"Her brother kept talking to his hand, and Tina's mummy got a lot of ideas for grounding him – you can use a different punishment each day. His mummy sent him to after-school sipology lessons, and he still goes because he gave his hand a name!"

Rupert slowed down he had had enough.

"You mean child psychology," corrected her Mother.

"Yes, that's what I said, aren't you listening?" Miana said.

"A name for his hand?" Mrs Curdy asked.

"Yes, No-one. No-one is actually a name, can you believe it?" replied Miana, proud of everything she knew about her friend Tina's brother.

"That's the same name Rupert chose for his hand, isn't that weird, Mummy? He deserves a punishment every day too. That's what I want." Miana turned to look at Rupert. Rupert crossed his eyes and folded his lower lip and poked his tongue out.

"Weirdo" she mouthed.

Rupert wondered if that book would also have some ideas about how to make Miana talk less, even better, he thought, not at all.

Rupert sat at the dinner table playing with his food. He had lost his appetite. He was thinking about the singing lessons he had mysteriously won but then his new birthday plan came into his mind, he decided to pretend that everything was fine so that no one would interrupt his plans.

"Did you read the letter about the singing lessons?" Asked Mrs Curdy while typing something on her phone.

"Mum, I'm no good at singing," he said.

"Well, you will be once you start the lessons. But I have something more important to tell you, and it can't wait," she said. Her hyper acting made everyone at the table stare and waiting for a bombshell to drop.

Oh, no, Rupert thought. A cold shiver went down his spine as he remembered his calendar and guessed what his mother was going to say. It was too obvious. Her being nice gave it all away. He quickly took a sip of water and told himself to stay calm.

"You know –" she paused, "your Birthday is coming soon and turning twelve is very special, and we must have a –

Don't say it, please, don't say it. Rupert prayed to himself and felt his body bracing itself for the confirmation. He swallowed a piece of chicken without chewing, feeling it going down his throat, but he couldn't stop his mother's lips. They started to pronounce, as if in slow motion, a terrifying word for him.

–P a r t y," There, she had said it.

Rupert gulped a mouthful of water. A deathly silence descended around the dining table. Mr Curdy put his glass of wine down slowly on the table, wiped his mouth and put the white serviette gently back on his lap. Miana gulped from her pink glass three times in a row, straightened her back and held her knife and fork correctly. Mrs Curdy smiled as if she had done the world a favour.

Rupert had been rehearsing how to answer for this moment ever since his last birthday party, but still, the words did not come immediately to mind. Eventually, he remembered.

"Can we do something simple, and I'll tell you who I would like to invite?" He said.

"Sorry honey, I've just sent a save-the-date message to everyone, but you should still be able to invite some special friends of your own if you want, the formal invitations won't be sent until tomorrow morning." She put her phone down, not meeting Rupert's eyes instead she focused on cutting the chicken on her plate. Rupert had been through it all before. He knew any argument would be futile. He closed his eyes resignedly and asked.

"How many invitations did you send?"

"Only eighty," she said.

"Only eighty, please tell me you don't mean eighty families," he said.

As if to confirm it, Mr Curdy interrupted before his wife could reply.

"I'm sure it can be changed," Mr Curdy looked at his wife, but she ignored him.

"It won't be more than three hundred people, some people always cancel at the last minute," she said.

Rupert felt as if a dense, grey cloud had already descended over him, threatening to destroy every living creature on earth. The cloud just went black.

"I can't – Not another party," Rupert was now burning with rage. His mind was full of images involving all types of food, decorations, and loud music. He could see the clowns, magicians, puppets and mimes. The house will turn into an unsupervised circus, with hundreds of people and not one familiar face. Too many presents, from: Someone, – To: Who cares.

Rupert could see Miana resting quietly, her feet tucked under her chair – her comments were not needed, not even the book of punishments, her silence was vital at that moment. Her mother was taking care of the situation but also, she did not want to be sent away and miss the fight that was coming up. Seeing Rupert being told off seemed somehow pleasurable to her.

"You'll love it," Mrs Curdy said.

"No, no, no, I said no!" Rupert thumped the table, pushed his chair back and threw his napkin on the table. "I'm sick of people trying to dress me up, combing my hair, fixing me with extra lessons. I hate playing the violin, I hate Mandarin, I hate singing, I want to be me, and I hate your horrible parties—"

Mrs Curdy froze and for once in her life she was speechless. Rupert seemed to have surprised everybody, including himself. He did not know he had the courage to speak to anyone like that, to shout like that and to lose control like that.

"Get to your room," She ordered and turned to Eugene. "Eugene, take him upstairs and make sure he stays there,"

"I know the way to my bedroom – I don't need help, and I'll happily stay there," and with that he left. Rupert could feel Eugene following him out of the dining room, but was stopped by Miana's shout of.

"Eugene, if Rupert doesn't want you, I do, and I want more syrup," Miana said.

Rupert went to his bedroom and slammed the door behind him. There was nothing inside his bedroom that he wanted. He then decided to go out again. Slowly, he tiptoed along the corridor and snuck down the back stairs. They were narrow and cold. He felt short of air every time he used them, which was not very often. It was the secret passage for the housekeepers as they were connecting directly the ground level to the kitchen.

Rupert went through the kitchen to Alan's bedroom. Alan was not there. He imagined that Alan would be in the gym. Before he turned to leave, he saw Alan's keys on the desk next to the calendar. He spotted a red circle marking his birthday. I hate birthdays, he mumbled. He helped himself to the side door key and left vowing never to come back, to live free, without anyone telling him what to do when to do it, or how to do it.

Rupert stepped outside the house on a cold and dark November evening. At first, he strode quickly along the street, wanting to get away from the house, feeling the heat of his rage burning his face, but when he felt he had gone far enough, he slowed down, put his hands in his pockets and felt the icy air refreshing his skin. Only one side of the road had streetlights, the other side was full of trees, casting dark, forbidding shadows across the street. In the distance, a small car seemed abandoned on the shadowed side of the road. Rupert started to shiver his trousers were not warm enough. A coat would have been nice, he thought. He wore a woollen shirt with a cardigan on top. Almost instantly, the icy weather started to creep into his bones. He kept on walking to keep himself warm, not knowing or caring where he was going. His hands thrust deep into his trouser pockets. The explosive moment he had just experienced was losing rapidly its intensity, but he kept on going. The cold wind piercing his skin gave him some doubts. Why didn't I think it through? He said to himself.

Not far from his house Rupert could smell a strange stench in the air, like a dead animal. It was as if it was coming from an open sewer drain. Looking straight ahead, he saw a figure standing in the shadows, wearing a long dark, hooded robe. By his side, there appeared to be a smaller figure, like an animal, but they seemed to be talking to each other in hushed tones. Where did they come from? Rupert wondered. As he got closer to them, he was able to just overhear their conversation.

"Are you sure his name is Rupert?" The animal looking figure asked.

"I read it on his crib," replied the human figure.

Rupert's eyes widened as he walked closer to them, they stopped talking and turned into the shadows.

Rupert stared at the ground avoiding any eye contact with whoever was hiding in the bushes. From the corner of his eye, he could see the oversized cat claws of the animal figure, scratching the concrete path. Rupert inhaled deeply and held his breath. He turned around and quickened his steps, hoping for that creature not to be set free.

The sound of his footsteps echoed in his ears, for a moment Rupert thought someone was following him. He looked up and saw that the human figure was now at the other corner of the street trying to hide, but he was on the bright side, and Rupert could see a white hood covering his face. How did he get there and where is the small figure, he wondered. Rupert looked back and realised that the man and his companion had not moved. He looked to the other side and saw the man without a companion disappearing around the corner of the street. There are two of you, am I seeing things?

It was dark and foggy but Rupert could see that the man's companion was a big cat on a chain, like a tiger. The animal pulled against the chain, trying to get free. And that stench, what is that smell? He asked himself. It was making him feel sick to his stomach.

Rupert could feel and smell the danger he was in now. He regretted having left home wishing he was safely locked away in the warmth of his bedroom, where he was supposed to be – grounded.

Rupert stopped walking. Realising there was no one around to help him and no place to hide. He turned back and noticed that the car that had been parked further down the road, started to move slowly towards him with its lights off. He began to walk away from it, quickly. But the car was coming on more quickly now – it was almost beside him. Rupert pretended to ignore the car, but as it drew up beside him, he noticed that, except for the driver, the car was empty. He felt trapped and confused. The car stopped beside him, and the driver rolled down the passenger side window. He stared at the window, paralysed, fearing the worst, not thinking, not blinking, not breathing.

"Get in the car," said the driver.

Rupert jumped.

Rupert could not see the driver's face, but he recognised the female voice immediately and quickly got in the car.

He turned to look back at the end of the road, but the man had disappeared into the woods leaving the fear and the smell lingering in the air.

"Uh, he … he … hello, Mrs Stevens, I was just looking for my, my cat," Rupert said. The lady reached for something in the rear seat. Rupert was shaking.

"Here, wear this," Mrs Stevens gave Rupert a thick sweater she had in the back of the car keeping her eyes on the street while Rupert put on the sweater.

"Thank you," he said.

Mrs Stevens set off and dropped Rupert outside the driveway to his house.

"How did you know I live here?" he asked.

"I didn't know, your searching eyes showed me," she replied.

"Thank you so much," Rupert said.

"Have a good night, Rupert. Remember, cats always come home on their own, so make sure you walk on the bright side next time."

She waited until he had gone through the gate.

Rupert watched the car disappearing around the corner. Walk on the bright side, he repeated – he was not sure what Mrs Stevens had meant to say it did not make much sense to him. That was close, he thought.

He ran up the hedge-lined driveway towards his house. A thundering noise came from behind the hedge along the driveway got his attention. Rupert turned to see what it was, but before he could get out of the way, he was knocked off his feet by a small, frightened deer that had burst through the hedge. He heard its steps in the distance as the animal disappeared into the thick bushes and quickly pulled himself to his feet.

"What just happened?" He asked himself without hesitation he ran up the driveway. The feeling of someone behind him proved his suspicion of being watched. He wanted to shout, but the words would not come out of his mouth, and there was that smell again, wafting from the end of the driveway. Rupert reached the house and headed for the side door, his trembling hand reached out for the handle but instead, he grabbed a small, warm hand.

"Aahh, ahh ahh," Rupert screamed, as did the person attached to the hand. Rupert looked up and saw that the hand belonged to Miana.

"Miana, what are you doing here? You scared me to death, get inside quickly,"

"Not before you tell me where you doing out there?" She replied.

"I went for a walk," he said.

"Well, I'm going for a walk as well then," she said.

"No you aren't, you're just spying on me get back inside it's dark."

Miana stood frozen to the ground, staring wide-eyed over Rupert's shoulder. Her eyes rolled up into her head, and she swayed on her feet before collapsing into Rupert's arms. Rupert held her tightly and pulled her through the door and into the house landing on the floor with Miana on top of him, protecting her from the hard surface he pushed the door shut with his feet.

"Miana, are you okay, wake up, wake up," Rupert shook her shoulders.

Alan came and rushed over to carry Miana to the conservatory and laid her down on a couch. He looked over at Rupert.

"What happened here, and what's that smell?" Alan asked.

Rupert shrugged his shoulders, unable to speak, and pointed over to the door. Alan went over and opened the door to look outside, coming back straightaway to where Miana was resting. He held her head and whispered something, trying to get her to wake up. Rupert could not understand Alan's words. He was still trembling. Miana woke up, just as her nanny, Clotilde, arrived.

"Ah, there you are, my sleeping princess – I was looking everywhere for you. You look tired," Clotilde said and curried Miana in her arms to her room.

"I saw something weird outside, a man, and an evil looking creature, then another man," Rupert said to Alan in despair.

"What were you doing out there, you shouldn't step out of the house without telling me, there is–" Alan stopped.

"I saw, it," Rupert said.

"Rupert, we need to talk about this later, but for now, you mustn't talk to anyone about it," he said.

Alan walked Rupert to his room quietly.

"You must try to get some sleep. There's something I have to tell you, first thing tomorrow morning," Alan whispered. Rupert knew that Alan was avoiding another confrontation with Mr and Mrs Curdy.

"Why not now?" Rupert whispered back.

"It's late, and you don't need any more fights with your family," he said.

Rupert did not understand why Alan would not listen. He went to his bedroom annoyed about it all. His first attempt to escape had been a total disaster, but somehow he felt even more trapped than before, and in a way, he thought, it was better to live with what was inside the house than with the unknown danger outside.

Rupert knew that his parents would not have noticed that he was gone. He closed the door behind him and locked it. He had never noticed the lock on his door before, but today, even though it had always been there, he found it instinctively. Rupert felt that he had left something behind, he did not know what it was exactly, but the sense of persecution stayed with him, he could not stop thinking about the strange man in the black robe and the animal attached to the chain and the smell of a dead animal that seemed to follow them around.

"He said my name. I know it was me, but how about the figure in white, were they together?" Rupert said slowly. "But why did Alan seem to be upset for the first time, what's going on?"

Rupert settled into his bed, leaving his bedside lamp on. He opened his little yellow book, closed it again, then switched the light off and lay awake. Strange shapes in the dark started to take weird forms. They appeared and disappeared as Rupert looked in different directions. He turned the light back on again to get rid of them. He knew it was just his imagination playing tricks on him. Rupert hugged himself. He remembered that the sweater he was wearing did not belong to him. It was Mrs Stevens,' his science teacher. He forgot to change into his pyjamas but he did not care and turned the light off again, instantly, the weird shapes came back again. He closed his eyes unable to get rid of the feeling that something, or someone, was watching him. Twice during the night, he awoke sure that eyes were watching him from deep in the darkness of his room. He tossed and turned in a restless sleep. I've put Miana in danger, but what did she see? Rupert muttered to himself, as he woke up yet again.

He got up from his bed and reached for his old favourite soft toy, Marci, which he kept on top of the cupboard where Miana could not find it, together with the birthday-notes, he had received from Marci and which he had kept over the past years. Rupert knew that Marci could not be sending him birthday notes, but he liked to think so. For some reason, Marci frightened Miana. She was convinced that the toy changed its size and shape. Miana thought the toy was ugly, as she could not tell whether it was a male or a female, she was certain that it was alive, and she had said so many times, but no one would listen to her. What nonsense, Rupert thought, as he clutched his old cuddly toy and finally drifted off to sleep.

Chapter Four

FOOBA BALL

Wednesday, 11th November

The morning light crept in through the window, rapidly invading Rupert's bedroom. It flowed over his floor rug, climbed his bed and finally onto his quilt, which covered him from head to toe. Rupert lay awake. The events of the night before were still vivid in his memory as if it just happened.

Who are they, why are they looking for me, he asked himself. He patted the bed with his arm, searching for Marci, but the soft toy was not there. That's strange, he thought. He distinctly remembered bringing the soft toy to bed with him during the night. Rupert felt the need for a cuddle and as had always been the case, Marci was his only candidate. He pulled the quilt down from over his head. The quilt slid to the floor. He rolled around slowly, undecided whether he would get up and start the day, or lie in bed for a while longer. His eyes were closed. They felt sore and itchy from the lack of sleep. Gently, he opened them and wiped the hair from off his face, but when he moved his hand away, his whole body froze with the shock at what was hiding behind the lights above his bed. Rupert rubbed his eyes and looked up again in the hope that it had just been a trick of the light. But when he looked again, the ceiling light was wrapped with what seemed to be a big piece of bright orange dough, with a pair of big, deep, glossy black eyes. For a second, Rupert thought it was one of Miana's toys, but there was no way in the world that Miana could own a toy that looked like that. Besides, it was orange – not pink. Rupert had never seen anything like that before.

The brightness of the eyes intrigued him. The strange thing seemed to be pulsating and it was staring at him as if it was urgently trying to say something.

"That thing looks as if it's alive," he said. The orange dough started to sag and looked as if it was about to fall to the ground. Rupert sat up quickly and jumped out of the way, just as the blob landed with a splat at the bottom of his bed.

Rupert stood rooted to the spot. Holding his breath and staring at the orange mess on his bed, he wondered what this thing could possibly be. He could tell it was facedown, as he could no longer see those deep black eyes, which had been staring down at him. His curiosity eventually got the better of him and he inched up carefully to the orange blob, as close as his nerves would allow him. He poked at it with his bare finger, poked, poked, poked, each time in a different place, he could hear his rasping breath, but the orange blob did not respond at all.

Perhaps it wasn't alive after all, he thought. Feeling more confident now, he gave it another prod with his finger. It did not move.

Rupert stood still, not knowing what to do next, when suddenly the orange blob began to change shape slowly as if it was a balloon being inflated, adopting the shape and size of a basketball. It rolled off the bed on its own and landed on the floor without bouncing, it rolled over again, slowly. Rupert backed away quickly and stood looking at the ball, which was now staring at him.

The orange ball closed its eyes tightly and with a loud popping noise, two arms grew out on each side of the ball, each with a hand with four chubby little fingers which looked like worms.

"What on earth?" Rupert mumbled. Then there was more popping, as two legs with chubby, wrinkly feet grew out at the bottom of the ball, each with only three toes on each foot but with nicely trimmed nails.

Rupert watched in disbelief as the orange blob morphed in front of him. There was another loud "pop" and a head started to rise on a long skinny neck carrying the eyes with it. The orange thing opened its eyes and stared at Rupert.

"What?" Rupert swallowed. As he did so, with a final pop, pop, pop, a pair of triangular ears appeared, a nose and then a mouth shaped into a wide grin. The orange blob was no longer a ball it appeared to be a living two-foot tall creature, complete with a face, arms, legs and feet. Around its' neck hung a chain with a triangular framed pendant, which was divided into several triangles each of which was empty.

Rupert felt that his brain was about to pop also. He opened his mouth as if he was about to shout, but closed it again. Strangely, and specially in light of the events of the night before fresh in his mind,

Rupert felt no fear, although what he had just witnessed was completely beyond any sane explanation. He looked at the window on his left, then turned his head to the right, he remembered he had locked the door. How did it get in. he wondered.

This would be a great sample for science, it'd be sure to get me into the Genius Club. He thought.

Rupert did not want to blink, just in case the little creature disappeared.

"Why...why...who..." he began, but couldn't get the words out – his tongue felt numb. The orange creature began to copy Rupert's facial expressions, except, making fun of him in an exaggerated and silly way.

"What are you?" Rupert asked, intrigued, pointing at the little orange creature. There was no answer.

"Who are you?" Rupert tried again and still, no answer.

"What do you want?" he tried again.

"One question at a time, please," the little orange creature replied.

Rupert's body and brain froze when he heard the little orange creature reply with a deep and calm voice.

"You can talk," Rupert shouted.

"You too," responded the little orange creature.

"Wait a minute... I mean, what... what are you?" Rupert asked. He scratched his head as he moved a step to his right to get a better look.

"I'm a Kuark," came the answer from the little orange creature, copying Rupert's voice and moving one step to his right also.

"A what?" Rupert said, stepping to his right, one more time.

"I'm a Kuark called Blake," said the orange creature, taking its turn to step to the right.

"Okay Kuark, tell me then, where do you come from?"

"Please call me Blake, I never came, I've always been,"

"What does that mean? Don't you have a home...like a planet?" asked Rupert, who was now convinced he was talking with an alien from outer space.

"This is my planet and my home," Blake replied.

"Well... if you're not going to tell me the truth, then you can just go," said Rupert, standing still.

Blake paused and seemed to be thinking about what Rupert had just said.

"Fine," it replied, "let's make a deal then, I'll answer your questions, but only if I think you can understand the answers."

"Fine," Rupert said.

"But not now, I'll tell you later," Blake said.

"No, tell me now, I want to know now please," Rupert blurted out.

A minute of silence passed with no sign of either of them given in. Rupert's eyes widen when he saw the smile that began to appear slowly on Blake's face.

"Oh, all right, all right, I'll tell you, but you have to promise me you won't tell anyone else," Blake said.

Rupert nodded his head in agreement.

"What am I – that was your first question, wasn't it? Blake asked.

"Correct," Rupert said.

"Well, I am the creation of my Master. He created me in his mind and then manifested me into his world – our world,"

"Who am I – the second question, wasn't it?" Blake asked.

"Correct," Rupert said.

"I am an imaginary being, my master's inner being," Blake said.

"What do I want – the third question?" Blake said.

"Correct," Rupert said.

"Nothing," said Blake, "so there you are...all answered...happy?" Blake rubbed his hands fast as if he was wiping some dirt from them.

"All right...Blake, tell me then, where did you get manifested? I've never heard of anything like you before, so it's not possible for you to be from here," said Rupert.

"I come from an invisible world here on Earth, another dimension. Humans call it Imagination, and that is the world that runs parallel to your world.

"That's not true. I've never heard of this before. You're just trying to trick me. Imagination is just things you imagine that are not real," Rupert said.

"Of course it's true," Blake said, "you, humans, take imagination for granted, you couldn't possibly imagine anything that's not in your brain already. You think you imagined it, but imagination is the place where you humans take ideas from and then store them in your brains."

"So what are you doing here then, I didn't imagine you?" Rupert said.

"I'm here on a mission, but more importantly, I'm your new friend, that is if you can catch me," said Blake, as he bobbed away from Rupert.

"I'll catch you in a second. You look as if you're way too slow and sleepy,"

"No one calls me sleepy," Blake said, standing in front of Rupert with its chubby little legs apart, hands on hips and belly down to its knees.

Rupert laughed as he stretched out and grabbed the little orange creature around the shoulders.

"There – see, got ya, on the first try," he said.

"Ah, but, for how long?" said Blake, oozing out from under Rupert's grip.

"Yuck, you're all slippery and disgusting," said Rupert as he held up his arms and looked to see if there was any gooey mess on his sleeves.

"No one calls me slippery," said the orange creature as it lunged forward, but Rupert moved away and Blake crashed into the table lamp behind Rupert, smashing it against the wall.

"Shh, be quiet," Rupert said.

"Tell me, why are you unhappy?" Blake asked.

"How do you know I'm unhappy?" Rupert seemed surprised.

Blake stared at Rupert without replying. Rupert began to feel uncomfortable just standing there. It felt as if Blake could read his mind and know what he was thinking.

"Tell me, are you a type of alien or something like that?" He asked.

"It's my turn to ask the questions, right?" Blake said.

"Fine," Rupert shrugged.

"Why are you so unhappy that you want to leave this family?" Blake asked again.

"What? How do you know that? Have you been spying on me like everyone else?" Rupert said defensively. Blake continued just to stare at him questioningly.

"Okay, I'll tell you why," Rupert replied grudgingly, "I'm forced to do things I don't like. Like studying more than anyone else and getting the worst results. I hate this house and everything inside it. I don't want to be compared to other kids. I'd rather hang out with kids in the street. They don't have to go to school. Everything they have is better than what I have even those that have nothing, and, I am grounded since the minute I wake up. To be more precise I am grounded right now," Rupert gave a big sigh as if he had just dropped a massive sack from his shoulders.

"Good, very good – I see what you mean, but what do you think these kids in the street want?" Blake asked.

"Nothing, I guess," Rupert said.

"Well, you're not a hundred per cent right – you know, in fact, you're zero per cent right, which makes you completely wrong. You're complaining just because you're a kid, and that's what kids your age are good at. Complain, complain and complain. So if that's how you're going to be, then I'm gone." Blake turned around and went in the direction of the door.

"Wait, please stay," Rupert said, "I won't complain anymore, or at least, not whilst you're around and, by the way, you can't use that door."

"Nope, if it's going to be, moan, moan, moan all day, I'm leaving and I'm using any door I want," Blake said.

"Oh come on … what did I say wrong? I'll do anything you want if you agree to stay," Rupert said.

"Now we're talking! What're you willing to do for me to stay?" Said Blake, rubbing his hands slowly together.

"Anything," Rupert said.

"Anything, huh? Now, let me think," said Blake as he put his fist on his forehead and pretended to be deep in thought. He tapped his head with one of his stumpy little fingers, cupped his chin and then rubbed his stomach.

"You will agree to go on a mission, your own mission, but I can't tell you what it is yet, we'll talk about it later," Blake said.

Rupert smiled, he did not believe in Blake words. He walked towards his closet, and, as if reading his mind Blake quickly ran past him, reaching the closet's drawers before him, almost knocking Rupert over in the process. With one hand Blake opened the top drawer then the second one and proceeded to throw clothes in all directions while covering its big black eyes with the other hand to give Rupert some privacy while he was dressing. Rupert laughed as he bent over to pick up the clothes that were strewn all around the bedroom.

"You mentioned a Master, do you have a master? Rupert asked.

"No more questions," Blake replied.

"So now, Blake, what am I going to do with you? If you're going to stick around – are you? Because if you are, I'm going to need to hide you or something,"

"Hide me? Why? No one needs to hide me. I can do it myself," Blake bent his head to touch his toes, until he became a perfect round shiny orange ball again, a mixture between a football ball and a basketball.

"Wow, that's amazing … very impressive, you are a Fooba ball. Please don't do that in front of anyone. You'll just scare people and embarrass me," Rupert teased.

Blake popped himself out again and stood perfectly still, his black eyes searching in circles as if there was something in the air.

"I won't, don't worry you'll embarrass me too," Blake said slowly, looking around as if he could hear something. He seemed to start floating then crashed into the wall, as if someone had picked him up and thrown him across the room.

Blake slid down the wall, slowly, until he reached the floor.

"Wow! What did you do that for – that must hurt?" Rupert said.

"It wasn't me… I'm okay, I'll explain later," Blake replied as he kept looking around. "That was uncool, totally uncool," Blake said, under his breath.

A knock on the door brought Rupert back to the reality of his life.

"Who is it?" Rupert asked, watching Blake transform into a ball again and roll into the corner beside the chest of drawers.

"It's me, are you up yet? Can I come in," Alan shouted.

"Sure," replied Rupert, he looked at Blake again, before turning to open the door for Alan.

"Are you okay after last night? Alan asked urgently, "I think we need to talk about it."

"Yes, I'm okay," Rupert said, quickly closing the door behind Alan.

Alan stared at all the clothes scattered around the floor.

"It's good to see you full of energy today," he said.

Rupert grabbed his school bag and walked out of his bedroom protecting his latest cool secret. Blake had arrived at the best moment, and nothing was going to spoil that, Rupert thought.

Rupert's day at school went on without incident. He had Blake on his mind every second of the day, he could not wait to get back home. He was the first to get out of school and raced to get in the car. Once at home Rupert got out of the car, leaving the door open behind him and ran to his room. Alan followed him as quickly as possible.

"What?" Said Rupert when he saw the intrigued expression on Alan's face. Rupert stood by the door waiting for Alan to leave, but instead of leaving, Alan looked around and focused on the corner where Blake was pretending to be a ball.

"Aha! I was hoping you'd be around, when did you get here?" Alan asked the ball.

"That's my Fooba ball, please don't touch it," said Rupert.

Blake rolled out of his corner towards Alan, who casually flicked Blake with his foot and caught it in his hands in mid-air before dropping the ball on the ground and trapping it under his foot.

"Fooba ball, hey, I like your new name," Alan said.

"Nope, he just made it up, I'm still Blake,"

Rupert was astonished that Alan seemed to know Blake. He closed his bedroom door and pushed the lock button, for the second time. He decided he like the clicking noise, it made him feel safe.

"How do you know about him?" Rupert asked, looking at Alan and Blake accusingly.

"It," Alan corrected, staring at Blake, who, by now had wriggled out from under Alan's foot, popped itself out again and stood looking up at Alan with an angry look on its face.

"Please don't say anything about him to anyone," Rupert begged.

"It," Alan repeated. "There's no risk of that, but there's something you need to know, and now that Blake's here, this would appear to be the right time." He looked at Blake, who nodded conspiratorially in reply. Alan sat down on the bed and looked over at Rupert.

"This is all about you – you had better sit down and buckle your seat belt because you are destined to go on a very rocky road my friend.

Chapter Five

THE MISSION

Rupert loved to hear Alan's stories, they were funny, full of action, often confusing, and the more he listened, the less he understood, but in the end Rupert believed in them. Alan's contagious enthusiasm made him sit to listen one more time. Rupert hurried to give Alan the ready signal to begin.

"Last night, Err," Alan said as he cleared his throat, "the man you saw on the street, with his evil looking creature – well, Err," Alan cleared his throat again. "He was in fact, looking for you. His name is Daltom, and that terrible foul creature with him, is called Begnon. They've been hunting you for almost twelve years, and now that they've finally found you, your life is in danger." Alan blurted out.

Rupert looked at Alan with dismay his eyes were round with terror, he could not move as he took in what Alan had just said. It was as if time had stopped. You're out of your mind, Rupert said to himself.

Blake looked at Rupert and then slowly turned his head towards Alan.

"Well, that's the introduction done, shall we tell him the bad news now?" Blake said.

"What do you mean, my life is in danger, do they want to hurt me, but, why – eleven years ago I would've been only a baby… and I haven't been hiding. What could I possibly have done to them?" Rupert said.

"You've done nothing. That's not the problem. It's what you are able to do, the reason why Daltom wants to get rid of you." Blake said.

"What is it that I can do?" Rupert asked terrified.

"Your mission, remember?" Blake said.

"Just wait a minute, before Blake gives you all the information he's supposed to, there's something about yourself that I must tell you. Alan pulled out a handkerchief and started to dry the sweat from his forehead. He stared at Rupert whilst pacing back and forth across the room in front of him.

"Well, I'm waiting – say it. You're making me nervous,"

Alan stopped his pacing, sat down on the edge of the bed rubbing the back of his neck and looked at Rupert in the eyes.

"Mr and Mrs Curdy are not your real parents..." Alan spoke incredibly fast, as if the words were exploding out of his mouth.

"I beg your pardon," said Rupert, "you're joking aren't you?"

"You heard correctly, I'm not joking. Mr and Mrs Curdy are not your real parents, I'm sorry..." Alan repeated.

"It's not true," Rupert looked across at Blake as if to see whether Alan was playing a trick on him, but Blake was looking down at the floor.

"Wait, are you telling me that I'm adopted or what, what do you mean, they're not my real parents?" Rupert's mind took off immediately looking for answers, comparing his physical features to the rest of his family. He could not find a resemblance. Instantly the list of un-likes was endless, his eyes stared vacantly across the bedroom and tears began to collect in the corners. Even though thinking about his miserable life and his wish to run away from his family, the news that he did not belong was surprisingly upsetting.

"Rupert, are you okay?" Alan asked.

"What? – Yes," He nodded his head and wiped the tears from his eyes.

"You were in danger as a baby," Alan said. In order to save you from the man you saw last night, your real parents sent you away with me. I had instructions to bring you to Mr and Mrs Curdy, and that's what I did. Your real parents' names are Vincent and Serena Star, and your real name is Rupert Star."

"This is insane, why are you telling me this now? I'd rather not know anything." Rupert put his hands on his stomach.

"I wanted to tell you but... Mr and Mrs Curdy were only supposed to be your godparents, but they thought it was much easier to pretend you were their real child – so things got complicated," Alan said.

This can't be true, Rupert thought, as the tears began to run down his cheeks.

"Why did they pretend to be my parents, they don't even like me," Rupert said, "It just can't be true. Who are my real parents and where are they?"

"Here read this," Alan gave Rupert a newspaper clipping which he had kept for twelve years, for just this occasion.

Most Successful Scientist On The Run. Said the headline in bold writing.

Vincent Star has fled from the authorities after being accused of murdering four young scientists in his laboratory, authorities...

"What? Is he—" Rupert closed his eyes. He saw a projector sliding words in front of him. You Are Grounded – Not Good Enough – Average Student – Poor Report – His Name is Rupert – You Stink – Murderer. With voices from his parents, Miana and strange voices calling him Murderer.

What is wrong with me, my life is only getting worse by the minute, I'm the son of a murderer, he thought.

"Vincent is not a murderer, he was set up by Daltom. He's not running from the police, he's running from Daltom. Daltom is the real threat... for everybody," Alan said.

Blake closed his eyes and nodded his head, "Alan, you're making things worse... stop this."

"Please, sit down and let me explain how it all began, that's the only way for you to understand why you are where you are," Blake said.

Rupert sat on his bed, hugged his legs and looked at the ground waiting for Blake to begin. Would it get any worse, he wondered.

"Vincent is the smartest scientist the world has ever seen. He made discoveries that no one of his age could ever have done. His incredible success caused his once best friend, Daltom, to become envious of him. So much so, that Daltom became Vincent's worst enemy. Serena, your mother, is also a brilliant scientist, but she prefers to stay in the shadows, she never used her real name on her discoveries.

"Where are they now then, are they alive? How come I never heard of them before" Rupert looked at Alan.

"They're still hiding, if Blake is here, it means that Vincent is still alive," Alan said.

"And my mother, why aren't they together, where is she? Rupert asked.

The day Daltom found their hiding place, up in the mountains, they went in different ways in order to make Daltom lose track of you. Your mother managed to escape with you." Alan explained, "On that day, I had gone to meet Vincent, but instead, Serena met with me and passed me her baby – you. She was supposed to come too, but she was injured, and Daltom was following her steps. She guided me telepathically to take you to the Curdys and that was the last time I saw her." Alan said.

"Did he kill her?" Rupert asked.

"She hasn't been in contact with Vincent after all this time, but somehow Vincent thinks that she's still alive," Blake said, "but they promised each other they would reunite when you turn twelve."

"Twelve? I'll be twelve soon," Rupert rushed to speak.

"That's why I'm here," Blake said.

"What sort of things did Vincent discover, how can they be my parents? I am not nearly as intelligent as you say they are, I'm just an average student with no special skills or talents and all I want is to run away from this family,"

"Vincent discovered how to balance the forces of good and evil, and you my friend are destined to reassemble the Eight-Pointed Star which is the only way to balance these two forces. Daltom wants to be the one who puts the Eight-Pointed Star together, in order to control the world but he can only succeed, if you're not in his way,"

"What is the Eight-Pointed Star? I don't get it," Rupert said.

"I'll explain everything you want to know, but here, take this and play it whenever you want. Vincent designed it for you. He believes that once you see with your own eyes what he is trying to achieve, you will believe in your mission," Blake put a cube the size of a tennis ball in Rupert's hand.

"What's this?" Rupert asked.

"Your mission, compact in a cube, the red button will show you how the earth will be destroyed. The green button will show you what needs to be done to save it,"

"I see," Rupert said.

"Vincent discovered that there was something unearthly compromising the existence of humankind. He then dedicated himself solely to finding a way to stop what he believed could be the destruction of humanity. He soon learned that a very powerful force, coming from a broken star was the cause and to fix the problem it was necessary to put the star back together again. The Eight-Pointed Star broke billions of years ago. Its' particles are too close to Earth and are causing problems – problems that soon will bring an end to humankind.

Blake took Rupert's hands with the cube in it and twisted it. A bright light with millions of small particles glided in front of Rupert's face. A star with eight points floated in the centre.

"That's amazing," Rupert was mesmerised. He felt as if each particle was touching his skin making it tingle.

"Technically, The Eight-Pointed Star can't be put together again, but its energy must in order to be transformed. The eight points of the star have moved in different directions, and each point has broken individually so that the pieces are now separately orbiting the Earth."

Rupert could see the star moving and its points pulling away from the core, as Blake was taking him through the explanation.

The first point to be reassembled has broken into eight pieces. Each piece represents a member of a team. Humans carry seven of those pieces, whilst the eighth piece, can be carried by either a Kuark like me or a Murk. I believe you came across a Murk last night, that creature with Daltom last night is a Murk. Murks come from the same dimension as I do. Except, they are evil.

"So we'll be looking for only one point and not the whole star?" Rupert asked.

"Correct, Vincent and Daltom are vying to put together the first point and it is only on your twelfth birthday that this incredible task can be achieved," Blake paced holding his hands behind his back.

Rupert was puzzled, trying to process all this information. He twisted the cube again, and the star disappeared.

"I still don't understand, I can never achieve something like this, you're wasting your time."

"You can change things Rupert, your parents sacrificed everything for you to be able to put The Eight-Pointed Star together, you can't let them down now," Alan said.

"But what do I have to do with all this? I don't get it," Rupert said, "I don't even know how to start, I'm not sure if what you are telling me is even true" He replied wiping the tears from his eyes.

"We all know that – that's why we're here to help you," Alan said.

"I'd rather look for my real parents, they are the ones to explain me all this I'm not interested in that silly star – it means nothing to me," he said.

"It meant everything to your parents and following the instructions will get you to find them. Rupert, you are the one who can stop Daltom by continuing what they couldn't finish," Blake said.

"Even if I wanted to, don't you know that The Eight-Pointed Star is only a myth, a story, not something to find, it doesn't exist," he said.

"It's only a story because up until now no one has been able to discover how to find it and how to put it together, it doesn't exist as a divine entity it lives within people – it'll all come together on your birthday," Alan said.

"But that's insane, my birthday is only few days away,"

"We have to start somewhere," Blake said.

Rupert twisted the cube again. The star was now occupying his entire bedroom. Seven points were outlined, and only one was clearly visible and cracked into eight smaller triangles like a jigsaw puzzle.

"Each point is an individual puzzle and each puzzle must be solved separately, taking into account that half of the star points contain good energy and the other half contain evil energy," Blake touched each of the outline points, and they disappeared leaving the one cracked right in front of Rupert.

"That's the reason why no one has ever tried before. If all the four good points are found consecutively, the Star will be balanced, and that will make it an easy task, but that's unlikely to happen. Daltom knows he has as many chances as Vincent, and that's why he's so ambitious to put the star together himself.

"The Eight-Pointed Star is universal. So each of its points can be found nesting anywhere in the world. The triangle puzzle we are looking for has a Masterpiece and a superhuman which must be blood relative, five humans and a Kuark like me, Blake pointed his finger at himself, this explains why you were selected," he said. Blake tapped the star point, and it broke into eight pieces floating on air.

"Superhuman?" Rupert said.

"I knew you were going to like that, I called them superhuman because they can understand more than a normal human, without a superhuman I would have never been here," Blake said.

"How do we find the pieces of the puzzle then?" asked Rupert, as if finding eight pieces would be an easy task. Making puzzles was one of his favourite distractions.

"The pieces are not visible by themselves, so the trick is to find a person who's the right member of the team and gather them together on the date set – and that is your Twelfth Birthday. The members will attract or repel each other when they are interacting. On the set date, and when all the members of the same team are together. Each triangle will appear on their right hand," Blake grabbed one of the pieces floating in the air and put it on Rupert's hand, the piece disappeared, and a light shone in the centre of his hand, "like this," he said. The pieces can't be mixed up because there will be a colour for each team. If by any chance a member of the evil team is on the good team, its triangle will appear on their left hand, so we must take care when selecting the four missing members of your team," Blake said.

"Four? I thought you said eight," Rupert said.

"Yes, I did say eight. But there's a Good team and an Evil team, we're in the Good team, and there are already four members," Blake said.

"So this is easy, we're halfway, aren't we?" Rupert said.

"Yes, we're halfway, except the evil side has only one member missing," Blake said and frowned.

"What? No way, who are the four members on our side?" Rupert asked.

"Well, there's Vincent–"

"But where is he?" Rupert asked.

"He promised to come back on your twelfth birthday, he will be there don't you worry. I know this is complicated and it's a lot to absorb, but little by little, all will become clear to you...so... just be a bit patient..." Blake said, "listen carefully because this is very important. Whoever completes the triangle first will be the founder, but there is a twist."

"A twist? It sounds like a game," Rupert said.

"You can see it as a game – a deadly game. The Masterpiece can only be replaced if the holder of the Masterpiece is dead," Blake looked down.

"Daltom is waiting because solving the puzzle is not all he wants. More than anything, he wants to kill Vincent," Blake said.

"Where are we going to find the rest of the pieces?" Rupert asked.

"They will come to you before your twelfth birthday. Just follow your instincts," Blake said.

"But I'm no good at instincts."

"The moment you felt dissatisfied with your life and decided to rebel against it that was the day the countdown to your birthday began. The same moment I sat by your ceiling light," Blake said, "you must pay attention to the people you interact with these days because one of them may be part of either team. We have to make sure that they're on our team and not on the evil one, as you can't tell the difference between the two unless you pay careful attention to your feelings. Not sensing anything is good, feeling nervous, alert or severe cold is bad, feeling good is good." Blake smiled.

"That should be enough for today. It's time to go and play some sport." Alan interrupted as he stood up and headed towards the door.

"Wait, I want to know more. How can we find the team if we don't look for them, I just sit and wait, this can't be?"

"Remember this, Rupert," Blake was now propped up against the wall. "There are no accidents or coincidences. All the people you meet during these coming days will play a part in this important mission, whether for the good or the evil team. They're waiting for the perfect time to become part of it."

"But, what will happen after we put the first point or puzzle together? Rupert kept on asking.

"Be patient, young man. You won't be missing out on anything, after all, this is all about you. Once the first puzzle is joined, it can never be split apart again. This team has an advantage, as they already have a percentage of the Star's power, encouraging them to continue to find the other seven points.

Knock, knock, knock, "Rupert, Mr Korviatello is waiting in the lounge," Mrs Curdy called from outside the door.

"What? I said I'm not going to take singing lessons," Rupert whispered.

"Just give it a go, you have nothing to lose," Alan whispered back.

"She isn't my Mum, I don't have to do what she tells me now," he said.

"It's not her fault. They were asked to help, and they did so, you must carry on as before and pretend you know nothing," Blake said, "and remember, the Curdys know nothing about the Eight-Pointed Star either, so it's recommended to keep it that way.

"All right, I'll pretend, but I'm looking for my real mum until I find her,"

"Vincent will answer that when we meet him," Alan said.

"Rupert, are you there?" Mrs Curdy yelled.

"I am, Mum. I'll be there in a second," Rupert hid the cube under his pillow.

She isn't my mum.

"Make sure you are not late, I must go now." Replied Mrs Curdy.

The loud noise from Mrs Curdy's high heels disappeared slowly down the corridor while Rupert kept on complaining.

"How can I be part of this important task when I'm forced to do these ridiculous activities? I hate singing – I never sang a song in my life, I always pretend to sing. I hate violin. I'm useless at languages, I hate clubs, ahh grrrr!"

"See you tomorrow, Rupert," Alan said.

"Why tomorrow? I'll come to see you when the music teacher is gone," replied Rupert.

"He's staying the night, so you'll be singing for a long time," Alan said.

"What? Why is Mum punishing me?" Rupert complained.

"She only wants what's she thinks is best for you," Alan said. Rupert gave Alan his worst look and left, slamming the door behind him.

Chapter Six

MRS STEVENS

Thursday, 12th November

Rupert stood in front of his bedroom window, mesmerised by the stunning sunrise. Orange, red and pink clouds blended together in the sky. He pulled the collar of his school shirt up and started to do the top button first. His ears were still buzzing from his singing lesson the night before. What a waste of time, he thought. He turned to his left and saw the cube that Blake had given him, on his bedside table. It reminded him of all the information he was given by Blake and Alan the day before, and now he was involved in a mission, which still did not seem real to him.

My dad made this for me, how clever is that, I wish I was clever too, he thought, as he weighed the cube in his hand.

An unfamiliar, and neatly folded sweater at the end of his bed caught his attention. It was navy, with a thin white stripe around the v-collar. For a moment Rupert was puzzled, but then, he remembered it was the sweater Mrs Stevens had lent him the other night. The housekeepers must have cleaned it and left it there, for me to return, he thought. His mind went back instantly trying to recall the details of what had happened that night, but it was still a blur, the darkness of the street and the rotten smell coming from Begnon dominated his thoughts. He refused to go down that path again and forced himself to stay focused. Rupert grabbed the sweater and stuffed it into his school bag, to return it to Mrs Stevens, before he forgot.

He pulled down his school tie from the closet, draped it around his neck and walked back to the window. The red sky invited him to stare. He held both ends of the tie, putting the wider end on the right side checking that it was longer than the other. He crossed the wide end over the other end.

"Blake, are you still here?" he asked.

"And where do you expect me to be?" came the reply from under the bed. Rupert grinned as he brought the wider end of the tie underneath the narrow end from left to right.

"It's going to be weird to look at Mum and Dad now, knowing they're not my real parents," he brought the wider end over, from right to left.

"You know what, your real parents would most probably have been the same, guiding you to be the best you can be in everything you do, but perhaps, you'd be just as resentful with them as you are now with the Curdys," Blake said tucked in, under the bed.

"Whose side are you on, then?" Rupert snapped, bringing the wider end under the knot to the centre part, faster than the previous steps.

"Mine," Blake teased, popping his head out of the bed.

"Oh forget it, I'm not in the mood," Rupert said, bringing the wide end down, passing the loop in front to tighten the knot. He stepped to the right and stood in front of a standing mirror. He stared at his reflection while adjusting the tie up by pulling the narrow end down gently with the other hand he moved the knot up until it reached the centre of his collar. His mind raced away, seeing hundreds of male and female faces run through his head, then it all stopped.

"I wonder what my real parents look like," he said to himself, "will I be able to recognise them if they were in front of me?" He pulled down the collar of his shirt and turned to face Blake.

"Can you tell me what Vincent looks like physically? If he's your Master, then you must know," he said.

"Of course, I do, it's easy to explain, but you have to believe me, as it will be as if I'm describing you, except, he is much taller, much older and much, much hairier."

"I'm serious," Rupert said rolling his eyes.

"Me too, you'll see when you meet him," Blake said.

"And Serena?" Rupert asked.

"I'm not allowed to intervene between you and your Mother, even if I wanted to." Blake said.

"I have a feeling that she's alive, and I'm going to find her," Rupert said, "I don't know why, but I just have this feeling."

"That may be so, and I hope it is, but for now, you've got to focus on the first-star point. Reassembling the first puzzle is your mission," Blake said.

"I can do both. Alan said that Daltom saw her last, so if he's looking for me he'll find me, and once he finds me, he'll tell me where my mother is."

"No, you can't get close to Daltom, or he'll kill you."

"He can't if he needs me alive to get the first star point,"

"That's not correct – he can still kill you and then there'll be no need for a masterpiece," Blake growled.

"But he's had the chance before, and he didn't do it, so he must want me alive," Rupert said.

"He didn't know it was you. That's why," Blake said.

If he gives me back my Mum, I'll give him the first point of the star on my birthday. Rupert thought.

Rupert left his bedroom and bumped into Miana who was standing in the hallway.

"Heel, sit – Good dog, not too fast. Heel – Stop." Miana ordered, but as usual, Jeeves just ignored her and went about his own business. Jeeves sat looking at Miana with a –just get me out of here– expression on his face. Rupert remembered that Jeeves used to enjoy the constant attention from Miana, but today he did not seem too keen on being bossed about, so, as Rupert walked by, Jeeves seized the opportunity and darted between Rupert's legs and sped off down the hallway.

"Eeoouu, you stink. Stop staring at me, Because of you, Jeeves has run away," Miana yelled.

Rupert smiled and carried on down the passageway, pretending to ignore Miana as he walked by, as usual, but all the while thinking to himself that she had forgotten about what she saw the other night.

"Let's go," Rupert whispered conspiratorially to Alan, who was waiting for Rupert at the bottom of the stairs, as he headed off towards the back door, avoiding going through the kitchen and the prospect of having to face his parents.

Later in the day, during his science class, Rupert approached Mrs Stevens to return the sweater.

"Not now please," Mrs Stevens, told him, as she continued to write the list on the board of materials they would be using for the next experiment.

She's strange sometimes, he thought to himself as he returned to his seat at the side of the classroom by the window.

The window beside Rupert's seat gave him a perfect view over the fields to the forest. From there, he was able to do his best daydreaming, while staring at the trees swaying slowly from side to side in the wind. Rupert was somewhere in another galaxy, as far away as possible with his thoughts. He was thinking about the events of the last few days. Then, a voice coming from far brought him back to the classroom. Mrs Stevens was standing in front of him. He had no idea what had happened as he turned to face the front of the class, the room was empty.

"Are you okay, Rupert? You haven't heard a word I said to the class, is there a problem?" she asked.

"No, I'm fine – thank you," he replied.

He quickly scrambled his books together and looked up at Mrs Stevens.

"Well, I suggest you sort out whatever it is that is bothering you and pay more attention in my class," she growled.

On the way to his next class, Rupert remembered that Mrs Stevens might have seen the mysterious man in the black robe or the one in white. He still had to return the sweater she had lent him, so he decided he would pay her a visit later on in her office.

When the class finished, Rupert headed off to Mrs Stevens' office. He knocked on her door.

"Come in," Mrs Stevens replied.

"I wanted to return the sweater you lent me the other night – thank you very much," Rupert said as he handed it to her, "I didn't know you lived in that area," he said.

"I don't, I was just visiting a friend. Did your cat come home?" She asked.

"Yes, he did," Rupert lied.

Rupert looked around the office. There were no pictures, maps, charts or anything like that on display and unlike all the other teachers, her desk was totally clear, apart from her notes from today's class, which she now picked up and placed in the top drawer of her desk. As she did so, Rupert caught a quick glimpse of a calendar inside the drawer, and he could have sworn that it was clear except for one date, which had a red circle on November 21st, but there was something else written beside it. That's weird, he thought. Why would she have a circle around my birthday? He left more intrigued than when he came in. She can't possibly know it's my birthday. I'm going to have to sneak back and check to see what she's written beside it. He said to himself.

Rupert joined his class, planning how he could get back into Mrs Stevens' room without her finding out. The best time would be at the break while the teachers went to the staff room for morning tea. That would give me plenty of time to quickly enter the office, check the calendar and be out again before she had even left the staff room.

During break, Rupert waited patiently at the end of the corridor until Mrs Stevens had left her office and disappeared into the teachers' lounge at the other end. He picked up the pile of books he had collected, as if he had been instructed to take them to her office, and walked casually inside. He opened the drawer and checked the calendar, taking care not to move anything. The calendar had only one date circled, and it was indeed his birthday, November 21st but Rupert's mouth fell open when he discovered a different name on the calendar.

"Daltom," he read. His body experience an instant shock.

There were old exam papers under the calendar. Rupert recognised his own writing and grabbed them. His hands trembling in the process, there was a pile of his exams all with full marks, but somehow, he had been receiving a copy of them in which he only scored low marks, marks which had given him the average-student label he was known for. Mrs Stevens had been dishonest with him, but why? He wondered.

Suddenly, the full weight of what this meant hit him, and he staggered backwards out of the room, almost tripping and dropping the pile of books as he went through the door. It all makes sense. She was with him that night. She's been watching me all this time. She'll be the one who'll take me to Daltom, he thought.

Rupert propped himself up against the wall outside the office and just managed to stop himself from falling over. He saw Mrs Stevens leaving the staff room. His legs felt too weak to walk away. His arms lost all the strength and the pile of books he was holding fell to the ground. He stooped to pick them up, just as Mrs Stevens returned along the corridor with a cup in her hands. She paused briefly beside him and sipped her drink. Her eyes fixed on her office door then she carried on by and went inside.

The last two classes of the day were with Mrs Stevens again. Rupert sat behind his desk, facing the front attentively. He started to tap the pencil fast on his science book. Mrs Stevens was late for her class and this was the first time in as long as Rupert could remember, that she was late. It worried him that she might have discovered he had broken into her office.

Just then, the door opened, and an old man walked slowly into the classroom holding a pencil in one hand and his reading glasses in the other. He was Mr Zhong the librarian, he only visit the classes when he had to deliver an urgent message to the students. Mr Zhong had been in the library for many decades, he wore his traditional Chinese gown, wore his long hair on a ponytail and kept his chin whiskers long.

"Children, listen, listen please," he said, "Mrs Stevens won't be here this afternoon, she has urgent matters to attend to, and has left instructions that you are to do revision, please let me know if you need any assistance, but I prefer if you don't." Mr Zhong sat confortable behind the desk.

There was an audible sigh from the classroom.

"Is everything all right?" asked one of the students closest to him.

"I understand there's an important meeting for next week's Science Elite Exam which Mrs Stevens is attending, you don't need to know more," Mr Zhong replied.

Rupert stopped tapping his pencil. She's Daltom's accomplice. She's probably meeting with him right now. He told himself.

On his way out, Rupert saw the new posters on the wall announcing the Science Elite Exam there was an extensive list of all the requirements and rules beside it, other children gathered around him to read.

"I wonder who will win the S.E.E this year," said one student.

"Only a genius can win it, our school hasn't won it for years," said another student.

I wish I could have the chance to do the test. Rupert said to himself, but he held no hope of being selected. He had always had the feeling that even though science was his favourite subject, he never seemed to get the grades he thought he deserved, and today he understood the reason why.

Chapter Seven

THE FROZEN DEAL

On the way home, Rupert was quieter than normal. He wondered what he could possibly have done for Mrs Stevens to cheat on his marks. He could not find any valid explanation other than she belongs in Daltom's team.

"Come on, spit it out – what happened today," Alan said.

"Nothing, why," Replied Rupert.

"I know you but if you don't want to talk that's fine, perhaps a bit of exercise will cheer you up," Alan said. They drove around stopping in the first football pitch they saw.

"We don't have a ball," Rupert said.

"Nope, but I can improvise," Alan went to the back of the car and emerged with a bright orange ball.

"Are you sure – can he?" Rupert felt for Blake.

"It, and, it will be okay. It's not human you know," Blake rolled his eyes making Rupert laugh at last.

Rupert kicked the ball without any enthusiasm. His heart was just not in it. Alan put a bit of power on a kick and Rupert missed it entirely, the ball bounced out of the park and rolled in front of a group of boys who had been standing and watching them for a while. One of the boys kicked the ball back.

"Thanks, d'you want to join us?" Alan asked.

"Nah," answered the boy.

"Can we?" The boy behind him asked.

"Come on, then – show us what you've got, I'll be the ref," Alan said.

"Definitely more than what you've got, you can't even kick the ball straight," said the youngest of them all.

There were five boys in all. One by one they joined the game. Rupert held the ball in his hands watching intently. He has never seen them before, they looked scruffy and unkempt, two of them have similar features as if they were twins but with different height. They joined the game on opposite sides. All of them wore worn out ski jackets. Discreetly, Rupert pulled his shirt out and ruffled his hair up and ran over to join them.

The match was played with intensity and both teams seemed as competitive as one another in their own rule-less world whilst passing the ball, kicking, falling and pulling shirts. There were no complains, only grunting noises. After the game was over, the five boys left as strangers, not even saying goodbye. Rupert stood with Blake tucked under his arm, watching as they disappeared down the street.

It was dark, and torrential rain was forecast for the evening. Rupert and Alan arrived home later than usual and Rupert was surprised to see that it was his father who was waiting for him in the kitchen this time.

"Where have you been?" he demanded, as Rupert came through the door.

"I can explain Mr Curdy," Alan said walking behind Rupert, but Mr Curdy put up his hand, cutting Alan off.

"You've missed your violin lessons, and your Mum has had to make up excuses for you again… what do you think you're doing?" Mr Curdy said.

"I'm not taking violin lessons anymore, or singing lessons, for that matter. From now on I'm going to do what I want," Rupert said.

"I beg your pardon," yelled Mr Curdy, "you'll do as I say, whether you like it or not, and you are grounded for the rest of the week."

Rupert ran up to his room, carrying Blake in his hands, slamming the door behind him.

"I'm not going to be grounded – I'm going to be gone forever," Rupert said.

"Bad idea, bad idea, you won't get far this time. Daltom is out there and this time you won't be so lucky, he knows who you are," Blake warned.

"But I'm not scared of him, this time, it's me who's looking for him. He'll take me to my real Mum tonight," said Rupert.

"No, he won't, and I'm not going to let you go," Blake argued.

"Can't you understand that I've been living a lie for all these years – that I deserve to know if my mother is alive," Rupert argued back.

"Once you help Daltom with the first-star point, if that's what you intend, then he'll have no mercy for anyone, and if your Mum is alive, he'll make sure that it won't be for long. And if you don't intend to help him, then he'll just kill you, so either way, you're dead."

Rupert ignored Blake's warning. He pulled on a sweater, his coat and beanie and left, leaving Blake pacing from side to side on his bed.

Rupert went down the servants' stairs again. He knew Alan would be in the gym, and the housekeepers were busy with their work around the house. He knew that he could slip out without anyone paying attention if he went through the kitchen. Morris was there, reading the newspaper. Rupert snuck behind him and went out of the house through the back door. He tried the side gate where Miana had fainted on Tuesday night, but it was locked, so he pushed his way through the bushes at the side of the house. His coat pocket caught on one of the branches, so that when he pulled himself free, he tore a large hole in the side of his coat. The sudden release from the tree branch made him miss-step into a puddle, which splashed water and mud up the leg of his trousers. By the time he managed to get out of the garden, he looked scruffy and unkempt, just like the boys he had played soccer with that afternoon. The street was dark and busier than it had been the last time he was out. He could hear people talking, cars passed by and there was the sound of children playing in the distance.

It started to drizzle, but Rupert did not mind, he was prepared for the weather this time. The wet grass muffled the sound of his footsteps. The wind was blowing softly in his ears. He pulled the beanie down to stop them from becoming too cold. In the distance, he could hear the sound of rolling thunder. Rupert started as a cat ran out from the bushes and across the street in front of him. He turned to see what had caused the cat to take fright, and his body froze when the lightning slashed through the smoky clouds lighting up the silhouette of a man in a black hooded robe, standing in the shadows at the end of the road.

"There you are Daltom," Rupert said to himself as he crouched down and hid behind a low hedge to watch him. Rupert wanted to gather himself before he walked over to demand the whereabouts of his mother. The rain was becoming heavier now, splattering the pavement and creating puddles everywhere.

Daltom patrolled along the road, he did not seem bothered by the rain, looking into each of the houses. Begnon appeared at the bottom of the road where Daltom had been standing, and hurried up to stand beside him.

"Master, your guests are in the park," Begnon hissed.

Daltom followed Begnon he was almost invisible in the blackness of the evening. Rupert took a shortcut through the hedges arriving at the park before them. He was intrigued to see who the guests might be and saw a group of people playing, pushing each other and whispering, all dressed in long, hooded raincoats. He came close and realised that they were only young children, probably his age – one of them came over, pulling a balaclava down to hide his face. Rupert pulled his wet beanie down further and his sweater up to cover his mouth, leaving only enough space in front of his eyes to be able to see. The child in the balaclava asked Rupert a question but he could hardly hear the words so Rupert nodded in agreement.

"Well, it's the wrong time to be here, you'll be in trouble if you stay around. A dangerous man is roaming around and he has a deadly beast with him, if it catches you, it will rip you open and eat you. You must leave," the boy said. Rupert saw the boy putting a horror look in his eyes.

"He is here now," the boy whispered as he pointed at a pile of bags. "Hide over there."

Rupert slid behind the bags, which were stacked up beside a rubbish bin, which smelt of manure, to his surprise, it was not as bad as the smell emanating from Begnon. With the moonlight reflecting through the clouds, Rupert was able to read the sign on the bin. Dog waste? He pinched his nose lying on the ground. Begnon came and stood only a few feet away from the rubbish bin, it sniffed and sniffed the air. Rupert only hoped for the Dog waste to help mask his scent.

"His name is Rupert – he lives in house number eight. I want him dead," Daltom said. The children had now gathered around him.

"Dead? We don't know how to kill," said one of the boys.

"Don't worry, that pleasure will be mine," Daltom casually explained, "all I want you to do is to spy on him. I'll take care of the rest. It will be as easy as it was with his mother and that will be an end to that stupid Frozen Deal."

Rupert squeezed his eyes tightly. The confession of Daltom killing his mother felt as if he had been stabbed through the heart. His tears dropped to the ground, taking with them all his hope of finding his real mother. He wiped the tears away with his hand. Slowly, he inched away and silently disappeared into the night.

As he walked home he thought of what he had heard and the anger bit into him – it began to take the form of a man, but Rupert could not imagine Daltom's face. It could be anyone, he thought.

Rupert arrived back at the house with his plans of finding his mother in tatters. There could be no question of his teaming up with Daltom now – not after what he had just heard, and now he had that group of boys to contend with as well. He walked slowly up the path and pushed his way through the bushes as he had done earlier, and snuck through the kitchen to the laundry. Quickly, he took off his drenched clothes, gave his face and hands a quick wash and put on some clean clothes which he found in the laundry room, so as to avoid any questions he would likely get as he went through to his bedroom.

As he made his way to his bedroom there was a flash of lightning which lit up the whole house, promptly followed by a clash of thunder which made the windows tremble as if the glass was about to break. Instantly, the house was thrown into darkness. By then Rupert was two-steps away from his bedroom door, he rushed quickly into to the safety of his bed.

"You're back earlier than I thought," Blake voice came near Rupert.

"Oh you scared me, I can't see anything, where are you?" Another strike of lightning outlined Blake's figure. He was standing beside Rupert's bed.

"You could have come with me to find out,"

"No, I couldn't. Begnon can sense my presence, just as I can sense his, and then you wouldn't have been able to hide when you needed to,"

"How did you know I'd need to hide?" Rupert asked.

"Because otherwise you wouldn't be here now," Blake replied.

"Alan's been looking for you," Blake said.

Just then, there was a knock at the door. Rupert saw small, moving light coming from the bottom of the door. It was Alan pointing at the floor his torch.

Alan told Rupert that the storm had knocked the electricity out for the house and that it was going to take a while to be back again, so everyone had gone to bed already.

"Alan, before you go, I have something to ask," Rupert said.

"You don't sound too good, what happened?" Alan asked.

"I want to know about Vincent and how he could ever be Daltom's friend?"

"It's a long story," Replied Alan.

"I want to know... I need to know something about them," Rupert begged.

"I know what you mean but the best person to tell you all these things is Vincent, and as he's not here the second best choice will be Blake, and I'm sure he'll be delighted to enlighten you with his knowledge. After all, that's what you are here for aren't you," Alan pointed the torch at Blake.

"All right, all right, just let me warn you that I can't tell you about Vincent without telling you about Daltom," Blake said.

"I don't mind. I'm ready," he said.

The wind was driving the rain faster now, hitting the glass window hard. A loud cracking sound interrupted as if the heavens had been torn apart. The lightening lit up the entire sky and Rupert's bedroom making him jumped off his bed and into his closet. The darkness was back but he could get his way around with the dim light from Alan's torch. Rupert opened the drawer and patted his belongings until he felt the smooth and silky texture of a package in his hand, he pulled it out, took the cover off and a small tent pop open in the middle of the room. Rupert threw his pillow and quilt on the floor, within seconds Blake and Alan joined him placing the torch on the floor pointing up at the roof of the tent and gave Blake a sign to begin.

"Vincent was a child prodigy," Blake started, "his gift was nurtured at home and at school by his parents and teachers, and with his genius he was able to get to the root of his researches, but also, expelled from his first school.

"Expelled? What d'you mean," Rupert asked.

"Vincent got expelled from his first school after he destroyed the entire laboratory because an experiment he was working on went wrong," Blake laughed.

He was a young genius seeking answers to questions no-one had asked before. His brilliance and fast thinking made it difficult for other children to keep up with him so he was a lonely child. Vincent did not mind this solitude and continued thriving on his own, until one dark and gloomy afternoon on a lazy, rainy day, in fact, the only day Vincent had ever got ill as a child, when he welcomed a little boy into his life. This boy was the opposite of Vincent in all aspects, except one – he was as intelligent, but in a different way from Vincent. He had no sense of humour and was unpopular with the other kids at school. It was hard to imagine how these two could possibly get on so well, but they did – that boy was Daltom. He was frail, and always looked sick. He had fair hair that was always long and unkempt and covered half his face. Daltom's voice was grave, as if he was much older than he really was, so everyone at school teased and bullied him. The children called him all sorts of names. Vincent felt sorry for him and started to protect him like a brother. Together they shared almost everything.

They both graduated from school at the age of twelve and continued their higher education privately.

At school, Daltom's results showed that he excelled in dangerous and destructive ideas. Therefore, the school denied him the opportunity to join Vincent in the young scientist competition for the prestigious Royal Blue badge and instead made him take additional studies, while they tried to sort out his problem. Vincent went away, and Daltom had to stay.

The teachers didn't understand that Daltom was as gifted as Vincent. It was said that Daltom had spent the first years of his life in an orphanage. Then he'd been put in several different homes, but always returned to their school because his foster families couldn't handle him." Blake paused.

"So he doesn't have any family," Rupert asked.

"He was welcome back at school because of his intelligence, and someone secretly took responsibility for him at the school. Daltom never knew who this person was. But Vincent was convinced it was the Chinese librarian. Four years after, Vincent returned to the school. He went directly to Daltom's dormitory, knocked on the door but got no answer, so he opened the door and found Daltom hiding behind the curtains, lying on the floor shaking. Vincent helped him to his feet and took him to the school nurse."

"Vincent went back to Daltom's room to wait for him, and he saw there a book on how to become powerful, mastering the world of the dark forbidden arts. Putting the book down, Vincent saw letters on the desk. He grabbed one and saw it was from Zairis Urn Kru, also known as Zuk, the master of the dark forbidden powers, who was serving a life sentence in prison, guarded by hundreds of men, both inside and outside his prison. Zuk is also watched by our kind. Even we can't trust him.

When Daltom returned, Vincent questioned him about the book, but Daltom denied any responsibility. They spent time together for a couple of months, but after a while they began noticing the vast differences between them.

"At the age of seventeen, the news of their splitting up again was not taken well by Daltom. But ten years later Vincent asked Daltom to work with him again,"

"Vincent's research and discoveries were a total success, and he had become a wealthy man. Daltom couldn't control his jealousy this time. So one by one Daltom stole Vincent's ideas so that Vincent found himself competing against his own work.

When Vincent confronted Daltom and demanded an explanation, Daltom refused to discuss what he had done. Vincent decided to go to his laboratory to protect a decade of discoveries, but unfortunately, it was too late. The lab was empty. Daltom had destroyed everything, a whole lifetime of research, his best memories, and his future discoveries. Daltom's master plan was perfect. He succeeded because he knew Vincent better than anyone else.

Daltom had left a note on the only door still standing, it was hanging from only one hinge which kept on moving, catching the eye of Vincent straight away. Meet me in the Batie Woods, if you want to see your workers again. The note said.

Vincent arrived at the Batie Woods to rescue the scientists but it was too late, four of his employees were already dead. Daltom had prepared a trap for Vincent and in the middle of his frustration Vincent had fallen for it. He found himself in a net, which Daltom had set as a trap. Daltom kicked and hit Vincent until he thought he was dead, leaving him to rot inside the net."

"How did he manage to survive?" Rupert asked.

"Vincent had known that Daltom was after something too dangerous and so had learned how to protect himself from the dark forbidden power, by training himself to die for a short time.

Twenty-four hours later, Serena, miraculously came out to the woods and found him. He was as good as dead, but with Serena's help, Vincent slowly regained consciousness. Vincent's recovery was slow, and he was very weak for a long time. It was a real miracle. Vincent had escaped death for the first time."

"You couldn't help him at all? If you knew all this detail, is it because you were watching, or is this part of your imagination?" Alan asked.

"I was there all the time, watching every step he made, but it's like being behind a two-way mirror. I could see him, but he couldn't see or hear me. I wasn't allowed in his physical life unless he opened the path and invited me in, and when Daltom attacked him, I knew he wasn't dead because I was watching him – if he had died, I would have disappeared, never to come back to this world," Blake said.

"After Vincent's recovery he had a feeling that trouble was going to come his way, so he decided not to complete his work. Vincent and Serena disappeared so that Daltom would think he was dead and Vincent was able to continue his work in secret and without the threat of Daltom."

"When Daltom confessed to murdering my mother he also mentioned a Frozen Deal? What's the frozen deal?" Rupert asked.

"The Frozen Deal is a pact between Vincent and Daltom, it was made in the village of Engelberg the day you were born."

"The day I was born?"

"When Vincent and Serena were expecting you, the power of their emotions so close to your arrival made it easy for Begnon to find them. Serena was in bed for two days prior to giving birth – Daltom provoked Vincent to fight. Vincent didn't put up a fight, even though he had sworn to himself that the next time he saw Daltom, he would make him pay for everything. Daltom was naturally furious that Vincent was still alive and had every intention of finishing the job, but at that moment, the baby cried for the first time. His crying echoed in the whole village. Vincent had missed the actual birth of his son, so instead of taking revenge out on Daltom, he offered Daltom anything he wanted, just to make him leave. Daltom didn't hesitate to express his demand. Daltom's ambition to control humanity was finally going to be fulfilled and so, without hesitation, Daltom asked for the Masterpiece to put together The Eight-Pointed Star. Vincent was not expecting that. He had no choice. That was the only way of saving his child, so he agreed, asking for The Frozen Deal' as the only condition."

"How come I didn't know all these details? I was the one delivering Rupert into this world," Alan complained.

"It's all your own fault, you were the midwife, then you went for a walk in the village and stayed forever, an hour later, you came back to say you were leaving," Blake said. Alan did not seem happy.

"A midwife," Alan mouthed.

"What else happened?" Rupert asked.

"Well, Vincent asked Daltom to give him sixteen years as The Eight-Pointed Star has to be reassembled slowly and on specific dates. Vincent was thinking about you, as you were too young to be involved. The youngest you could be part of the project was twelve, but Vincent wanted you to be sixteen years old to be safe. Daltom knew that it was the most powerful discovery on Earth. He only agreed to twelve years, and on the exact day at the exact time he was going to come back for it. Vincent had no choice but to accept.

Daltom knew that the baby had arrived. Begnon managed to get into the house, so, to distract him, I came out to provoke him, but he almost destroyed me.

Meanwhile, your own Kuark was watching your moment of birth, which is our duty, and he will tell you full details with his version," Blake said.

"Oh, no," Alan cried.

"Are you alright? Did I say something wrong? You're looking pale," Blake asked.

"I'm fine. My head hurts, a bit, but that's all," Alan replied.

"Tell me, how have they found me?" Rupert asked.

"I was aware that the moment I came to you, Begnon would find me, and so he did,"

"So this is all your fault otherwise, they wouldn't have found me," argued Rupert.

"When a Frozen Deal is made a day is given to us for each year waiting, so I wasn't the only one able to find you, twelve days to your birthday – I came right on time," Blake said.

"No, you didn't, they found me before you did," contradicted Rupert.

"I was there when your little pink human came to annoy you, she was also part of the plan," Blake said.

"Okay you two, it's almost midnight – we'd better get some sleep," Alan said.

Chapter Eight

THE OTHER SIDE

Friday, 13th November

"Alan I'm ready, let's go," Rupert whispered outside Alan's door giving a big yawn. He covered his mouth with one hand, but could not stop his stomach from rumbling. Rupert had decided not to have breakfast as to avoid another encounter with his parents. He was still grounded, but he did not care about the fights, or about his school grades, or even Esteban Lambert.

With only five hours sleep, he was surprise he felt well rested. The idea that he would be able to get his Kuark had given him a sparkle in his eyes, it seemed like a wish had come true. A wish he had never wished for. Rupert loved the idea of having company at all times, someone unique which he had created himself and with whom he could talk to, whenever he wanted to and that he could make disappear anytime he wanted to be alone. He could not ask for more.

A firm knock on the door from Rupert eventually got Alan up on his feet and he poked his head out of the door.

"Rupert, what's going on? What's the hurry?" Alan asked.

"No hurry, just that I want to go to school now," There was a louder rumble from his stomach. Alan rolled his eyes.

"You're hiding from your parents, aren't you?" Alan said, "and, you're starving, your stomach sounds like a volcano."

Rupert thrust his hands deep in his pockets, then he turned his head slowly, he thought he might have seen something out of the corner of his eye.

"Let's go now I—" He turned his head sharply this time, someone was spying on him again, and it was hiding behind a plant in the hallway, he could clearly see the tip of someone's shoes, small, pink and shiny. There was only one person in the family who would wear those types of shoes.

"Stop spying on me, I hate you," Rupert shouted at Miana.

The leaves of the plant moved unnaturally, Rupert heard a loud scream followed by little steps scurry away. Miana ran back to the kitchen shouting for help. Rupert chased her. Miana made it to the entrance hall where his parents were just getting ready to go out. Rupert had no choice but to face them. He looked at them as Miana explained what had just happened. Rupert just stood there, waiting for whatever punishment was going to be dished out.

"Well," said Mrs Curdy, "I'd rather stop all this fighting and concentrate on the party. Miana can exaggerate sometimes. She's all right. What do you think, honey?"

Rupert thought he was hallucinating.

What on earth? He heard a voice inside his head.

"That's not fair, punish him, he scared me to death, and he chased me down the stairs, punish him, Mum, punish him now," Miana complained, but no one seemed to be paying any attention.

"There are five spare invitations, so I thought you might want to invite some of your school friends," Mrs Curdy asked Rupert.

"So, there are more invitations," Rupert said.

"Well, lucky you," Mrs Curdy looked at Rupert and gave him a stiffed smile, before turning to face the wall mirror and beaming at her own reflection. "Oh! You're going to have such fun. It'll be a day everyone will remember," she began to fiddle with her false eyelashes and made some strange faces in the mirror. Her voice sounded distorted.

"You're not grounded anymore, how about that," she said. Miana opened her mouth in disbelief.

"But mum…" Miana protested. Rupert was equally surprised with this turn of events.

"Thank you, Mu… Mum. By the way, I'll be back a bit late today, I'm taking part in a race after school, over the Other Side." Rupert had planned an entirely different speech, so he had to improvise. He looked at his father, but Mr Curdy would not look him in the eye.

"What? Am I invisible, grrr," Miana went to the kitchen, slamming the door behind her.

"The Other Side, Oh well – I don't have time to go there and cheer for you this time, I'm afraid," Mrs Curdy said, "next time perhaps."

Rupert left quickly. Cheering? He thought. His mother had never been to any of his activities and Rupert knew that she would never come close to it.

"We'd better go, Rupert – it's getting late for school," Alan said.

"Okay, I know that Mum's behaviour is weird, as in suspiciously weird – but I don't care. I'm missing school today,"

"What...Why? I don't understand why are you looking for more problems? Do you enjoy being in trouble?" Alan complained.

"'Trouble' is my middle name," Rupert said.

"I'm sure it is," Alan said.

"Where do you want to go?" Said Alan as they drove off in no particular direction. Morris drove out of town and into the closest village.

"Stop, look, I knew they were going to be here, those are the same boys I played with the other day, drop me off in the next street." Rupert felt an impulse as to run to them, but instead he wacked casually back and went over to the boys, leaving Alan under strict instructions to stay in the car. Alan disagreed and stood within a decent distant. Rupert wished he could be trusted as he was meeting boys his age, what could they possibly do he thought.

"Hi," said Rupert standing on the side of the pitch.

"D'you wanna play?" Asked one of the boys, rubbing his hands together and blowing air into them.

"Sure, I have the whole day" Replied Rupert enthusiastically.

"So do we, we have the whole day, every day, forever," said the youngest boy.

"You don't go to school?" Rupert asked.

"Are we gonna play or are we gonna talk, I don't wanna talk," said a boy Rupert remembered being called Justin from the previous time.

Rupert struggled to remember their names, but as they played, he was attentive to memorize them and by the end of the game, he knew them all.

"Elmer, where do you live?" Rupert asked. He guessed the boy was about the same age as him. He was the same height, but a bit slimmer. His light brown hair was down to his shoulders with a white, round patch of hair above his right ear. He brushed his hair to the side, but it kept on falling over his eyes.

"On the streets," Elmer replied.

The streets? Rupert said to himself.

Elmer's younger brother was called Marlow. He wore his hair in a ponytail. He had the same white hair patch but it was partly covered. He seemed quiet and would not look Rupert in the eye.

"How about you, Matias," Rupert asked.

"Same," Matias replied timidly. He looked younger than the others. He was a couple of inches shorter than Elmer and Marlow. Matias had black hair and dark twitching brown eyes. A pale scar, about five centimetres long under his right ear stood out on his skin. He had thick lips and a flat nose.

"He doesn't like to talk much, just leave him alone," said the youngest one called Fastor, before Rupert could ask Matias anything else. Fastor seemed to be younger and shorter than Matias but he looked heavier than the others as he was carrying a few extra kilos around his waist.

"And you are Justin – I heard your name being called a lot," Rupert said to the last boy to be questioned whom appeared unfriendly.

"That's right, I'm Justin and I don't like you," Justin pushed Rupert with both hands. Rupert landed on the floor and as Justin was about to kick him, Elmer got in the middle and stopped him.

Rupert stood up, cleaned his hands on his trousers and said nothing. He felt confuse, he thought he was being friendly but was not scare. The other boys stared at him motionless as if nothing happened. I guessed that's the way it is.

He could not understand how they could be friends. Each one seemed different from the other, perhaps that was good, he was also different, and like them, he did not feel that he belonged anywhere.

Rupert saw Alan pacing back and forth and finally he came and stood by his side.

Fastor started to run around like a mad goat, jumping on top of the public benches, his arms up in the air imitating an aeroplane.

Elmer came over to Rupert to say that they were leaving. He seemed nicer than the others, and clearly the leader of the group. Rupert liked him instantly and decided to invite them to the race on the other side. Elmer rejected the invitation, making excuses about the weather, whilst Matias begged him to participate. But Elmer pulled him aside and talked to him quietly. Rupert overheard the word police. He gazed at Alan, who seemed alert and had overheard the conversation too.

"Well, let's meet tomorrow then," suggested Rupert.

"Deal," replied Fastor, running off to the main street.

"Maybe you'd better go with him," Alan said pointing at the boy.

"He won't go far, he's too slow," said Elmer. The four other boys ran off, trying to catch Fastor, who was already weaving his way between the cars along the busy road.

Rupert had never had more fun in his life. He hoped that at least four of the boys were the ones he was looking for to complete the puzzle. That would be so easy, he thought.

"You're not thinking…" Alan said.

"I am," Rupert laughed.

"You still have more than a week to make the final call, they aren't only street kids, these kids are thieves," Alan said.

"No, they're not. I don't choose them, if they're the ones, then that's it," Rupert said.

"Well I guess you're right," replied Alan.

Rupert felt relief at the thought that his team might already be completed. The day was going a bit slow for Rupert he was looking forward to the race, although he was puzzled with the fact that he had never raced on a Friday before. That was the day the state schools raced, unfair. He thought, what a way to end the week.

"By the way," Alan said, "don't listen to any comments during the race. The kids from the Other Side are well known for losing their tempers easily."

"I'm not scared – I'm in,"

"Err, well," Alan cleared his throat.

"What," Rupert said.

"Nothing, I forgot what I was going to say," Rupert gazed at Alan.

A wide bridge connected the two parts of the city. Beneath the bridge flowed the river Rhone, as it exited Lac Leman. Each side of the bridge was referred as The Other Side. It is over this bridge that most races started and finished. Rupert had never raced here before. The beauty of the shores of Lac Leman is sufficient in itself to transform any activity into a fantasy one. The bridge has a pedestrian walkway on each side and a magnificent view over the Alps. It was a mysterious thing to Rupert, that by just crossing the bridge, people spoke of going to The Other Side, as though maybe one side was good and the other was evil. But there was no such thing as a good or evil side. It all depended on whether the person observing had good or evil thoughts.

Alan pulled out a pink vest for the race, and Rupert noticed that there was a daisy sticker beside the number. Rupert started to warm up as they got close to the meeting point.

A group of girls passed by, followed by a smaller group wearing the same vests, that's awkward, Rupert thought.

After ten minutes of jogging and passing the female competitors, some of them accompanied by their mums or grannies, Rupert needed to ask some questions to confirm his suspicions.

"Wait a minute. Where are the boys, is this a girls race? I shouldn't be here," he argued, "I'm going to be disqualified,"

"The race was originally meant to be only for girls, but they changed the rules and boys are now allowed," explained Alan.

"Except only you heard about it, so only I have turned up," Rupert nodded his head.

"I just wanted to distract you. I thought you've too many bad days in a row. Besides, I know how much you love sport, so enjoy." Alan said.

"Thanks," said Rupert sarcastically.

"Hello, Dominique," said Alan to a young girl as she ran by him.

"Hi, Mr Bodden," the girl replied.

"Mr Bodden?" Rupert said to himself.

Rupert knew that Alan was a martial arts teacher, and he loved helping out the schools. That was the best way for Alan to kill time until Rupert returned home from school. Alan had never spoken about it, and Rupert had never asked.

Close to the starting point they came across a narrow street hidden between two big buildings. Alan looked up as if he was looking for something. Rupert's eyes followed Alan's gaze. The houses had balconies and most of the people were waiting to watch the race. On one of the balconies a young girl sat staring at the road. She moved close to the balcony, her hands gripping onto the balcony bars to look down at the parade. She was on a wheelchair.

"Hi Marion, how are you doing?" Alan asked.

"Hi, Alan," replied the young girl. Her hair styled in two light brown plaits that hung down to her waist. She had big sapphire blue eyes and was wearing a black sweater, red scarf, beanie and thick winter gloves resting on the blanket draped over her legs. Rupert noticed that the girl did not call Alan by his surname like the other girls had. As he looked up he felt his legs suddenly felt weak, his heart beat faster and he lost balance but he did not understand why. He did not see the step ahead of him and tripped, falling to the ground. He got himself up slowly, keeping his head down.

"Oops! Sorry, let me introduce you, Rupert, this is Marion."

"Oh, hello Rupert, finally, I meet you," she said.

"Hello," Rupert smiled and looked inquisitively at Alan.

"I've heard a lot about you," Marion said.

"If what you heard came from him, please don't believe any of it," Rupert pointed at Alan. He experienced an unsettle feeling and thought about what Blake had said when meeting people who may be part of the puzzle. She cannot be part of it, he thought.

"We'd better keep going. See you later," Alan said.

"Later," Marion replied.

Rupert carried on jogging towards the start of the race, recovering fast from that embarrassing moment. Alan stayed on the side of the road. The starting point was crammed with girls. Rupert hated every minute of it. He looked at Alan to show him his frustration, but Alan was bouncing his body whilst listening to his headphones.

"Good evening, ladies and gentlemen, boys and girls. We are here once again today to race one more time. Today's charity beneficiary is the Joshua Home. The elderly people who live there want three bicycles for their gym, and we hope with your participation, they will have what they want. We hope not only to reach our old age but to be in good shape to ride those bicycles too. It's fantastic to be able to help them accomplish one more dream in their later years. Thank you to all of you and now let the race begin." A man's voice announced over the loudspeakers.

The starter pistol cracked in the air and the contestants set off across the bridge like a ray of different shades of pink and into the town. They wore floral patterns outfits with big bows on their hair. The girls were more talkative and louder than Rupert had anticipated. Rupert hated that he was the only boy.

Rupert noticed that two girls he had not seen before were getting awkwardly close to him and were running now beside him. He quickly looked from side to side and his mind could only register the contrast in the colour of their hair; one had fair red hair up to her shoulders and the other one thick dark brown hair. What on earth do you two want? He said mentally.

"Oh, Lesha, stay close, mummy's boy is going to let us win," said the red-haired girl with small eyes, wearing prescription goggles. She was stockily built. Her name was Gaelle and looked as if she was around twelve years old. Rupert saw when she pointed at him to her friend.

"This is a nightmare, this can't be real," he repeated to himself over and over again. He wished he could disappear.

"What did you say, oh, there's a boy?" her friend Lesha shouted, exaggeratedly pretending she had not seen Rupert. Lesha was tall, with big brown eyes and long unbelievably messy brown hair. She wore long blue leggings. Rupert looked at her and thought she was different, scary and loud, but different. She seemed athletic and perhaps a bit overconfident. He thought.

"Show us what you've got, boy. I bet your mummy will be cheering, and ready with an energy drink to make you go faaaster." Lesha shoulder barged him.

Rupert tried to ignore them, then, he felt someone running right behind him. He knew it was more than one person judging by the chat and giggles. He refused to look back.

"Don't do that, you'll get caught," said one of them.

"No I won't," replied the other one.

Rupert overheard the whispering and felt his feet tripping over someone else's feet, his body landed flat in a puddle of mud, and out of bounds for the race.

Rupert could not believe that someone had just done that to disqualified him from the race. Those sweet, female figures were actually monsters inside those shiny costumes. Monsters with angelic faces and silky hair, except for Lesha, who didn't have silky hair at all, he thought.

He was pulling himself together when Alan arrived.

"Oh my, what happened?" Alan asked.

"I just tripped over," he said.

"Well consider yourself disqualified?" said Alan, "You do know the rules, don't you? You weren't allowed to step out of the road line."

"My body was out but my feet were in," Rupert argued.

"I've been there before, trust me," said Alan, "Oh, hello Lesha, where is Gaelle?"

"Right behind you," said the red hair girl.

Rupert looked at the two girls but kept looking ahead. He knew that these were the girls who had tripped him up. He also heard snaps from a phone while he lay on the floor. He closed his eyes feeling small and mortified.

"Here this is…"

Rupert ignored Alan, trying to introduce him and stepped out of the race. The two girls overtook him and were now fifty meters ahead. Rupert kept his eye on them.

"There they are, lets get rid of them," said another girl running past Rupert with her two friends following her. They had jet-black hair, and wore gothic style clothes with black leather wristbands on both arms. Rupert lost sight of them for the moment but when he reached the corner, a group of people had gathered in a circle.

Rupert recognised the red hair lying on the floor and stopped to confirm his suspicions, he saw the girl's nose covered in blood, her arms grazed and her hair was full of mud. But his suspicions were wrong. The red-hair girl that was being helped was very similar to Gaelle, but it was not Gaelle.

"You've got the wrong girl," someone whispered behind Rupert.

Rupert turned his head. He saw the girls in gothic looked they were having an argument. Rupert suspected they were talking about

Gaelle. He looked again but there was no one there, they had disappeared into the crowd.

"Are you all right, for a moment I thought it was you who had fallen down?" Alan asked Gaelle.

"Hi, Alan," said Lesha, "it was Sonia and her gang, I saw them, they confused that poor girl with Gaelle." Said Lesha. Lesha's voice sounded husky and gentle to Rupert, unlike the way she had spoken to him a short while ago.

"Rupert, meet Gaelle and Lesha," Alan said.

"We've met," Rupert said sharply.

"Oh, is this Rupert? Oh, sorry about earlier, we were just joking," Gaelle said, while wiping her nose. Rupert gave her a long stare and then turned away. The girls giggled to each other, covered their mouths with their hands and went back to the race.

"How come everyone knows my name?" Rupert asked Alan.

"Well, I spend most of my time with you, so when you are not around all I have to talk about is you."

The race carried on with Rupert wishing to finish the race running outside the white line next to Alan.

"Who do you think will win the race?" Lesha asked Gaelle.

"Take a guess," replied Gaelle looking as if she had just pushed the fast button, speeding up to win the race one more time.

"Liar, you said you didn't care about winning today." Lesha complained.

"I can't help it, I love collecting trophies, Gaelle replied, she finished one metre ahead of everyone else.

"And today's winner is..." Silence took over as participants and spectators listened intently. "Number eight, Miss Gaelle, this is wonderful. Six races in a row this year– how do you feel, young lady?" Asked the man with the microphone, pointing it closer to Gaelle.

Rupert and Alan turned around to head back to the car park. It was becoming dark, and Rupert looked up as they passed the balconies, but there was no sign of Alan's friend, Marion. There were a lot of people still on the streets, parents looking for their girls, and girls screaming as they greeted each other because they had not seen each other for a few minutes. Rupert was quiet and started to enjoy overhearing the girls' chatter.

"I've got her this time," said one of the gothic girls passing Rupert.

A few blocks away a whistle blew in the distance.

"What was that?" Rupert asked.

"Rupert, try to keep up with me. One of my students is in trouble," Alan said.

"I'll be right behind you," Rupert said.

The two sped up while Alan kept on whistling to answer the call and followed in the right direction.

"The race is finished," someone shouted at them. Within seconds, Alan was on the same street as Lesha. Gaelle was lying on the floor beside her and seemed to be unconscious.

"She's dead, she's dead," Lesha cried.

"No, she isn't," Alan replied.

Alan picked up Gaelle and started to run while Rupert and Lesha ran behind him. Rupert had to keep up with Lesha. She ran like a hare, he thought.

Gaelle was taken immediately to the to the emergency ward of the nearest hospital. Rupert had never been in a hospital before or at least not that he could remember. He did not say anything he had only just met them in the worst way he could ever have imagined. Lesha cry unstoppably and would not reason with anyone.

"She's going to need a lot of rest, but she will be okay," the nurse said.

An hour later, a doctor came walking out slowly, with a look of little hope, Rupert saw Lesha holding her head with both hands, her red eyes were staring at the doctor approaching him down the corridor.

"Are you the relatives?" The doctor asked.

"Yes, Doctor, we are," Lesha replied immediately.

"It's strange, I have to say, she has bruises all over her body, but there are no broken bones. She's conscious but is in a deep sleep at the moment, unfortunately she must stay the night as a precaution but she will be allowed company. We haven't seen anything like this case before." The doctor explained.

"I'll stay with her?" Lesha said.

"I'll come tomorrow morning, Lesha. Everything's going to be ok – trust me," Alan said.

"Who could have done that, you must make a police report," Rupert said.

"We have to wait until Gaelle wakes up, Lesha is not going to tell us anything," said Alan.

"Why not, they were together, weren't they?"

"Lesha is different." Alan nodded his head. Rupert gave one step backwards.

"Oh don't you worry, she's not a monster or anything like that. She's just stubborn. She has problems with a girl called Sonia and every time they see each other, there is a fight. But now they've decided to pick on Gaelle."

"When you say fight, you mean pulling hair and staff like that, right?"

Alan laughed.

"Both Gaelle and Lesha are black belts," Alan said.

"Ha, funny," Rupert looked at Alan. "Are you serious, how can that be?" Rupert teased.

"I trained them," Alan said, "what, you thought I was joking?"

"Weren't you? They're as mean as can be…" Rupert stopped he didn't want to tell what they had done to him. Black belts… he wondered.

"They may look mean, and can say mean things sometimes, but they are good kids – don't judge them by their appearance,"

Rupert listened to Alan's words. Those two girls seemed to be closer to him than the rest. I wonder why?

154

Chapter Nine

GARDEN IN A BUBBLE

Saturday, 14th November

"Stop that!" Rupert shouted.

Blake jumped stopping instantly to face Rupert. His eyes wide open, holding his round belly with both hands standing completely still.

The sound of Blake padding on the floor as he paced from side to side on Rupert's bedroom put him on a bad mood. His constant fidgeting distracted Rupert in his attempt to read the book, which Mrs Curdy had left on his desk. He was staring absently at the pictures, making little progress in turning the pages. The book was titled The Hidden Wonders of Chillon Castle. Rupert guessed that somewhere, in his school calendar there was going to be a trip to this place, which is the reason why Mrs Curdy knew about it.

That's why she bought it, to see if I could excel in something at school. Rupert concluded. He slammed the book closed, put it on his bedside table and stood in front of his window. He needed to think and make decisions, feeling the pressure of a task given to someone with no skills and very little intelligence and that person was him.

"You have questions, don't you, and you don't know how to ask, because you think you're not allowed to think like that about your friends," said Blake standing behind Rupert.

"You're scary. I don't have friends. I only have...wait, how do you know. You can't get in my thoughts. I didn't give you permission to do that. That's trespassing," said Rupert staring at Blake eye to eye.

"I couldn't see your thoughts even if I wanted too, but your body language says it all. And you've been speaking to your Kuark. I can't help but listen," Blake said.

"The only Kuark I talk to, is you...but about that, I do have something to ask you,"

"Told you," Blake said.

Rupert had met too many people and they all seemed different. He could not make up his mind who was good and who was evil. He wanted Elmer and friends to be the goodies, but he knew that Justin

156

did not like him. Justin is dispensable I only needed four of them not five. And the girls, all of them are for sure evil, except the girl in the wheelchair, but what could she do? Nothing, he thought.

"When will I be able to bring my Kuark?" Rupert asked.

"It all depends on how much you and your Kuark want to be together, I'm sure he or she has appeared already in a dream, that's the easiest way, sometimes you humans talk to us every day," Blake said.

"He, it will be a he, I've had enough of girls, and I haven't talked to any imaginary friend, I always speak to myself," Rupert said.

"That's what you think, but you never talk to yourself, when you say something out loud you are responding to your Kuark. People believe that you are losing your mind, but you must be very clever to be able to capture the conversations of your Kuark,"

"I wonder what my Kuark will look like," Rupert said.

"That's up to you. You'll be able to give it any look you want," Blake said.

"Oh, I see," replied Rupert, checking Blake out.

"I know, I know – Vincent wasn't stylish enough when he brought me, even though I begged for a new look. He refused, with the excuse that I'm cute," Blake twirled around like a ballerina.

"That's a ballet dance." Rupert laughed, "You've been watching Miana practising her ballet dancing,"

"No, that's how I stretch," Blake replied, indignantly.

"Well, I'm going to see Alan, he's waiting for me, I'll see you later." Rupert left his room, walked down the hall, passing Miana's room and his parent's room and stood at the top of the stairs to listen to that soundless moment. He smiled as he tried to freeze the moment. He heard the common sounds coming from the housekeepers' quarters. It was a pleasant moment, something he had not noticed before.

"No, I'm not hungry," he said to himself, and stopped dead. "Wait, I'm talking to myself again or did I – am I answering to my Kuark? No, I wasn't, I'm having a mental conversation," Rupert continued down the stairs. "It's not my Kuark, oh why do I listen to Blake, he's giving me the wrong information," he said to himself. And as he was about to leave the house through the kitchen door, he almost crashed into a small cage, which contained a black rabbit that was eating a piece of carrot in the corner.

"Whose is this" Rupert asked. He bent down and peered into the cage.

"It's Miana's new pet," Clotilde replied.

"Why, what's wrong with Jeeves?" Rupert rushed to ask.

"Nothing, this is Miana's second pet," she replied, "Miana found it in the garden."

"Do you mean our garden?" Rupert asked.

"Yes, out there." Clotilde pointed out to the bottom of the front garden where the fountain was.

"You'll find more if you keep looking. Wild rabbits usually come in herds so there is bound to be more somewhere," Rupert said, just as Alan came into the kitchen.

"One's enough, besides this one's a female bunny and it looks as if she's pregnant," Clotilde said, "I'm going to take it to my room and use some shoeboxes and towels to create a perfect delivery room for Mrs Rabbit."

"Are you sure you want to keep it? He asked. Hoping that Clotilde would realise that she was putting herself in trouble by keeping an animal without asking his parents.

Clotilde nodded her head whilst cuddling the rabbit close to her face.

"I was about to come and get you," said Alan. I'm going to check on Gaelle before we meet your new friends, what d'you think?"

Rupert knew he did not want to see Lesha and Gaelle, but felt that he had to, as they were Alan's friends. Maybe he would be able to discover something, pretending he was fine with their behaviour from the day before.

"I was going to ask you about her. Do you think she's okay?" Rupert said.

"We'll have to find out, won't we?" Alan said.

The hospital was only fifteen minutes away, on a narrow road heading towards the Jura Mountains. The mountain chain looked like a protective wall keeping people under surveillance. The building appeared neat and clean, surrounded by open green areas. Next to a park with tall trees, and a well–trimmed, two-meter high hedge, perfectly pruned. Rupert entered the hospital's reception area and behind him came a man caring an injured boy in his arms. The sound of his crying made Rupert's hair stand on end. His only prior experiences had been with Miana, but he had never seen a child crying with a real reason. The nurse that assisted them the day before was on her way out. She looked at Rupert and came to see them and explained that Gaelle had recovered overnight, and her grandmother has just picked her up.

"Well that was easy," Rupert said.

"It wouldn't be that easy if I tell you that Gaelle lives in an orphanage and Lesha lives with her aunt. Someone is lying here, who could be pretending to be Gaelle's mum and why?" Alan said.

"Why didn't you say anything? Your friend just got kidnapped," Rupert said.

Who on earth would want to kidnap them, they would only scare the kidnappers away. Rupert thought.

"The nurse said they've only just left, so let's search this area."

"They can't have been kidnapped. There's no one to pay a ransom for them. Let's split up, but if you see anything, call me straight away please," Alan said.

Rupert went out through the back exit of the hospital, which led to a park area. He walked through a large corridor decorated with pot plants. On the right-hand side, a crowd of people had formed walking around aimlessly. Rupert followed the path connecting the street to the park and saw more people arriving. Too many people to be in a park at this time of the day, he thought. He noticed that everyone seemed to be busy, and were not paying any attention to him. It was as if they could not see him. He climbed onto a bench, and from there, he was able to spot Lesha's hair.

"There you are," he said.

Rupert thought of calling Alan, but he changed his mind. He knew that he would lose sight of Lesha if he did so. He walked slowly mingling with the people in the park. Lesha seemed to know where she was going. Lesha stopped for a moment to meet Gaelle. Rupert did not see where Gaelle came from, but she was not alone. A female figure wearing a long white gown joined them. Rupert could not see her face, as it was hidden under a large summer hat and big sunglasses. She looked like a bride in her white satin dress, with lots of sparkling bits all over it.

"They seem too friendly to say that they had been kidnapped and in no rush to escape, so I'd better go and get Alan." He said to himself.

The girls turned their heads from side to side as if they were hiding something or hiding from someone. Rupert ducked and waited a few seconds he knew they were up to something evil. His curiosity went up a level he was intrigued with the three figures. They walked in the direction of the nicely trimmed hedge together with the mysterious lady.

Rupert could not make the decision whether to go or to stay. Staying was more tempting than he could imagine. He watched the three female figures walk along a path he had not seen before. He hurried in the direction of the path and stood in the same place they had stopped before they entered, the path has disappeared and there was some glitter on the grass where the path had been.

"This is so weird, I knew there was a path here I can't wait to tell Alan." He mumbled. He managed to squeeze between the bushes bumping his head on what seemed to be a glass wall. He patted it, pushed it and knocked it, but the wall didn't move.

"What's this?" Rupert said taking a step back.

He could see the three blurry figures having a friendly conversation. Rupert could not hear a sound coming from the other side of the glass wall. He walked along the wall, sliding his hand on the glass until he was able to get a clearer view. He breathed on a spot and wiped it with the end of his sleeve. His view improved a little. Even though the mysterious lady had her back to him, Rupert was still able to follow the conversation. His only talent, which no one, not even

Alan knew about, was that he had taught himself how to lip-read. I knew it was going to come in handy one day, he thought. He held his face as close as he could to the wall right on the clean area he just prepared with his shirtsleeve. His nose slightly touching the cold glass with his hands cupped on each side of his face, he was able to see clearly now and focus on Gaelle and Lesha's lips.

The mysterious lady held each girl by their hands as they stood in front of a wooden bridge, which arched over a pond full of lily pads.

"We've got some news. We saw the boy yesterday, he is weak, perhaps he is ill," Lesha said.

I knew it they were spying on me.

He sidled along the glass wall until he was able to get a view of the mysterious lady's face.

"Close your eyes and keep on walking," she said as they stood in front of the bridge. Gaelle and Lesha held on to the curving handrails. They crossed the bridge slowly, and as they came to the other side, they quickly stopped.

"You can open your eyes now," The lady said. Rupert saw that the last step of the bridge was glowing – it was the entrance to an enormous garden covered by a gazebo that shimmered and sparkled as it caught the light.

Where has all this come from? Rupert could swear that, the gazebo had not been there a minute ago.

"Amazing, we've only crossed over a bridge, yet this is like another world, it feels like my swing," Lesha said.

"This reminds me that you promised to take me to see your swing," Gaelle said.

"We have no school on Wednesday, I'll take you then," said Lesha.

"Deal," said Gaelle.

"This is like a dream, a different sort of world," said Lesha.

"It's the same world, only in another dimension," said the lady. Rupert remembered Blake having said the same words.

Lesha and Gaelle walked slowly and stopped in front of four enormous arched windows. In the first window, Rupert could see the wonderful red and gold leaves dangling from the branches, some gliding their way down, others already scattered on the ground. The window next door seemed wrapped in sparkling cotton walls, with the evergreens standing tall and strong in the background. In the third window birds flew across the meadow, crispy green trees with branches dangling down and covered with fruits. Wild flowers moved playfully as the wind gently pushed them Rupert could almost smell them. The fourth and last window was glowing. A simple glance at it was enough to feel the heat and dryness of the place. There was not a spot with even the smallest shade to hide. The ball of fire in the sky was threatening to burn it all to ashes.

The longer Rupert watched the clearer his view became. The glass wall also seemed to become flexible, as if it would give way if he exerted any pressure against it, so he would be able to cross over to this surreal world. But no matter how hard he pushed the glass would not give way.

Resignedly he admitted to himself. They'll have to come out sooner or later, and I'll be waiting here.

The two girls stood in front of the arched windows. Gaelle was standing on top of the scattered yellow leaves trying to catch the leaves falling from the trees. Lesha passed in front of the next window and stood in front of the spring window.

The garden shone like a jewelled gallery encrusted with life. Light sparkled everywhere. Rupert surrendered, mesmerised by the dazzling view in front of him. He sat and rested on the ground to contemplate the beauty, which he could see, but not touch.

Rupert spotted an area of sparkling sand, which looked as if it was a bed full of tiny diamonds Gaelle rested on it and closed her eyes.

"What is this place?" Lesha asked. Rupert missed what Gaelle had said before she lay on the bed.

"My world inside a bubble," The lady said, "a fraction of my divine world, that's all I was granted after giving up my enchanted path. Here is where I can connect with my kind." The lady walked close to Gaelle turning her back to Rupert.

"She is a witch, but why does she wear white instead of black?" Rupert wondered.

"Can anyone visit?" Lesha asked. Rupert was finding it difficult to keep up with the conversations with only seeing one side at a time.

"Then, how is it that Gaelle and I can see it?" She said. Rupert began to crawl along the wall to get a better angle so he could see the lips of the mysterious lady.

"Because you– The lady turned around and Rupert missed the rest of her words.

"I can't wait to tell Gaelle when she wakes up," said Lesha. The lady started to turn again. She was explaining something.

"Gaelle shouldn't know yet that she is part of it," the lady said.

"Why not?" Lesha said.

"...Daltom," The lady had turned again, and when she turned back, Rupert only got the last word of her sentence.

The lady put her arm around Lesha's shoulder, and they both watched as the birds flew from one tree to another.

They are part of Daltom's team. She seems scary to me. Rupert thought.

"... You turn to Daltom's side, too." She said.

Oh I see, Gaelle is part of Daltom's, but Lesha is not there yet, Rupert thought.

A hedgehog brushed against Rupert, which made him jump. The hedgehog shuffled away but not before it pricked Rupert with its spikes, causing him to shout out loud. Rupert stopped himself quickly. The mysterious lady looked straight at him, she took a few steps in his direction and opened her arms.

The glass wall disappeared together with the three figures, and was replaced with a garden with common plants and trees.

"Rupert, where have you been – are you all right?" Alan came running.

"I'm fine, I just got pricked by a hedgehog, but it's all right now, but you won't believe what I just saw," he said.

"What did you see?" Alan asked.

"Over there, there's a glass… well, I saw an amazing garden full of gems and other shiny stones. Both Gaelle and Lesha were in there, talking to a woman…" Rupert listened to himself and slowed down, wishing he had never started a conversation he could not even believe himself.

Alan stood there listening intently while Rupert explained what he had just seen. He could guess by the look on Alan's face, that he was concerned. Alan looked over at the hedge. He pushed himself through the hedge and back again.

"I can't see anything," he said.

"How did you pass through?" Rupert asked.

Rupert followed him through, but the glass wall and the dazzling views from the garden had disappeared.

"Are you sure you didn't dream about this?" Alan asked.

"I swear I saw…" He stopped, then opened his mouth again to say something, but thought better of if. There was no way he could prove what he saw.

When Rupert arrived at the park to play football that afternoon, he thought he was too early as none of his new friends were there yet. He kicked the ball against the fence as he waited. Twenty minutes later, Elmer and Matias turned up walking slowly. Rupert passed the ball and Elmer held it under his foot.

"What's up?" Rupert asked. Matias looked down at his shoes, leaving Elmer to do the talking.

"Where are the others?" Rupert asked.

"We changed our plans. We're not playing anymore," Elmer said.

"Next time then," Alan said.

"Okay, no problem. Thanks for coming," Rupert pretended he did not care, then turned away and kicked the ball as hard as he could across the pitch.

"Hang on a minute, what happened?" Rupert turned back to Elmer and Matias.

"Well, Fastor was caught by the police yesterday. He was caught pick pocketing." Matias spoke fast before Elmer could stop him.

170

"Where is he now?" Rupert said.

"He's at the minors' detention office, but he'll soon be sent back to a hostel – and we'll be caught too if we get too close to him," Elmer said.

"Is there anything I can do to get him out?" Rupert asked.

"No, you're also a minor, besides you don't want to be involved with someone who has a detention record, and that's all of us," Elmer said.

"Alan can do it," Rupert said.

Rupert did not want to lose a potential member of his team and he knew that by helping one of them, they would help him when he asked them to be part of the puzzle.

"Fine, you'll have to show me where he is. I will drop you off at home first. I don't want you involved in this," said Alan.

"I'm already involved, so I'm coming with you," Rupert said.

Everyone jumped in the car. Morris' face showed his disapproval. Elmer and Matias were dirty and smelly. They drove for twenty minutes until they reached the minors' detention office.

"Over there, I can see Justin and Marlow," Elmer shouted.

"Can I get out here?" Pleaded Matias.

Matias was dropped off fifty metres before their final destination.

Rupert walked into the office, holding Blake with both hands. A tall officer in his late fifties came close to Alan, while Rupert waited in the corridor.

"Good afternoon Sir," Alan said.

"Officer, Pfister," The man showed Alan his name embroidered on the pocket of his khaki shirt, as he quickly scanned the corridor and stopped as he focused on Rupert.

"Who are you," he asked, "a new member of the gang? It'll take no time for you to look just like them, despite your fancy clothes."

After a short wait, Fastor was eventually brought into the office and left to stand beside Officer Pfister, who remained seated behind his desk, with a frown on his face and Elmer's letter in front of him. Fastor smiled at Rupert and then at Alan, and straight away he started to bounce up and down.

Once in the park, the boys divided themselves into two teams and played together again, this time, happier than before, as if they were celebrating Fastor's freedom. They played with complete disregard to the rules, cheating and pushing and pulling each other while laughing at themselves.

After they had settled down for a drink, Rupert gave each of them an invitation card to his birthday party.

"I don't like birthday parties, but this one looks as if it's going to be fun," said Rupert.

"Costumes?" Elmer shouted.

"We have no costumes, can we come disguised as homeless people," said Justin making them all laugh, "but aren't you too old for a costume party?"

"No worries. I'll help you guys with the costumes," said Rupert, "I just want you to come."

"I love parties," Fastor said.

"You've never been to a party in your life," Matias said.

"That's why," replied Fastor. Everyone laughed and threw their empty water bottles at him.

Rupert said goodbye to the boys, watching them as they vanished around the street corner.

"What are you thinking about?" Alan asked.

"I was wondering, when are we going to tell them about the puzzle?"

"You need to know a bit more about them, don't you think? We don't even know for sure that they're part of it."

"Officer Pfister will know all about them. We should ask him," Rupert said.

"That's good thinking, we'll do that right now," Alan said.

Morris took Rupert and Alan back to the Minors' detention office. They found Officer Pfister, just where they had left him. He looked surprised to see them.

"Something told me that you were going to come back. Are you looking for a job?" the officer directed his question to Alan.

"No, we're just curious about those boys," Alan said.

"Let me warn you," said the officer, "these five kids are difficult to control, the country of birth perhaps had an influence on them, their age, their difficulties I don't know – but it's something."

"Where are they from? I thought they were from here," Rupert said.

"They're from all over the world, but they have been raised here since they were only three and five in Little Heaven's orphanage, they've been together for quite a while, If you are trying to help them, I wish you good luck, you are going to need it.

"I'll see what I can do. Thank you for all this information," Alan said.

Rupert arrived home covered in dirt from playing football. He hoped to sneak into his room and clean himself before anyone saw him, but just as he was about to reach the safety of his room, he heard Miana shout.

"Eeeoouu…. what on earth happened to you?"

"I had the best time of my life, little sis," Rupert said proudly.

"And I will have the best time of my life too when Mummy sees you and tells you off," Miana said.

"Don't you worry about me, little sis. I'll have a shower and dress up in my best shirt, and guess what, Mum will be so proud of me, remember, I'm the birthday boy. Have you bought my birthday present yet?" Rupert teased.

"Yes, a pink hairbrush, because that's all you deserve," Miana said.

Rupert escaped to his room laughing, thinking that Miana was quite clever coming out with that answer. He realised that Miana could be annoying, but living at home without her would be pretty boring.

Chapter Ten

BLACK RABBITS

Sunday, 15th November

"See that? My best shot," shouted Rupert.

"Is that all you've got? Watch this," replied Elmer as he kicked the ball, lost his footing and fell backwards. Rupert saw in slow motion when Elmer landed in a puddle, splashing mud all over Rupert's clothes.

"Let's play catch," Matias said.

"Catch is for fools," Justin said.

"No way, catch is for fast runners – Let's see who's the fastest here," Elmer said, lying on the ground in the mud making mud angels.

"All right, all right, let's see who can catch me first," said Rupert as he started to run, but he had under estimated the depth of the mud he was standing in, so his feet got stuck and he was unable to get anywhere and in a matter of seconds, he was captured by his friends. Elmer and Fastor held Rupert's arms while Matias and Justin held his legs. Marlow was doing the countdown to drop Rupert in the biggest mud puddle Rupert had ever seen. They dragged him all through the ground. He was laughing so hard that he found it impossible to keep his mouth shut to avoid swallowing any mud.

Rupert had never been more thrilled, he could clearly hear his own laughter, and everyone else's. Then one by one, his friends started to disappear, like bubbles bursting in the air. Rupert laughed even more. They then appeared wearing smart, clean clothes, laughing and pointing at muddy Rupert. His world was perfect, and he just wanted to freeze that moment. He opened his eyes, looked around accepting with disappointment, it was only a dream, the best dream in his entire life.

Feet on the pillow, quilt on the floor, right arm dangling over the bed with the knuckles of his hand resting on the floor, Rupert had slept like a baby. He dragged his quilt back over him as he smiled, revelling in that lazy moment. He tried to force himself to fall asleep again and continue his dream, but all he could do was repeat all the images over and over while he lay awake. What a way to wake up, perfect for a nice quiet Sunday.

The housekeepers were getting ready for their Sunday off, each of them had their own activities and they were ready to go.

Rupert was lolling around in bed, enjoying the peace of his room when a sudden noise shook his whole body. His skin covered in goose bumps, his hair stood on end, his ears were buzzing and in pain. His heart was speeding up, reacting to the disturbing noise coming from outside. He got to his feet as he recognised the high-pitch scream.

"Catch it, catch it, that black rabbit is mine," Miana was hysterical, screaming at the top of her voice from her bedroom window.

Miana' shouts worked as well as any fire alarm in disturbing the peace and quiet of a Sunday Morning, Rupert thought. Only Clotilde and Rupert knew of Miana's new pet, but at that moment, the entire family, as well as the housekeepers and neighbours, were about to find out there was a rabbit in the Curdys' home, a wild one. The house helpers were running in different directions, trying to catch Miana's black rabbit.

"Over there – get it," one of the housekeepers called.

"Catch it – Catch it." She pointed at each direction she looked at confusing everyone willing to help. There was not, one, wild rabbit – there were hundreds of them, coming in and out from everywhere. Rupert saw Clotilde rushing inside the house.

"Good idea, hopefully she will calm down," Rupert said whilst putting on a tracksuit. He ran downstairs to help, but was in such a hurry that he went out in bare feet, so he had to run back upstairs to fetch his shoes. On his way out, he overheard Miana quarrelling with Clotilde. He stood still just outside Clotilde's room peering at Miana.

"I told you to keep it in the cage – I told you," Miana complained.

"I did, Miana, let me show you," Clotilde pointed to the cage in her room.

"What! They're disgusting – they're all naked. Where's their black, shiny fur? They look horrible," Miana said. Rupert covered his mouth and stayed quiet as he tried to resist laughing.

"Their mummy will lend them some of her fur until their own bunny fur starts to grow, which will only be in a few days, and then they'll be all beautiful and fluffy,"

"But I want them black and fluffy now, can one of them be pink?" she asked.

"No, it can't. You need to be patient, you'll be the only girl in this town with three black, fluffy bunnies to play with," Clotilde said.

"Fine, but I don't want to touch them until they're all fully dressed. They look all wrinkly. Why are their eyes closed? Lazy bunnies," she shouted.

Rupert covered his ears he had heard enough and went to help catching the rabbits. He heard scratches and a wimpy noise from the bottom of the door. He guessed it was Jeeves begging to join the fun. Rupert let him in. His back legs were running faster than his front ones, so he slipped a couple of times before he took control and started to bark while chasing them.

Eugene asked for the helpers' attention and told them to stop chasing rabbits and to enjoy their well deserve rest. He explained to them that the Animal Care was going to arrive soon.

They all seemed to agree with Eugene but no one left until the Animal Care arrived.

"Fine," said Eugene as he received a phone call from the Animal Care driver, confirming their van was already by the gate.

"Rabbit stew, Cajun roasted rabbit, *Coelho fricasseed*." Pascal was in the kitchen putting some rabbits in a sack, while naming some rabbit dishes he could cook. Rupert had never seen his house in such turmoil.

Rupert noticed that all the rabbits were the same size and colour – they were black with no lighter patches and no spots, all of them ran and stopped at the same time, their heads also moved in a synchronised way, like robots.

"Crikey, what's all that noise, it's Sunday, the neighbours will be calling the police anytime now." Mrs Curdy's voice sounded like a loud whisper. Her gaze did not focus on anyone in particular. Rupert noticed that she was not wearing her glasses, so she had not seen what was actually happening, but he also knew that she was going to be down any minute, and not only him, but everyone else would be told off.

The Animal Care van arrived. The sliding doors opened on each side and out jumped six men wearing white bunny suits, each with a net to try and catch the rabbits. Another van arrived shortly afterwards with small cages to take the captured rabbits away.

After several hours of collecting and packing, the house seemed to be free of all the rabbits. Mr and Mrs Curdy came to speak with the men from the Animal care.

"Where did all these rabbits come from?" asked Mrs Curdy, without even saying – hello.

"Bonjour, Madame. What a mysterious case, wild rabbits, dig burrows in fields and forests, but they're usually scared of people, so this type of case doesn't happen often. There're too many, and I'm afraid the rabbits may have been living in your garden for quite some time. I suspect there is more than one burrow here, as they usually live in large colonies." Said the man in charge of collecting the rabbits.

"Of course, there's more than one – anyone can see that. There are hundreds of them," Mrs Curdy snapped.

"Take as long as you need. But just make sure you find them all and make them disappear," Mr Curdy said.

"I'm afraid this may take a week or two," said the man.

"What! We can't move out just like that," Mrs Curdy growled, "you can take a couple of days, but no more than that."

"That's impossible Madame, we have to stop the spread of these animals immediately. In cases like this, it's essential that the house is clean thoroughly. I'm sorry to tell you that the family must move out for a while," the man added.

"Well, that's also impossible, we can't move just because some stupid rabbits invaded our house," Mrs Curdy said.

"I'm afraid you have no choice on this. This infestation also affects your neighbours and the rest of the village, so if you don't move by choice, you will be forced to do so," replied the man.

The man looked at his notes, wrote something on it, tore out the page and handed it to Mrs Curdy.

"You have four days to evacuate the premises," he said.

"You have no rights," she growled.

The man left, leaving Mrs Curdy mouth opened and with eyes of terror.

Rupert quickly calculated the day, they were moving out on Thursday, only two days to the party. Mum is going to make someone pay for this.

"Mummy, mummy," called Miana, entering the room, "you've got to see my three little wrinkly bunnies – They have no fur."

Rupert turned his head fast in the direction of Clotilde. He saw Clotilde close her eyes and her shoulders drop with resignation, waiting for Mrs Curdy to explode with anger and fire her from her job. Rupert felt Clotilde's pain and he knew that the other housekeepers were feeling the same. He also knew that Clotilde loved her job as to put up with Miana, there was no other explanation. He thought. But his mother was in charge and she always has the last word. Rupert sighed while he waited in agony to hear Clotilde's sentence.

"Which three bunnies? Who on earth brought these animals into the house?" Mrs Curdy's horror face gave a slow gaze at all the housekeepers to find the guilty one. No one looked her in the eye.

"Wanna see them? Wanna see them?" Miana insisted.

Mrs Curdy held Miana's hand and walked slowly in front of all the housekeepers, stopping in front of Clotilde.

"Show me where they are, honey," she asked Miana, as she stared at the nanny. Clotilde stood still, avoiding any eye contact.

"In Clotilde's bedroom, come, I'll show you." Miana looked at her mother's face and seemed to understand that perhaps it was not a good idea to have told her about the furless bunnies. She slowly let go of her hand, stood with her head down and started to cry.

"Mum, let me explain," said Rupert, "we found a rabbit yesterday it was wandering around looking for food. Clotilde helped us to catch it. I begged her to keep it, as I need one for an experiment on a science project. This morning she found out the rabbit had delivered babies overnight. Perhaps the other rabbits were looking for this one. Maybe we should move out."

"Honey, but your birthday is on Saturday," said Mrs Curdy as she turned to face Rupert.

"Well, I never told you before, but I always wanted to have my birthday party in a real castle, for instance the Chillon Castle, you know, the one all your friends talks about. Why don't we move there and have the party there as well?" Rupert could not believe what he was saying. He could not shut his mouth, but he seemed to have no control over it, his brain was condemning each word as he said it out loud. Rupert saw Alan cover his mouth with one hand and then he vanished behind the rest of the helpers. He heard the sound of a chair being dragged across the floor, followed by a heavy sigh. Rupert could only see his legs and the big mane of hair over them. Rupert guessed he must have said something terrible for Alan to behave like that.

Tears ran down the faces of the cleaning ladies as they stared at Rupert. Eugene stood taller with his chest out, Pascal dropped the sack of rabbits, but luckily it had been secured with a knot, while Morris dropped his jaw so that his mouth hung open with a steady gaze on Rupert. Miana did not seem to understand what was going on. She looked up and made as if to say something.

"Keep quiet Miana, please," Rupert begged silently. He saw Clotilde squeeze Miana's shoulders to stop her from ruining the moment. Miana rolled her eyes in confusion.

Un chateau! How exquisite," Mrs Curdy replied in her squeaky voice, looking up at the ceiling. Rupert immediately guessed that she had already started planning how to decorate the castle.

"Right, I have a lot of phone calls to make. There's no time to waste. I need to let all the guests know. These stupid rabbits aren't going to ruin my costume party, I mean, my son's birthday,"

"I'm not your son," Rupert bristled.

"Why are you all still here?" she said, "don't you all have Sunday off, go on, off you go and leave us in peace." The housekeepers did not hesitate and left instantly.

A feeling of relief ran through Rupert's body, he relaxed his shoulders, closed his eyes for an instant and gave a shy smile. He new he was going to pay dearly for what he had just said. He saw Mrs Curdy leaving the kitchen, her husband by her side and Miana sobbing behind them.

Alan kept his head down as Rupert strolled towards him.

Alan made a grunting noise as he lifted his giant frame from the chair. Rupert was waiting for Alan's complaint. There was no excuse. He had messed everything up.

"I have to say, I'm proud and impressed with the way your fast thinking helped Clotilde, but why the castle? We're just six days away from having to put the puzzle together, what on earth were you thinking?" Alan said.

"I have no idea. I couldn't control my words, they all came at once, and well, it is what it is, I guess. Oh dear, what a mess," Rupert said.

"It'll be hard work to clean it all up," Alan said.

"It's too late Mum has started the preparations already. I need to go for a run now," Rupert said.

"You should have run before, instead of speaking. A castle? Come on then," teased Alan.

"Excuse me master Rupert," Eugene called returning in a hurry.

Rupert turned around and saw Eugene holding a square package with both hands with a glow looking in his face.

"This is for you, an early birthday present from all of us, including him," Eugene looked at Alan. Eugene held a gift, wrapped in silver paper with a red ribbon. He stretched out his arms and handed it to Rupert. His feet rooted to the ground.

"No please, you shouldn't and it's not my birthday yet," Rupert said.

"We know, but it just felt right. Also, it won't be mixed with the hundreds of other presents coming your way." Rupert walked closer to Eugene, took the present and thanked him.

"Please give my thanks to everyone," Rupert spoke aloud, he knew that the rest of the housekeepers were behind the door listening.

"Well, are you going to open it?" Alan said.

Rupert tore the wrapping paper. His face beamed when he saw the images on the box.

"A drone? – Wow, six-axis gyroscope, radio system, built-in camera, 100m remote control distance. Great choice, thank you so much," Rupert hugged Eugene and went to his room. He left the drone on his bedside table and went back down again.

Alan left with the rest of the housekeepers but not before offering Rupert his company, Rupert declined the offer, wishing to be on his own. He saw everyone leaving and stood in front of the gates. He stared at the heavy iron gates moving slowly and before the two leafs completely closed together, a rabbit, which seemed to be hiding behind a pot plant, dashed out in between. Rupert looked around to make sure his parents could have seen what he saw. He rubbed his hands and blew air to warm them up, then pulled out his gloves from his tracksuit pockets and put them on. The sun, which was blocked by an enormous cloud, was fighting its way out. Rupert came close to the gate and saw that the rabbit, which had just escaped through the gates, was sitting only a few metres away.

"You're lost aren't you," he said. The rabbit jumped and disappeared into the bushes.

Rupert used the side gate and went for a run. He ran slowly while he was on the side of the road, for two hundred meters, then he sped up, listening to his own steps on the pavement. He was looking for the entrance to the walking trail, which he knew inside out. He kept on thinking about the black rabbits and the way they moved. An imaginary wall seemed to appear beside him as he ran. He shook his head, stopped and closed his eyes for a second. When he opened his eyes again, a black rabbit on the side of the road was staring at him.

"Can't find your friends little fella," he said. The rabbit hopped back into the bushes, stopped, looked at Rupert again and made a little hop, this time as if inviting Rupert to follow him. Rupert knew that, in the direction the rabbit went, there was no trail and it was difficult to walk with the amount of pieces of wood and sticks on the ground. I better go back, he thought.

He turned around to make his way back. The rabbit appeared again, hopping and waiting as if inviting him. Rupert decided to follow the rabbit, then another identical rabbit joined and the two directed him to an abandoned wine cellar.

This is someone's property, I must go, he heard chatting noises close by, then saw a group of people fleeing from the cellar covering their mouths with their hands. He stepped out with the intention of checking the place, but stopped in his tracks when he saw a small figure walking out of the cellar. Rupert stood behind a tree and within seconds, the stench of Begnon went up his nose. Rupert peered around the tree slowly and saw Begnon standing upright on two legs. Begnon was sharpening its long blade-like claws, which protruded from its paws, against a tree. For the first time, Rupert was able to see what Begnon really looked like in the daylight. Begnon seemed to be trying to hide from the sunlight. Its eyes were closed tight against the light, and its head turning from side to side, searching as if trying to catch the scent of something. He sniffed the air a few times and started to walk slowly in Rupert's direction. Rupert's legs were trembling he was unable to move. A rabbit quickly ran from the opposite direction and Begnon chased it. A hooded man walked out slowly from the cellar, holding a black rabbit by its ears and threw it into the bushes.

"The rabbits will force them to move out of the house, and the boy's dreams will take them to the castle," Daltom said.

"Ingenious," Begnon said.

"We're getting closer and closer to destroying the stupid father and son – but we're missing one person," Daltom said.

"How about Sonia," Begnon replied.

"Idiot! Sonia has no skills – not even to scare a chicken," said Daltom.

"I'll eat the chicken," Begnon said.

"This is serious," Daltom snapped, "we'll have one last meeting soon, I must convince the girl, she can do more damage than she could ever imagine."

Rupert saw them disappear into the distance, Begnon continuously sniffing the air. Daltom's words repeated in Rupert's ears, his suspicions were now confirmed. Gaelle is the girl Daltom's talking about. He thought.

"Well that explains where the rabbits came from and why we are having my birthday in a castle. None of it was an accident."

Chapter Eleven

THE NEW STUDENT

Monday, 16th November

Mondays were the least favourite day of the week for Rupert. It was a day to keep a low profile and made no decisions. For his first lesson he sat comfortably at his desk. The view from the window tempted him to let his mind drift off. But he wanted to stay focused. The images of the black rabbits, having his birthday party in a castle and the race with the girls kept teasing his mind. He no longer trusted these abstract thoughts, as he did not know whether they were his or whether Daltom had planted them in his sleep. His mind turned to thoughts of Mrs Stevens. After his latest discoveries, he knew that she was somehow involved with Daltom.

"Good morning class," Mrs Stevens, said and waited for the students replay, "today we're going to the Planetarium."

Rupert started his breathing was suspended for a split second.

What…Where did she come from… The… The Planetarium? He could feel his own facial expressions his eyes open as big as they could. He was going to be officially allowed to be out in space. His thoughts were out of control, he wanted to get up from his chair to do cartwheels with excitement and shout out loud, yes, yes, yes, but he knew he was only allowed to do it mentally. He stayed still controlling his emotions not to let them out in public and waited, because it was Monday, and this simply could not be true.

So much had been said about this amazing place but what amused him most was to hear that virtually all the research had been kept secret. Whether it was true or not, it sounded extremely cool and was on top of Rupert's impossible-to-do list. Trips to the Planetarium were unheard of even though the building was an annex to the school it was never open during school hours.

Mrs Stevens was holding an envelope and opened it in front of all the students.

"Before we go I'll let you know who will be representing the school in the Science Elite Exam this year," she said.

She looked at Rupert. He lowered his gaze, pretending to scribble in the note pad on his desk in order to avoid looking back at his teacher. He knew he would not be one of the chosen ones and her look was only to say – you're not one of them. After he had discovered his real exam marks in her office, Rupert knew that Mrs Stevens was going to mark him down again, he knew now that she would stop him from succeeding and it was all because of Daltom.

Mrs Stevens opened the envelope and read out the names.

"Adam Crozet, Martin Morel, Oskar Wurgler and … Rupert Curdy." Mrs Stevens paused before she called Rupert's name. She stared at her list, as if realizing she had made a mistake. Her lips moved, reading the names again to herself in silence.

It is Monday. It must be a mistake. The voice in Rupert's head spoke before he could digest the news. He could hear the hushed complaints of his classmates around him. Then a silence descended on the classroom. Rupert felt uncomfortable. He was as surprised as everyone else but even more surprising, was to hear a name he had never heard before and which no one seemed to notice.

"Rupert? It must be a mistake he shouldn't sit the Science Elite Exam," Esteban Lambert said, "I've got better grades than him on every single subject."

Esteban enjoyed pointing out his brilliance compared to Rupert. His uniform was always impeccable. His shoes shone brightly and his hair was highlighted by the liberal use of hair jell. A mole on his chin stood out on his face but not as much as his jealousy towards Rupert.

Rupert stayed very still, alert and focused, agreeing in silence with Esteban, unfortunately, there had been a mistake, a big one.

Mrs Stevens listened to Esteban, her eyes meeting each student. The students remained quiet, waiting for her reply. She said nothing. Instead, she walked towards her desk took a pile of papers and began handing them out to each of the students. It looked like an exam paper.

"To give everyone a chance, there'll be a test, right now," she explained as she handed out the papers, "If there is anyone else who can finish the test with more than ninety per cent, that person will take Master Curdy's place," she stared at Esteban Lambert.

"Excuse me," a student next to Rupert held his hand up. Mrs Stevens looked at him with her eyes and body waiting for what he had to say.

"There's no one called Oskar Wurgler in our class," said the student.

Everyone seemed to agree with him, while they looked from side to side looking for an unfamiliar face.

"I...I am Os kar, Oskar Wurgler," came a timid voice from the back of the class.

The students turned to look at the child seated in the furthest desk in the last row of the classroom.

Where did he come from? Rupert thought.

"Indeed, however, we have a new student in our class. He has been highly recommended to the school. Oskar is qualified to do the Science Elite Exam. I thought that Oskar had been introduced already. Oskar please accept my apologies and come forward," said the teacher.

Oskar stood up and kept his head down as he shuffled his way slowly to the front, he held his hands together and gently turned to face the class. A collective sigh came from the students as he raised his head and looked at them.

Rupert noticed that Oskar was looking directly at him. The boy had a long scar on the left of his face, which extended from his eyebrow down to the bottom of his jaw. His golden-brown eyes lacked any light. His eyebrows were pointing at his temples. His light brown hair was short and had been badly cut, his translucent skin, made him look ill. Oskar surprised Rupert by smiling at him. Rupert smiled back. The rest of the class stared on in stunned silence.

How can he be chosen to participate in the most important test for the school, if he has never been here before, Rupert thought.

Rupert felt sorry for Oskar when he overheard comments by the other students, some more nasty than others, but all unnecessary.

Mrs Stevens sent Oskar back to his seat and finished handing out the test paper. She gave everybody the sign to start. One by one, the four chosen students finished their tests and walked out of the classroom whilst the others were surprised by the school bell and were forced to hand in their unfinished tests.

Later that morning Rupert walked past the lavatories on his way back to his class, when he heard banging noises coming from inside. He rushed in to see what was happening and heard snivelling noises coming from one of the stalls inside the bathroom.

He walked close to the cubicle so he could pay close attention, then again he heard snivelling noises, this time muffled as if trying not to be heard.

"Hello, is everything okay over there?" Rupert asked.

There was no reply.

He noticed that the door was not locked and gave it a little push. The door opened a bit and from there he could see a student. He pushed the door aside and there was Oskar Wurgler, the new student. Rupert did not know what to say. Oskar was sitting on the toilet wearing a paper crown, his face was bruised and his shirt torn apart. Rupert helped him out and asked who had done this to him, but Oskar would not say anything.

Rupert slipped his arm under Oskar's and helped him to his feet. He could feel Oskar's ribs on his hand as he put his arm around his body to support him. His head only reached Rupert's shoulders.

Together they walked to the Nurses' Room, where Oskar was told to lie down whilst the nurse looked at his bruises. The nurse was interrogating Rupert about what had just happened. Oskar finally explained that he had been washing his hands, when three students had surprised him by pushing him into the toilet where they smashed his head against the seat. He began to sob lightly as he explained his ordeal to his audience. Rupert was not convinced by the story.

After the nurse had tidied up Oskar's injuries, Rupert and Oskar left the nurse's office together.

"Thank you for helping me," Oskar said with a wheezing, throaty voice. Rupert looked at the scar on Oskar's face. It was nasty, and it could be seen where the stiches had been made, as if with a thick needle. He imagined that it was from a car accident or something like that, but he would not dare to ask. That would not be polite, he thought.

"It's not true is it – no one hurt you? Why are you lying, you can get people in trouble, " Rupert said.

"You're clever, I like that," Oskar replied, "well it wasn't three students, it was only one, he wanted me to tell him who stole his dog, but I can only use my powers to see the whereabouts of people, not animals.

Powers? People, who are you? Rupert wondered.

"What do you mean, you have powers?" he asked.

"Not real powers, I can only see when someone has gone missing and the surroundings but nothing dangerous, don't worry," Oskar said.

"That's… that's really cool, would you do that for me…tell me where a person I lost is?" Rupert asked.

"Of course, of course, I can do that, but don't tell anyone else, this must be kept secret.

Oskar put his arm over Rupert's shoulder as he agreed to help him. Rupert felt confused but happy at the same time a complete stranger has given him hope to find out where his real mother is.

"So you only started today?" Asked Rupert.

"Well, I only started classes today, but I've actually been here for a week now," replied Oskar.

"How's that – I haven't seen you before," said Rupert.

"But I've seen you every day," said Oskar.

Oskar's words made a current ran down Rupert's spine, making his hair stand on end. He did not like to hear that he had been spied on, first in his house, then in his street and now at school.

"What d'you mean, you've seen me every day,"

"I saw you arriving, sneaking into the teachers' office, playing sports, and leaving with your big friend," Oskar explained.

"Why, why would you do that?"

"Because I like you," Oskar whispered in Rupert's ear.

Rupert's mind went blank. A horror movie was starting to play out in his head but Rupert shut it off. Not now, this is serious. He felt that his privacy had been invaded. Everyone seemed to know everything about him.

"Don't be scare, I only want to help you," said Oskar.

"Scared, why, why should I be scared?" Rupert swallowed. He was trying to hide his emotional turmoil. He was definitely not scared. He was petrified.

"Well, everyone seems scared of me," Oskar said, "but if you want to find your mother you have come and stay over at my house that way we can also study for the test?"

"Sure, that'll be fun, wait, how do you know is my mum I am looking for?"

"I don't, I just took a guess, see I'm sure I'll be able to help you out and remember, don't tell anyone about it, promise?"

"Promise,"

"Here, this is my address. I'm so grateful that you saved me. You're my best friend, thanks," Oskar said.

Oskar turned and walked off, leaving Rupert alone to contemplate what had just happened. Rupert dragged his body to his first Astronomy lesson in the Planetarium. He remembered thinking that if this day ever came he was going to be thrilled. His happiness was going to be contagious and the experience was going to stay in his mind forever. That day was today, except the good feelings had lasted only a few seconds, or at least until he learned that someone was spying on him at school, someone like Oskar Wurgler. Can he really find out where my mum is? I guessed there is only one way to find out, he thought. Rupert walked among the other students waiting to be called back, expecting all this to be a false alarm, then he found himself in front of an elevator he also did not know existed.

In two groups, the students went in the elevator up to the Planetarium. As they passed through the doors to the lecture theatre, the dimmed lights made Rupert feel as if he was in a cinema. Mrs Stevens closed the doors behind her and showed the students to their seats following the strip lighting on the stairs. After a few minutes of safety instructions from Mrs Stevens, the students were shown all sorts of stars and constellations. They were then invited to go to a private booth and choose a planet, a star or a galaxy to study individually. The students were told that they must use the headphones as everyone was meant to produce an individual report.

Rupert was absorbed by the dazzling images and seemed fascinated with all the splendour and enormity of the universe. The students were able to observe, moons, planets, stars and galaxies.

"Excuse me," Rupert raised his hand, "there are no headphones for my monitor."

"Oh yes, we are missing one, in that case, use this monitor Rupert," Mrs Stevens said.

Rupert walked slowly, *It has to be Monday, that's why nothing works.* The voice in his head reminded him.

"You can make your selection from the files on the right, you mustn't touch anything on the left." Mrs Stevens said.

On the left-hand side of the screen, there were files with numbers and star names. Rupert was familiar with some of the names but there were too many to read them all. He could not decide what he wanted to look at. He wanted to see it all, but he only had forty-five minutes, and had already wasted fifteen just playing with the equipment. His fingers kept on moving the cursor on the screen in front of him towards the left side, the area where Mrs Stevens had warned him not to go. The files on the right hand side were mainly planets and he was familiar with all the planets and minor planets already. A voice in the back of his mind kept on reminding him that there was a side he was not allowed to enter. How tempting. He squeezed both his hands into a fist to concentrate. His mind telling him he could not do it. The voice in his head called him a wuss. He could take it no longer and allowed the cursor to explore the forbidden side of the screen. He started to read the name of the files wondering what Mrs Stevens is hiding in them.

As he came across a file called EPS, he became intrigued. He stopped the cursor on the name and it read, Eight Pointed Star. His eyes widened as big as they could for the second time during that Monday. *Double click*, shouted the voice in his head. Rupert looked around to see if anyone was watching. He could not spot Mrs Stevens anywhere. He double-clicked on the file and in seconds he was absorbed by the magical world, which opened in front of him. A cosmic sound gave him a tingling sensation all over his body. He loved it.

A notification box popped up on the screen. Second and last view, make sure you will not be disturbed. Once the viewing is finished place the cursor at the end of the last word and the file will delete and will never be seen again.

"Are you serious?" Rupert said.

It's still Monday remember? Said the voice in his head.

Rupert shook his head and put his pen at the top of the keyboard. He was about to do something he was not supposed to, but it was Monday, after all. His nerves started to betray him. He jumped as he felt the gentle touch on his lap he guessed that his library card had fallen off. He left it there. Sweat began to build on his forehead, knowing that he could be watching something that potentially he would regret later. He explained to himself that up until now, he had done everything he was told, except for today, he was going to do the opposite. His hand trembled as he moved the cursor close to the file, then as if an exterior force had possessed him, he pressed Enter.

The narration began instantly with a slide of outer space images.

–The Celestial Masters of the Universe continue to watch Planet Earth with concern. They have become alarmed and desperate as they are losing all hope of saving our dying planet, unless something is done to repair the destruction which was caused billions of years ago and which they kept secret ... until now, and this is how it happened.

In the most magical days, at the dawn of time, a time when the Universe was still young and transforming itself. There were billions of cosmic explosions taking place throughout the Universe, all caused by space particles, the size of small planets ricocheting of one another. These blasts lit up the cosmos as if an enormous box of firecrackers had been set alight. But all this activity had come at a price, it was absorbing energy from the Universe without control, creating a void into which particles of matter were being drawn at impossible speeds; comets were being dragged into the void, with their tails stretching out across the heavens behind them.

The Celestial Masters knew that the Universe could not sustain this level of activity – That, it would be only a matter of time before the inevitable would happen. Unable to prevent it, they watched on helplessly as the fastest and youngest comet of all sped relentlessly towards the most luminous and most mystical star of all. The comet hurtled blindly into the star, fracturing it to its very core, bursting with a blinding explosion, spraying out shards of itself, as if they were shrapnel from a nuclear bomb.

The celebrations stopped instantly. The light of each celestial body dimmed, leaving an empty sensation in the Universe and a broken star, lost in space.

Nothing in the Universe has changed since then, the emptiness still exists, making every celestial body lonely, mourning the loss of the Star. Its luminosity would have been visible to the naked eye throughout the Universe. It was the one and only, The Eight Pointed Star.

The Eight-Pointed Star was the balancing element in the Universe. It was characterised by possessing good and evil energy in equal proportions, and by its ability to keep those two forms of energy in perfect harmony. After the collision, each point of the Star was split into pieces in the form of prisms. The pieces were attracted to the Earth, and had remained in its orbit for millions of years, so that their good and evil energy had been influencing all living creatures since.

With the arrival of humans, these two kinds of energy took a greater hold of the goings on, on Earth. Humans are capable of absorbing both good and evil energy in large quantities, allowing them to become incredibly powerful, however with some humans able to absorb more energy than others, it is the cause of the eternal conflict between good and evil that blights mankind's very existence.

Mankind is unaware of the phenomenon, which is causing the trouble, but they are familiar with the Star's name as the Eight-Pointed Star appears in many children's mythical stories all over the world. Unfortunately, in those stories the Star is seen as a force for evil.

The Celestial Masters of the Universe were desperate to fix this unfair situation on earth, but they knew that the Earth had already been compromised by the two competing forces and how they influence and encouraged its' living creatures to fight amongst each other. They concluded that the only solution was for the Star to be put together again, so that it could restore its natural harmony, except, this time, with only one type of energy. They realised that the Star would never be able to return to its celestial path and even worse, that it may never be a Star again, but it would become part of Earth: as a protector, if put together by good forces, or as a destroyer, if put together by evil.

The Celestial Masters of the Universe knew that they could not intervene directly, as once they came close to Earth, there would be no way back for them into their magical realm. Once on earth, they would become mortal, adopting a human body. They knew that they must help humans to find the eight points of the Star to become part of Earth, for better or for worse, in the inevitable celestial wars that would come to Earth in the future.

They knew that there was still a chance to save Earth. But it also required the most dangerous idea of all. To give mankind the smallest and least celestial help, a divine particle that would come to Earth and remain to help influence them from the beginning to the end of their lives. Only in that way, would it be possible for the Star to be reassembled. But what could they send, how small, how intelligent? There were many questions to be answered and decisions to be made and the final outcome was to send to Earth Mini Celestial Beings – The Kuarks and Murks.

Kuarks and Murks exist in a parallel dimension to mankind, carrying good and evil energy. Their task is to help mankind in their responsibility of reassembling the broken Star. Kuarks and Murks can be as powerful as they want, which is something of which they are totally unaware, and which the Celestial Masters of the Universe have decided to withhold from them.

Kuarks and Murks have been evolving in parallel with mankind for thousands of years in their own world. As the Celestial Masters of the Universe are unable to foresee which humans are good, and which are evil, they send a Kuark and a Murk to be with each human, when they are born. These Mini Celestial Beings compete against each other from the outset, with the victor becoming the Mini Celestial Being for that particular person for the rest of their life. There are no exceptions. Each human has a Kuark or Murk from the time they are born. To most of mankind, they exist only as a thought, a dream, an imaginary friend or a crazy idea, but there are a select few people who are gifted with extreme intelligence, who have been able to coax their Kuark or Murk into their world and manifest them as a physical being. In this form, together with

210

their 'master' they are able to become a team formidable enough to carry out this most important task of protecting the Earth.

But even with all this help, the Celestial Masters realised that is still not enough, as the Earth seemed to be heading fast towards destruction. Taking it upon itself, one of the Celestial Masters decided to sacrifice its' celestial realm to become mortal and to help humans put the Star back together again, although its identity remained a mystery.

The teams able of carrying out the task have finally been found. Although there is only one Masterpiece to reassemble the first point of the star and change the myths of the Star into history, this masterpiece is a celestial master descendant and his name is Rupert Star.

The cosmic sounds started again and the lights at the planetarium went on. Rupert quickly removed his headphones and turned to leave. He saw that the rest of the students were by the entrance so he ran off to join them. When he arrived he remembered that he did not put the cursor at the end of the last word as the instructions commanded to delete the file.

What a mess, the voice in his head said.

"I think I left my pen behind can I go and fetch it?" He asked Mrs Stevens.

"Make it quick," Mrs Stevens said.

"Here, you left your pen behind," Oskar said as he held the pen up in Rupert's face. Rupert stared at him, not knowing what to say.

"Thank you," he blustered.

"Oops, I think I also left my library card, I'll be back in a second," Rupert ran back to the monitor. The distance from the door to his cabin, this time seemed further than the first time. He stood in front of the monitor and his eyes widened one more time.

File Deleted Successfully was flashing in red on the screen. His hands reached his head instantly and he squeezed his eyes as if in pain.

He picked the library card up from the floor and walked back to join the class. Who had deleted the file? He asked himself.

Did Oskar read the EPS file? Rupert could not ask Oskar, he would put himself into the hands of this mysterious boy, and perhaps he may not know anything about it.

Probably the file deleted automatically, but probably not.

Rupert remembered he must trust his instincts and at the moment, his instincts were telling him to stay away from Oskar. But he is going to tell me where mum is.

Chapter Twelve

MASQUERADE

Tuesday, 17th November

A nice quiet day for Rupert, he did not see his family at breakfast, and nor had he seen Oskar for the whole day. Oskar had been on Rupert's mind since he had left the planetarium. He was having doubts about Oskar being able to tell him where to find his mother and was mortified, as he remembered accepting Oskar's invitation for a sleepover – he wished he had kept his mouth shut, as he seemed to only get himself into trouble every time he said something.

Rupert heard the school bell go off. School was finished for the day and a nice quiet evening was all he needed it. From the distance, he saw the family car. He walked slowly towards Alan as he came around the car.

"Why is everybody here?" He asked.

"I knew you would forget," replied Alan, "we have an appointment at Masquerade you'll be ok, don't worry."

Rupert's head turned fast to stare at Alan.

"But…"

"No, not buts, please stop thinking about your previous birthday parties, it's ruining you," Alan said.

"I'm not thinking about the parties. I'm thinking about the shop. It creeps me out.

"But you have never been there. I don't understand what's the big deal?"

Rupert did not need to physically be in Masquerade. To his misfortune, he had happened to be close by every time Mrs Curdy mentioned the shop name, which was more often than he expected. Each time more highly attentive since the day he picked up his school bag, and underneath he found a full head mask attached to a short hair wig, Rupert was scared to death as the head looked so real that the image kept on visiting him most nights in his dreams. Since then, Rupert had a clear image of what to expect if he was to ever visit Masquerade.

Rupert got into the car and remained silent. He knew that no part of their conversation was for discussion in front of his parents, and to make matters worse, Miana was squashed in between them pretending to be invisible. He wanted to tell Alan that he was certain that his street friends were the missing members of the puzzle and nothing was going to change his mind. But now he must wait to be alone with Alan, making the journey to Masquerade agonisingly long.

"Have you got a costume in mind?" Mrs Curdy asked.

"Nope," Rupert replied.

Mr Curdy stared at his wife. He fidgeted a bit. Rupert knew that he was trying to distract her to avoid a car fight.

The custom made costumes were only for the family members. Mrs Curdy had decided that the housekeepers should only be wearing the traditional witches' and vampires' costumes, so she could distinguish them easily from the rest of the guests.

Rupert knew that whatever costume his mother chose for him, would make him look ridiculous, so for him, it was a lose-lose situation. He decided that to avoid any more confrontations with his parents, he would not complain.

Rupert saw Mrs Curdy checking on her phone, he could hear the ring of the phone she was calling.

"Giuseppe, darling, did you manage to find the crown for Rupert?" she said.

After a few seconds of silence, he heard Mrs Curdy continue.

"In that case, order it now and make an express delivery. All the details should be taken care of ASAP – we're running out of time..."

"A crown?" Rupert did not wait for Mrs Curdy to finish her conversation.

"I'm not going to be disguised as a prince or a king with the party held in a castle. How ridiculous, everyone will tease me, no way, I'm not dressing as a king."

Mrs Curdy hung up and looked up at Rupert.

"But you will be the centre of attention of this party and each castle must have a king. It's your birthday, after all," explained Mrs Curdy.

"That's right. It's my birthday after all, and I should be the one choosing my own costume," Rupert said.

"Okay, you can choose," said Mrs Curdy.

Rupert saw Alan looking at him in shock.

I didn't mean that, Rupert's said mentally.

"We've arrived," shouted Miana.

A large green flashing sign with black writing over the front door, left little doubt as to the business carried on inside Masquerade. It was the only shop for party accessories, in Geneva Old Town, in a narrow, winding street. The street was well known for second-hand shops, amulets shops, and antique decorations – somewhere Mrs Curdy would never usually venture. At the entrance to the shop, a human statue stood completely still, impressing the family while Miana asked him repeatedly to move. The human statue seemed as if he was made out of stone. Rupert looked carefully and was able to notice his breathing patterns. A minute after the statue put himself into an alive-mode and went to mimic a pedestrian across the road. Rupert understood that his job was to try and entice people into the store.

"If anything, this person can only scare people away," Rupert said.

As soon as the Curdys walked inside the shop, an employee switched the open sign to display the closed side, one hour earlier than what the sing said.

The curtains were drawn down and the effect lighting went on. The employees started to parade bringing boxes, which seemed lightweight. Rupert felt every single hair on his body. It was as if he had entered his own mind whilst asleep. He knew that from now on his dreams were going to be full of details, so goodbye to the foggy, blurry stories, his eyes were scanning all the horrible costumes before his eyes. He has been here before, perhaps most nights in the middle of his nightmares.

The employees were coming in and out, looking up and down at him. Rupert guessed that they wanted to see who was responsible for all their hard work over the last two weeks. A few seconds later, the wooden floor started to creak with the sound of giant footsteps getting closer and closer. The Curdys gathered together to the beat of the creaking noise. Rupert saw Miana holding tight to her dad's leg. Rupert squeezed his eyes tight and shook his head. He hated the idea of adding a sound effect to his dreams.

A plump lady welcomed the family. She was wearing a black and red can-can dress that looked ridiculously uncomfortable. The black feather in her head kept on bending forward making everybody move their heads up and down following the rhythm of the feather. Mum seemed to be her most precious client. Rupert thought. The plump lady wore bright makeup making her face look happy at all times. Her whole body sparkled as if she had covered herself with magic dust. Her name was Ms Glitter.

"Mrs Curdy, welcome to Masquerade," she kissed Mrs Curdy on both sides of her face without touching her cheeks, "what a lovely family you have brought with you today – I must say your dress is divine."

Mrs Curdy wanted to be disguised as a Renaissance lady, as that had been her dream costume ever since she was a little girl. She had mentioned it many times.

"I can see you in it already. You'll look stunning. Let's begin the fitting," said Ms Glitter.

Rupert rolled his eyes.

Ms Glitter clapped her hands twice, and her employees moved around faster as if following strict commands, Ms Glitter walked slowly in front of each member of the family. She stared at Alan – looking him up and down.

"I have the perfect costume for you," she said, grabbing Alan's dreadlocks and rolling them in her fingers. Alan stood still.

"Meet the girl," Rupert teased.

"And I finally meet you," said the lady. Rupert froze.

Rupert saw hundreds of masks, feathers, wigs, hats, swords, all types of accessories and many lines of costumes all hanging in front of a wall of mirrors which made the shop look like a carnival inside a bottle. Rupert had never seen so many costumes in one room. It was a lot to take in. His imagination could never stand a chance in this outrageous place.

He finally relaxed and was wandering around with Alan, laughing at some of the silliest costumes. A potato chip, a giant bottle of ketchup, a standard lamp, and a punching bag were among some of the strangest.

"Well that's stupid – if you dress as a punching bag, guess what everyone is going to do," said Rupert.

He noticed a calendar on the wall just behind the counter. It was marked with a big circle in thick red ink for Saturday.

Not again, he thought and turned his head to the hats display. Alan had brought Blake along with him disguised as the Fooba ball. Rupert spanned the ball around on the tip of his fingers, tossing it to Rupert.

"Are you good at it?" asked an employee looking at the ball.

"I'm okay, I guess," said Rupert.

Rupert pointed at a rail of costumes protected in plastic bags.

"How about all those costumes over there? They look as if they're all ready to go,"

"They are indeed, all ready to go," said the employee.

"There are hundreds of them, surely they can't be for Halloween, that's long gone." Rupert said.

"You're right, all these costumes you see here ready to go are for your party. It's only a few days away, isn't it?" said the employee.

"Sorry, I don't get it," Rupert paused, "are you telling me that all these costumes are for people coming to my party?"

"Correct, you must be the most popular fellow these days. We've hired out more costumes for your castle party than for Halloween and all the fancy dress parties put together." The employee added one more costume to the rail and went to fetch more merchandise from the storeroom.

Rupert looked at him with terror in his eyes. He opened his mouth. He did not know what to say. The employee carried on stocking the rail with costumes, he sang, and whistled and Rupert stared with resignation.

"I can't believe all this is happening because of my birthday. It's as if I am the most famous person in the entire world – and the truth is that I don't even know who I am," Rupert said, "I'm sure that Mum has sent at least a thousand invitations,"

Alan sighed in agreement. Rupert started to slide his hand between the hangers, browsing through the nametags.

"I wonder who's coming. I bet I don't know anyone," said Rupert.

"You'll ruin the surprise," Alan said.

"The surprise has ruined me already, these people aren't coming because of me." He randomly grabbed a tag and read it out loud.

"Oskar Wulgler – What?"

"Wow, how does Mum know him? That's creepy, he's just arrived, so she's probably invited the whole school, but then why did she give me only five cards for my school friends? She knew I wasn't going to ask anyone. This is a total disaster," Rupert dropped Blake on the floor.

"Relax and stop making such a fuss. Look on the bright side. You won't be stared at because you'll be in a costume," said Alan.

"Why do you always carry that stupid orange ball everywhere?" asked Miana, who by now had dressed herself as a butterfly.

"Not now Miana, just keep on flying as high as you can," said Rupert.

There was nothing for Rupert to do in Masquerade, except, to wait for his turn to be fitted. Rupert kicked the ball gently against the wall several times. He heard voices coming from somewhere nearby. He stopped and looked around to see if anyone else had noticed. The voices were coming from the changing rooms. He could hear someone talking softly and then others arguing.

Rupert picked Blake up from the floor, and walked by a glass vitrine displaying horror masks, they look too realistic but not unfamiliar. He thought. He moved closer to the changing rooms and listened intently to the words coming from inside.

"That one's mine,"

"No, it's too big for you," someone else whispered back.

"There are people hiding in one of the changing rooms," Rupert whispered.

"But the door was closed behind us when we came in, it must be the staff, you're not scared are you? Blake said.

"Why should I, don't be silly," Rupert lied and went to check on Alan.

A few minutes after, Miana began to shout.

"Oh gosh, why did we come here, I hate everything in this place." Rupert mumbled guessing that Miana has discovered the horror mask inside the vitrine.

Miana was standing in front of the changing rooms screaming as if she was still in her house searching for the black rabbits. The shop staffs rushed to assist her and with the same shocked attitude they stood in front of the changing rooms.

"Stop shouting," came a voice from the changing rooms.

Rupert stud static as his mind experienced a moment of confusion as he recognised the voice of Justin. That can't be, he thought. Quickly, he covered his face with an American Indian mask. The rest of the staff ran towards the changing room capturing a group of kids, who had broken into the shop. Rupert stared across at the kids, surprised to see his friends looking for trouble. He elbowed Alan to alert him knowing that his Mum would disapprove of his choice of friends. Rupert was mortified thinking that he was going to be told off and humiliated in front of them and they were not going to team up with him to put the puzzle together.

"What should we do with them?" asked one of the employees.

"I can help you, Ms Glitter," whispered Alan, "I can take these boys out, and I promise you that they won't ever bother you again,"

Rupert over heard Alan's words.

"Oh, you're my hero," said Ms Glitter.

"Giuseppe, let the guard take care of them." Ms Glitter said.

Rupert saw when Alan put on the sheriff's mask and picked up a few sets of plastic handcuffs from a glass display cabinet. He handcuffed each of the boys and attached a rope to their arms, keeping them all together. Rupert snuck out of the shop and followed Alan. Elmer was begging not to be taken to the police. His pleas almost made Rupert reassure him, but Rupert waited until Alan had taken them to safety. A couple of blocks away Alan pushed them into a corner. Elmer put his hands in front protecting the rest.

"It's all my fault, please don't hurt them," he said.

Alan took off his sheriff's hat and mask. Rupert stayed hidden, he heard the sound of relief from Elmer and friends when they realised it was only Alan under the mask. Rupert nodded his head and smiled.

What on earth did they think they were doing, he said to himself.

Elmer ran to catch up with the other boys while Rupert stared at them disappearing down the narrow streets.

"Kids… I don't remember behaving like this myself. Man, they're a handful," Alan said, "It's cold, let's go back,"

"I'm coming, just a second," Rupert said.

Rupert stared at his friends as they walked together in the middle of the stone street, they seem happy laughing and moving in a silly way. I bet they are laughing about the silly punching bag. Rupert smiled from a distance.

"I wish I was with them," he said.

He turned around and found that Alan had left already, he made his move to leave, giving just one more look at his crazy new friends, but then he saw a familiar shape walking in the direction in which Elmer and his friends had gone. He called Alan softly, but Alan was too far away by now to hear him. He knew it was Begnon and decided to follow the creature keeping a lookout for Daltom. Rupert could see that Begnon was watching his friends and they have not noticed. The street took them to a small arched bridge. Rupert saw when they stopped in the middle of the bridge resting against its railing.

"What? Don't stop there, guys, come on, run." He wanted to scream but he sat there biting his fingernails whilst fearing for the safety of his friends. His view was not as clear now. The night was falling quickly at this time of the year. The boys seemed to be searching for something inside their rucksacks and then started to put a cloth on top. With difficulty Rupert managed to see that they were now each wearing a long hooded robe. They sat down, putting one hand on their faces, as if they could smell the stench from Begnon.

Rupert watched Begnon's creepy walk stopping at times to sniff the air as he continued to get closer and closer. He spotted a light from a small lamp moving towards the bridge.

Someone's walking by, that'll scare Begnon away. Run, please, run, we need you alive, run. He repeated over and over in silence but it was pointless. He began to sweat, as he feared he was about to be a witness to a horrific crime.

The man came close and stood, facing the boys. Begnon came slowly and stood behind the man, guarding the street. The boys sat very close to each other and neither Daltom nor Begnon attacked them, it seemed to Rupert as if they were having a friendly conversation.

"Wait a minute, what's going on here, this isn't an attack, surely not. It looks more like a meeting and not the first meeting." Rupert felt weak, his world had fallen away, his trembling hands, covered his mouth as his eyes watched in horror.

Rupert's memory started to display images from the other night when a group of boys had met Daltom and Begnon close to his house. The two scenes were almost identical. Rupert knew that his mind was not playing tricks on him this time.

Cautiously, he continued to spy on the boys while they talked to Daltom. They stayed for a few minutes but Rupert couldn't hear a word and they were too far away for Rupert to read their lips.

Few minutes later, Begnon had jumped into the bushes and Daltom went across the bridge, one of the boys run back in the direction of Rupert whilst the others waited for him. As he got closer Rupert recognised Elmer, he watched quietly as Elmer picked a bag from the floor and run to be reunited again with his friends.

"Thieves," he mumbled.

Rupert walked slowly back towards Masquerade. A devastated feeling invaded his heart. They betrayed me and I thought we were friends.

"Rupert, what took you so long, is freezing here, you look as if you just saw a ghost. Are you okay?" Alan asked.

"Worse than that, I saw Elmer and his friends meeting with Daltom and Begnon, They knew who I am all this time, they are members of his team." Rupert held his head with both hands. "I was convinced they were part of our team."

"I doubt they are, they don't look smart enough to be part of it, hurry, get inside. I'm going to check that we are not being spied on by Begnon."

Rupert stayed, pacing up and down there was no hope now in putting the puzzle together.

"You're next," said Ms Glitter.

"No, I'm fine, thank you," Rupert said.

"Your costume is fantastic Rupert, here, try it on," Mrs Curdy said.

Rupert looked at Ms Glitter and said nothing.

"He refuses to dress like a king," complained Mrs Curdy.

"No doubt he is a king, but he's not the king you might expect," Ms Glitter replied, holding pins in her lips and keeping an eye on Rupert.

"What kind of king do you think he is? A king is a king, isn't it?" Asked Mrs Curdy.

"Mum I'm here," Rupert said. Mrs Curdy continued as if she wanted Rupert to hear her conversation.

"That's right, but he is the king of kings, leave it to me – I have the perfect costume for him," Ms Glitter whispered.

"He doesn't know what he wants… Do you have a Venetian mask to match this dress?" Mrs Curdy asked.

"Of course, there is always a Venetian mask in Masquerade. I'll be right back." Ms Glitter left Mrs Curdy contemplating her costume in front of a wall mirror, and she approached Rupert again.

"You don't seem excited about your fabulous party. The look in your eyes tells me that there are other things you'd rather be doing – Come with me," said Ms Glitter with a soft voice, keeping eye contact with Rupert.

Rupert remembered Mrs Curdy saying that Ms Glitter used to work as a child psychologist and was an expert dealing with kids, especially the difficult ones. Rupert dropped his shoulders and followed Ms Glitter without complaint.

"Try this on, and let me know if it fits, and, most importantly, whether you like it. The costume won't fit if it doesn't like you either." Ms Glitter handed Rupert a dusty old box, leaving her fingerprints on the surface. She closed the door behind her. Rupert heard her loud steps vanish back into the shop.

Rupert thought about her last words, she thinks I'm a little child, then shook his head he did not understand what she had meant to say. Neither the dust nor the box bothered Rupert. However, the content inside was his biggest problem. He wished the box was empty. There was nothing he would hate more than to be in disguise.

Rupert put the box down on the seat in the corner of the changing room, wiped the dust away from his fingers, put his hands on his hips and with a heavy sigh he stepped backwards, away from the box.

"No way am I going to try on the costume inside this filthy box. Why do I have to keep doing things I don't like? Why doesn't Mum understand that I'm way too old for these types of parties?" he mumbled.

A few seconds later, the box shook. Rupert jumped. He turned his head fast he was not seeing things but he was not sure. The box shook again as if there was something alive inside it.

"Is that you Blake?" He asked.

There was no answer.

His mind had no explanation, or any idea, not even an image. It was blank. The box was closer to the door than he was and it kept on moving then it stopped for a moment. Rupert got closer to the door, his heart raced a bit, but his curiosity forced him to lift the lid carefully to have a peek inside and when he opened it, his eyes beamed, he blinked and rubbed them hard with his hands.

"It can't be. It just can't be," he said, "this is awesome,"

"How on earth did Ms Glitter know that I didn't want a costume, and yet, I would do anything to have this one," he said.

Rupert had read that an unknown person had once made the most mysterious costume. This person had dedicated all his life to creating a multi-character costume. Somehow, the costume seemed alive and could become anyone the wearer wished. No one ever saw the creator's real face, as he was always in disguise being someone different every day. The creator of the costume disappeared not long after he'd achieved his dream and no one ever found his body and the costume was never found. There were many theories about what had happened to him, but now, the story did not matter anymore. Rupert had that costume in his hands.

He tried the costume on, but nothing happened. He looked like a boy inside a featherless chicken oiled up and ready for the oven. He remembered that he had to think and see who he wanted to be. He looked into the mirror and thought of being Blake and then he became dressed like Blake.

"Incredible, this is perfect," he said silently.

"I want to see Rupert. Is he dressed like a king?" Miana asked Ms Glitter, who was waiting outside the changing room for Rupert.

"How is your flying going? You must be an expert by now," said Ms Glitter. Rupert could hear the conversation and was grateful for Ms Glitter to send Miana away.

"I'm the best, you wanna see me? I can do flips and circles," Miana said.

"Oh, I'd love to see you, just give me one minute. I'll be right there, shiny butterfly." Ms Glitter managed to send Miana away to let Rupert out.

Rupert came out the fitting room with a grin on his face. Ms Glitter seemed anxious to hear his comments.

"This is amazing. How did you get it?" he asked.

"I'll answer all your questions once the costume is returned," said Ms Glitter.

"Can I take it now?" he asked.

"I'll make sure that the costume is with you by Friday," she said.

"But—"

"Don't worry. No one will see it or know about it. It's our secret,"

"Thank you, Ms Glitter," Rupert said.

Rupert had found something he did not know he was looking for, the most mysterious costume for the most unwanted party. Being delivered to his house was the best way to hide it from his mother. Rupert wondered how Ms Glitter knew about it, it seems mysterious to him.

"Thank you for getting rid of the thieves," said Ms Glitter to Alan.

"It was harder than I thought," he said.

"Don't go away, I do still need some measurements for your costume, everyone has been taken care of, except for you," said Ms Glitter. Rupert laughed.

After a long time of costume fittings for Alan, the family finally left the shop. The journey back home was forever long and most unpleasant for Rupert. Everyone in the car was talking about the feathers, sequins and butterflies. Rupert closed his eyes and leaned backwards. His mind confused with a mixture of thoughts and bittersweet feelings as he kept on seeing the image of Elmer and friends meeting up with Daltom.

Back in his room, Rupert lied awake, thinking how quickly his life had changed. He was involved in a mission that seemed out of this world, new people, fake friends, and deadly enemies. He thought. The last few days had been intense and confusing, and his head was loaded with tasks he must deal with, but he didn't know how to start.

"Who am I?" he asked himself. He knew it was going to be difficult to fall asleep, but he did not want to close his eyes to find a mysterious figure disguised in one of the hundred costumes he saw at Masquerade. He realised that his life had become a real dream or perhaps his dreams had become real now that finally he visited the place where most of his nightmares were hosted.

Accepting his reality he took out his favourite board game from his bedside table, sat on the floor and played, resting his elbows on a pillow. He saw Blake lying by his side pretending to be sleep.

"What do you think you're doing?" he asked Blake.

"Keeping eye on you to make sure you do exactly what you're supposed to do," Blake replied.

"…and what is that, may I ask?"

Chapter Thirteen

SOLITAIRE

Wednesday, 18th November

Rupert had assembled the drone he was given by the house workers and had mastered flying it around his bedroom. Unfortunately its battery only last twelve minutes. He practised landing it whilst getting familiar with the controls. The camera mounted on the drone meant that he was able to see part of his room he had never seen before. He saw a large collection of paper planes covered in dust on top of the wardrobe. He had made one plane each time he had been put in time-out.

Dressed in his school uniform, he estimated he had another two more hours until sunrise. It was only five thirty in the morning. What is wrong with me? He asked himself.

Most children his age would have to be dragged out of their bed and told hundreds of times to get ready, but here he was, dressed up and ready, with two hours to spare, and nowhere to go. He held the drone with both hands, walked to the window and looked out to the garden. It was dark, quiet, and empty like his feelings at that moment. The image of Elmer and the other boys meeting Daltom appeared abruptly in his mind. Quickly he looked for a distraction and found the drone in his hands. He imagined it flying out of the window, but he knew that there was nothing out there he wanted to see.

"I wish I had had this drone the day I saw the girls meeting that mysterious looking lady," he said, then his mind brightened up with an idea. He remembered the conversation between Lesha and Gaelle. They were going to meet today. Knowing that the state schools did not have classes on Wednesdays and Lesha was going to show a swing to Gaelle. That's a trap, he thought, that's my only chance to spy on them.

Rupert crept out of his bedroom, tiptoed down the stairs and went trough the kitchen door, using the light on his phone, he found the key to the side-gate and out he went, carrying his school bag with only his drone inside it.

"A bit too early for school, isn't it?" Morris said in a low voice.

Rupert jumped. He closed his eyes tight, dropped his shoulders and turned around slowly to face Morris.

"I was only–."

"No – You don't have to explain to me anything, wherever it is you're going, you shouldn't go alone, it's still dark," Morris interrupted Rupert.

Morris stood in front of Rupert, waiting, with the car keys swinging on his index finger. It occurred to Rupert that he was not the only one rising so early and with nothing to do.

"I want to play with the drone you all gave me for my birthday, it's amazing. Also, school starts today at nine." Rupert said.

"As I said, I don't need to know, just tell me where you'd like to go and I'll take you there," Morris said.

"I…I am going to Lesha's house, d'you know her," Rupert said, "I'm not visiting her, I'm just…" Rupert felt stupid. He knew that he was only a child and visiting a young girl at that time of the day was not appropriate.

"I see, well, it's your lucky day, there's only one Lesha I know about, and I've taken Alan there a few times before. He likes running through those woods, and, by the way, that's on the other side – It's a long way to go just to use your new toy, don't you think?"

Rupert stared at him in silence.

"–But, I guess the views around there are spectacular, and the perfect place to fly your new drone, let's go."

"Thank you."

They both snuck outside and once they had passed the front gate Rupert Asked. "Why are you doing this Morris?"

Morris paused for a moment before replying.

"Because, I see you're a boy who begs for an adventure. When I was ten I had almost a hundred adventures, some dangerous, other very dangerous and most of them led by my old man – you're almost twelve now and you have none of that. I not only drive you know, I observe too."

"Thank you, for observing," said Rupert, thinking that Morris was risking his job, if anyone found out about it, but he was not going to remind him of that, he liked the idea of being adventurous.

Rupert took the drone out of his bag, and instantly his mind took off and flew with it, seeing the trees and the hiking trails, but he could not see what Lesha and Gaelle were doing, they were a mystery to him.

I will be able to see what those two are doing, meeting the witch maybe?

"Errr" Morris cleared his throat. "Are you excited about moving to the castle? I bet you are,"

"Well, officially we move into the castle on Friday. But as we must evacuate the house on Thursday we will stay at the guesthouse for a day. Mum doesn't want us in the Castle, unless all the decoration is finished and she has given the approval,"

"I see – It will be something you'll never forget, to celebrate your twelfth birthday in a medieval Castle – I must admit that I'm not keen on living there with all those stonewalls, long staircases, heavy noisy doors and mostly, probably, ghosts."

"You'll be all right Morris. It's only for a short time."

They drove into the village of Mont-Sur-Rolle where Lesha lives. The houses looked small on the slope hills with an astonishing look down onto the glacial waters of Lake Geneva. The wooded cliffs covered by an enormous green blanket of vineyards, which had been recently cropped. Rupert put his face on the window and spotted the walking trials signs. That's where I'll be hanging out today, he thought.

"Lesha's house is the smallest up that hill. The one with the green door and green shutters," Morris pointed at the house, "at the top of the hill there is a deep forest, don't go in there, you'll get lost, follow the narrow path down to the village, I'll be waiting at the village farm."

"I won't get lost don't worry, thanks again Morris." The sunrise slowly enhanced the sky and brightens up the path. Rupert looked at his watch and realised that he had less than an hour to spy on the girls.

He waited close to Lesha's house, hiding between the cropped vineyard until she came out, doing up the buttons of her coat, rushing as if she was late for something. Fifty metres down the road she met with Gaelle. Rupert had his drone ready and followed them. But he kept on losing the signal. He remembered that the drone only had one hundred metres of coverage and twelve minutes of battery so he walked faster now and then to maintain the reception on his screen.

"Are you really going to show me your amazing swing," said Gaelle.

"Of course I will, follow me," replied Lesha.

Rupert was using his earphones, needing to use both hands for the controls. His eyes were fixed on the screen, and he wasn't watching the ground.

"Did you hear that?" Asked Gaelle.

"I did, it was only the wind, don't be scared, this place is safe I'll show you. You check over there, and I'll check over here," said Lesha.

Rupert closed his eyes tight.

A second noise was heard, Rupert's drone has landed on top of some dry leaves, he made it take off again but he fell to the ground while catching it to hide it from the girls.

"Rupert!" both girls shouted.

"What are you doing here? Leave immediately," Lesha said.

"Why's that? You two know everything about me, don't you?"

"All we know is that you are a spoilt little boy sick of living a good life," said Gaelle, while Lesha stared at him.

"Leave – you're trouble," Lesha shouted.

"I saw you two talking to a weird lady in the park by the hospital, and she knew I was there. Is she with Daltom?" The two girls looked at each other in disbelief.

"We don't know who Daltom is, don't be stupid. You came here to provoke us, to get information, how silly. We're done with you, now go away, or else…"

"Or else what, are you going to use your martial art skills on me," Rupert challenged.

"We don't need it this will do," Lesha pushed Rupert but he did not stumble. Instead he bent over and put Lesha over his shoulder. Lesha kicked and punched. Rupert dropped her on a pile of grass whilst Gaelle stared in amazement with her hands covering her mouth.

"There, you talk too much," he said.

"Ahrr, I thought you were smarter than that," Lesha said getting up, dusting her hands off on her clothes and grabbing Gaelle from her arms to shake her out of her surprise. Gaelle seemed to have loose her voice, as Lesha dragged her away.

They jumped over into the woods by the playground and began following the path to Lesha's secret swing.

Rupert quickly set himself up with the drone and got it to start again.

"Quick, he won't be able to find us," Lesha said.

Rupert smirked to himself.

"There it is," said Lesha, pointing to a swing made out of an old car tyre, suspended from the branch of a willow tree in the middle of nowhere. Rupert could hardly see the surroundings. He lowered the drone, but there was no sign of a swing.

"This is it? Where is it," Gaelle asked.

Rupert climbed a tree and sat on a thick branch, his legs gripping the trunk.

"Stop just here – I'll be right back," Lesha said.

"I hope you're not playing a trick on me, I'm scared, this is a bit too high and there's nothing down there," complained Gaelle but Lesha was long gone.

"Hellooo," Lesha went Whoosh!

"How did you get in, I want to try," shouted Gaelle.

After a few minutes, Lesha came back, out of breath and with her hair twice its usual volume. What on earth happened to her? Rupert laughed.

"Do you want to try it?" offered Lesha, looking around, as if she could see something. Rupert moved the drone so that it was facing the direction of Lesha's gaze but saw nothing.

"Nope, perhaps some other time," replied Gaelle. Lesha looked again. She rubbed her hands on her arms.

"Let's go now. I don't like this place," said Gaelle.

Rupert could see Lesha and Gaelle walking towards him, when suddenly he lost the reception of his drone, he moved the control buttons, but the image did not come back. It can't be the battery I only used it for five minutes. He saw the two girls passing close to him and held his breath. Once they were gone, he went to fetch his drone but all he found were its pieces scattered on the ground. He spotted a black wire protruding under a rock. He lifted the rock to uncover the little engine of his drone smashed into very small pieces. He was puzzled as the drone was found in the opposite direction of Lesha and Gaelle. He suspected that someone else was watching them.

Fresh shoe marks were visible in a muddy area. I knew it, but who could this be? He wondered. The shoe prints were heading in the direction of the swing. The sun had lit the top of the trees showing different shades of green on each side of his path. Rupert could see to his right, the way back to the village, and to his left, the footmarks showing him the way to the deep forest. He remembered Morris' words – you will get lost. But Morris had said something else – an adventure. He felt an impulse to follow the footprints leading into the deep forest. It's probably nothing, he thought.

Grunting noises coming from close by got Rupert's immediate attention. He rushed to where they were coming from and stopped dead when he saw a girl cutting the rope holding Lesha's swing in pieces with a big sharp knife. The rope was still attached to the branch on the ground. The girl took the tyre with her and walked quickly towards the village. Rupert vaguely remembered the girl. He knew he had seen her before but could not remember where.

Rupert waited until he was sure the girl had gone and went off to meet Morris. When he arrived at the village farm he spot a group of people gathered in a circle. He wondered what was happening and he came to see with his own eyes, as he got closer he spotted Lesha and Gaelle in the centre of the group.

"It can't be. I know where my tyre is – even Gaelle saw it. You might need glasses soon, sir," Lesha joked.

"You're the only Lesha around here, and I remember seeing you paint your name all over it, consider yourself very lucky the rope has been cut almost through by someone, you could have swing to death next time," said the man. Rupert imagined he was the owner of the farm.

"It can't be! Rupert was the last person we talked to," Lesha shouted, looking very upset. She ran away from the crowd with Gaelle following her closely.

What, what do I have to do with all this? Rupert thought.

Rupert walked fast through the group of people. No one there knew him except for Lesha and Gaelle and he did not want to be accused of something he had not done. A few steps from the car, Rupert turned sharply as he caught something out of the corner of his eye. It was the girl he had seen a few minutes ago cutting the ropes of Lesha's swing with a knife. The girl was wheeling herself in a wheelchair. It can't be, Rupert realised that he had seen more than he expected, and all without the help of his drone. He got in the car and let Morris take him to school.

After an uneventful day at school Rupert met Alan outside school as usual.

"So, how was your day, you left in a hurry this morning," Alan said.

"Yes, I didn't want to disturb you," Rupert replied.

"You never disturb me, although I did manage to sleep in – which reminds me, is this the address for the sleepover you have today?" Alan showed Rupert the paper with the address he had given him the day before.

Rupert closed his eyes and dropped his head backwards. The image of Oskar in his mind was as clear as if he was looking at a photograph. He said he could tell me where my mother is, but why it doesn't feel right. I sure made a mistake by accepting his invitation. A big sighed came out of him, he rested his head back on the car seat and closed his eyes. After fifteen minutes on the road the car slowed down and the ride started to feel a bit bumpy. Rupert opened his eyes to find himself in a place he had never been to before. After passing a small neighbourhood, the car came to a full stop outside an abandoned looking house.

"Is this his place? It looks a bit lonely," Alan said.

"It's fine – there he is, by the door," Rupert said.

Oskar was standing by the entrance door, a small rusted wrought iron gate was squeaking with the wind. Rupert saw when Alan put his hands on his ears. He remembered that the sound of the metal latches were painful to Alan's ears.

"Is it that bad?" Rupert asked.

"You've no idea," said Alan, "here, Blake may come in handy if you get bored with your studying – you and your new friend can go outside and kick Blake around, I'll be giving some lessons this evening." Alan joked.

"I wish, but he doesn't strike me as a sport person. I wonder who you will be training," said Rupert in a sarcastic way, referring to Lesha and Gaelle. Alan grinned and left.

Rupert legs were trembling as he walked towards the house, the over grown plants and abandoned look of the entrance gave him a rough idea of what to expect inside. He looked back and saw the tail of the car disappearing. He remembered he did not have his phone. Oskar waited for him at the entrance. He looked scarier than Rupert had remembered. The house was quiet, and no one else came to greet him. It felt like a Halloween evening. Soon Rupert realised that Oskar was on his own. He had never been home alone – his only reassurance was having Blake with him.

"Where are your parents?" Rupert asked.

"They'll come soon," replied Oskar.

Oskar's house was a small chalet with dark brown beams, a high ceiling and pointed roof. The window shutters were closed-tight. The amount of dust collected on the window frame showed him that these windows stayed closed day and night. Rupert could feel the stuffiness in the air. The lighting was less than ideal. Rupert pressed a switch on the wall, but nothing happened.

"Don't waste your time. Nothing works here. If you need a light, we have a lamp over there," Oskar pointed to a corner in the living room. "The other one is in my bedroom. That's all we need."

A strong toxic smell was coming from the kitchen. Oskar went to check it out.

"Is everything all right?" Rupert asked.

"It's fine," Oskar replied without any fuss.

Oskar's bedroom was the attic converted into a room. It had a bed, and an old mattress on the floor. Rupert guessed the mattress was for him. Lots of books were scattered around the floor.

"Well, are you going to tell me where mi mother is?" Rupert asked.

"It doesn't happen like magic, I must go to sleep and in a dream my questions will be answer," Oskar replied.

"What? I thought, you…"

"Don't worry, I'll tell you where to find your mother."

They sat on the floor mattress and started to study for Friday's test. The hours went quickly and before they knew it, it was ten o'clock. Oskar surprised Rupert with his knowledge. Rupert was tired but felt completely awake.

Rupert examined the room and under a big pile of books, he spotted a wooden box with its lid wide open. Inside the box was Rupert's favourite board game, Solitaire.

"Oh, you play Solitaire? I have a set just like yours. It's my favourite board game," said Rupert, pulling the box out from under the pile of dusty old books.

This board had the exact same carving design around its edges as Rupert's, the same colour wood, and the marbles were crystals with numbers and writing inscribed on them. Just like the one he has. The words were so small that anybody wishing to read them would need to use a powerful magnifying glass.

"If that's your favourite board game, you must spend a lot of time alone, like me," said Oskar.

"Where did you get it? I haven't seen another one like mine. You can't buy it in the shops." Rupert said.

"How do you know that?" asked Oskar.

"I was told that only a few copies were ever made," said Rupert.

"This one isn't mine. It belongs to... it belongs to my parents," said Oskar.

Rupert knew that Oskar was hiding something. His whole body could feel it, his head itch, his skin kept on tingling and he felt a bit uncomfortable at the conditions in which Oskar lived.

"Do you mind if I open a window?" asked Rupert.

"Sure, no problem. I'll be on the sofa for a while. You get some sleep. I'm used to staying up till late," said Oskar.

Rupert looked at his watch again.

"It's almost midnight and your parents aren't back," he said.

"They'll be here anytime now. You aren't scared are you?" Oskar asked.

"Course not, goodnight," Rupert lied.

"Goodnight," Replied Oskar and went out of the room.

Rupert was more scared than he could ever imagine, but it felt better lying about not being afraid than admitting his fears to Oskar.

Somehow he felt as if he knew Oskar, there was something in the way he looked at Rupert, which made him feel guilty even though he had only known him for a few days.

"Rupert, Rupert," Blake whispered.

"What is it, Blake? Are you okay?" Rupert noticed that Blake's eyes were bigger and brighter than the day he had first seen him up on his ceiling light. The moonlight coming through the window enhanced the brilliance of them.

"We must escape from here. There are no parents. This is Daltom's house. We can jump out of the window and get away before Daltom returns," whispered Blake.

"What...this can't be – what makes you think that, we're trapped," Rupert felt ill, his hands held his head, the walls were turning around he could not believe what he had just heard.

"Are you sure this is Daltom's place, can you sense Begnon?" he asked.

"No, but it doesn't feel right," Blake was trembling.

"Oh no how did I let him fool me, we must pretend we're going to sleep,"

"Bad idea, you will be dead by dawn, and me, I'll be eaten," Blake complained.

Rupert walked to the small lamp, took the bulb out and broke it. He hid behind a wide beam sitting on the floor, his chin resting on his knees. What can I do, what can I do. His mind went blank, the voice in his head disappeared, and the sound of silence shouting in his ears, there is not place you can hide today.

Two hours later, Rupert heard a loud bang from someone entering the house and slamming the door closed behind, followed by a loud clattering noise as some keys were dropped onto a glass table.

"My plan has worked, I've got that boy you want. He's trapped upstairs in my room. See, I'm better than that foul beast of yours – where is it, sleeping as usual?" Oskar said, out loud as if he wanted Rupert to hear him.

"Begnon doesn't sleep, he's always working for me, are you sick of living?" said Daltom, "come on then…show me what you've got." Demanded Daltom.

"It was easier than I thought, I made him believe I've been hurt, and he came to rescue me, are you sure he is the one, he looks inept?" Oskar said.

Blake quickly took the chain that he wore around his neck and slipped it over both Rupert and himself and then put the triangle frame inside his mouth. Instantly, they were invisible.

"This chain will keep us hidden from Daltom and the boy, but Begnon will be able to sense me," Blake whispered.

"What are we going to do now? How can we get help?" Rupert asked.

"Maybe you can use telepathy like Vincent and Serena. Alan has been learning, so he may be able to receive your call," Blake whispered.

"But I don't know how," Rupert said.

"Think, concentrate and speak with your mind to the person you want help from, whilst you see them in your mind." Blake said.

"I can't. Why can't you use yours?" Rupert asked.

"Because the first one to sense me will be Begnon."

"But he's not here." Rupert Whispered.

"He will be here any minute, and if I use any of my powers, he will see us immediately. This chain will keep us hidden, but not for long. I only have two minutes left," Blake explained.

"We're dead... if only I knew how to use telepathy." Rupert was doing his best to concentrate and to call for help, but it occurred to him that even if he could communicate with Alan, it would still be useless as it would be too late for Alan to arrive in time. Then, Rupert heard a word in his mind, *Solitaire* but he did not recognise the voice.

Rupert turned to Blake who was looking at him as if it was the first time he had really seen him.

"I heard that too," Blake said, "but don't even think about it. You must not play with that Solitaire board."

"I know what to do, let's get closer to it" Rupert whispered.

"You don't know how to use it, let's just hide. There're only three days to your big day. That board is dangerous, and you don't know what could happen if you use it incorrectly," Blake said.

"Don't worry. I've read all the marbles. I know how to do it," Rupert said.

"No, you haven't, one of the marbles on your board is fake, so you don't know everything about it," Blake said.

"I figured that out, but this board is complete, I'll be fine." Rupert said.

Rupert took the Solitaire board and rearranged the marbles carefully. After a few seconds, they found themselves in front of a transparent bubble.

Rupert had opened a portal to another dimension, the imaginary world where all Kuarks and Murks waited until their human host was able to bring them into this world.

"Come on – let's get inside," Rupert pushed Blake into the bubble.

Rupert could not see a thing inside the bubble. A bright object started to move in their direction. It stopped a few meters away. To Rupert, it looked like a small group of fireflies. Blake held Rupert still until the bright object went back the way it came, disappearing into the darkness.

"You should know that if by any chance the portal was opened to this world and a Murk was able to leave without having a master to control it, this would break the rules that had been set by the Celestial Masters, and there would be big consequences. But even worse, if Begnon sensed the portal was open and followed us into the imaginary world, he will kill you and eat me."

Rupert heard Daltom and Oskar coming into the bedroom and turned around to see into the bedroom. The flickering reflexion of a torch on the wall got clearer. Rupert heard a small click. He imagined that Oskar was trying to put on the lamp.

"Begnon should decorate the other side of your face with his claws for this." Daltom said, pushing Oskar aside.

Rupert stayed quiet. He could see the silhouettes of the two bodies standing in the room.

"You are wasting my time, I never asked you to bring the boy or anyone, my plan is working perfectly, I only need you for Saturday, and then you will go back to the dungeon," Daltom said.

"Please give me a chance, I want to live up here with you, it's too dark down there," Oskar begged.

"Get used to it. It's not going to get any better," Daltom replied.

"We can't stay here for too long Rupert. The longer this portal stays open, the greater the risk of something catastrophic happening beyond our control," explained Blake.

Rupert heard the front door close followed by Oskar's cursing words. He now had to wait until Oskar fell asleep to sneak out. He came again to the bedroom, went to the window and looked down, he closed the window and shatters and left.

"There's no way that we're getting out of this bubble right now. Oskar probably thinks we have jumped out of the window, so he's not going to look for us." Rupert said.

"It's more dangerous to stay here in this bubble, than out there." Blake then pushed Rupert out of the bubble.

"What did you do that for, we were safe there," Rupert complained.

"No we were not, close the portal now," demanded Blake. Rupert closed the portal by rearranging the marbles again. His safety depended of the darkness of the room. He waited until he was sure Oskar had fallen asleep. At five o'clock he opened the window slowly and squinted outside but could not see how high he was. He hung onto the window ledge and landed on a small balcony. Rupert saw Blake looking down at him. Blake grabbed his hands and it stretched his body helping Rupert to land on the ground safely. He ran beside the hedges in case Daltom returned. The street was empty and the cold, damp weather began to pierce his bones.

Two blocks down the road Rupert heard a flip noise, it sounded like the noise that Jeeves makes when he uses his dog door. Within seconds a dog started to bark from inside the hedge. The dog started to run in the opposite direction and it appeared in front of Rupert only few meters away from him. It growled and started to run ferociously towards him. Rupert felt his arms trembling then he saw Blake vibrating slipping from his hands. Blake landed on Rupert feet twice its size standing between Rupert and the dog. The dog skipped but could not stop on time and crashed into Big Blake. The dog shook his head and left wimping back to the hole in the hedge where it had come from.

"That was amazing, how you do that," he said.

"Not as amazing as your knowledge about the portal," said Blake, "you are ready for Saturday. You know more now than I could ever suspected."

"I read the writing on each of those marbles ages ago and studied their meanings, but couldn't make any sense of it. It wasn't until you told me the confusing story about the Eight-Pointed Star, that it all became clear to me – Look, there's Alan," said Rupert.

"What's going on, am I late, why are you outside? Isn't Oskar coming with us?"

"No, let's go quickly, we've got to get out of this place," Rupert said.

Alan sped away looking confused.

Rupert sat in the back seat slowly he let his body slide across the seat, closed his eyes and fell asleep. He slept in the car for two hours. When he woke up Alan was staring at him.

"What's just happened, are any of you able to talk?"

"Nothing, we couldn't sleep well so I left early." Rupert said, "I have to go now, I'm running late for school,"

iCASTLE

Thursday, 19th November

With only two hours sleep, Rupert's concentration felt less than ideal to be at school, but he managed to stay out of trouble even after falling asleep three times at his desk. His eyes were red and felt burning.

It's Thursday, something is happening today, he vaguely remembered. An enormous stone building came to his mind. He remembered that the day had come for him to move to the castle.

He strode out of school and rested his body against the school fence.

"Oh, I didn't see you," He said, when he spotted Alan standing in front of him.

"You look–"

"Exhausted," said Rupert finishing Alan's sentence, "I know."

"I heard kids never sleep on the sleepovers, but this one almost killed you. Look at your face, you need a good rest," Alan said.

Rupert could not agree more, indeed, he was almost killed. His birthday felt more like his mourning day.

"So how did your martial art classes go yesterday?" Rupert asked casually whilst putting his seat belt on, his only intention was to change the subject. He knew that with his lack of concentration, the truth about Oskar was going to slip out and if Alan knew the latest discoveries about Daltom he would not let him go to the test on Friday.

"Well, I've good news and bad news for you, what do you want to hear first?" Alan asked.

"Good news, of course,"

"Well, I think Lesha, Gaelle, and Marion are probably members of our team in the puzzle,"

"You've got to be kidding me, what makes you think that? What can they do, and anyway, who's Marion? You're confused, I asked for the good news and this is the worst news you could've given me." Rupert shouted.

"Wow, that certainly woke you up. I worked it out, there's no one else available and sometimes, hating someone may be that you actually like them.

"You're totally wrong,"

"And Marion is the girl in the balcony on Friday at the race, don't you remember?" Alan said.

Rupert's memory brought him two images of two different places with Marion on it. How come, I only saw her once he wondered. He could remember clearly the girl at the balcony on a wheelchair. Then, slowly his mind presented him an image of the same girl at the farm. His memory had just given him a shock – that's where I saw her – But his mind was not finished yet, another image showed up, this time promising intrigue and scandal as the image appeared with sound. He could hear the grunting noises Marion was making when she was cutting off Lesha's swing.

"Wait, it has to be a mistake, she–" Rupert stopped himself. He took his time to analyse the people he had come across up until now. He knew that Lesha and Gaelle were close to the mysterious lady, trying to convince them to be with Daltom. Marion was clearly Lesha's enemy but Alan seemed to really like her, and if three of them are in the good team where is he going to place the mysterious lady. Perhaps it is best if I tell Alan about the things I know, or perhaps not, what should I do. He wondered where was the voice in his head when he really needs it to make a decision.

"I think I remember her now but will she be ok, she's in a wheelchair," Rupert said.

"I know what you mean, but Marion was a gymnastic champion, she had a martial arts black belt, and she's incredibly intelligent. Her legs problem is a trauma, which she is overcoming, and she will soon start walking," Alan said.

Rupert was completely awake now. He was glad he did not intervene when he saw Marion in her moment of rage with a knife in her hand whilst cutting off Lesha's swing. He had no doubt now that those girls were all bad, evil bad. He felt that his team was going in the complete wrong direction.

"Have they known each other long?" Rupert asked.

"No, not long, although there's no love lost between Lesha and Marion. Lesha accuses Marion of all sorts of things – the latest is from yesterday. Lesha says that Marion had destroyed a swing she has hidden in the woods – but they've worked out they differences now," said

Alan, "poor Marion, she wouldn't be able to go deep in that forest, I go there regularly, and I've been lost more than once, but Lesha says that the farmer had described the girl bringing down the swing, and the description matched Marion in every way, a bit unfair don't you think?"

Rupert changed his mind again. He could not trust Alan, as he knew that Alan was blinded by the goodness of Marion and he was the one training all those girls. He realised that all these twelve years Alan had not taught him any martial arts skills at all. Rupert felt betrayed. He decided to keep to himself all the information he had collected lately regarding Oskar and Marion, and solve the mysteries himself, or perhaps wait until everyone was going to be in the same place pretending to be someone else. How convenient. He thought.

"What does Marion think of that?" Rupert asked.

"She knows she's innocent, that's why she doesn't argue back," replied Alan.

Rupert listened attentively to Alan and his mind at the same time. I know that Alan has more sympathy for Marion than for Lesha and Gaelle together, but perhaps because he thinks that Marion is at a disadvantage. But to me, Marion is the one to be worried about. Lesha on the other hand is transparent. She is ready to defend herself. She knows more than Alan thinks. But can she be on the good side. I would not want her on my bad side, that's for sure.

"How about Lesha and Gaelle are they on the team just because they're also good at Martial Arts?" Rupert asked.

Alan laughed.

"Being black belts is the bonus," Alan replied.

Rupert swallowed.

"So this means that all of them will be coming on Saturday, how are they going to enter without an invitation? Mum is controlling that,"

"Leave it to me, I can sort it out," Alan replied.

Rupert gazed out of the window and noticed that they were driving away from Geneva and in the direction of Lausanne. The next village was Montreux, Rupert only knew from reading the motorway signs. He did not remember ever being there before. A few minutes later, Rupert could see a big old stone building. He stretched his neck to double check, as the building seemed familiar to him, even though he had never visited a castle before. He found himself crossing a small bridge over the shallows of the lake. The castle was built on a little Rock Island on the banks of Lake Geneva. Set in an impressive layout, an oval shape with two different faces. The mainland-side of the castle was used for defence. The Lakeside presents the battlements, with three spiky towers the tallest being in the middle. There were no arrow-holes or any defensive walls. Trees and loose rocks served as a decorative feature.

Welcome to Chillon Castle he read on a street sign, "I know this place, now I know why Mum gave me that book to read, it's the only book she had ever bought me," Rupert said.

"Indeed, she wanted to make you familiar with it. This is Chillon Castle, you probably heard its long and fascinating history, you can't complain it will be your temporary home, where you'll celebrate perhaps the most important of all your birthdays," Alan said.

Rupert peered out and saw the ruins of some columns by the side of the road. He could see the most impressive medieval castle – its ancient walls had many stories embedded in them, like an exciting old open book.

"My house is a mighty castle!" Rupert heard himself whistle in excitement.

The car stopped in front of the Castle, Rupert felt small and fragile in its' shadow. The ancient stonewalls loomed over him, and when he looked up he could see the round shape of the towers and the severe battlements looking at him. The history and the mystery of this building were breath taken. It felt surreal to Rupert. Amazing, was all Rupert could say.

"Choosing a castle to celebrate my birthday was the best mistake I've ever made," he said, "It's enormous and older than I thought,"

"Ideal for a party," Alan joked.

"Where's the entrance?" Rupert asked.

"Leave that to me," Alan said.

Alan put in some earplugs, took a small remote control from his shirt pocket and pointed the device at the castle. With a creaking noise, an enormous drawbridge started to open in slow motion. A rusted chain came down from the top, holding each side until the mechanism had lowered the drawbridge over the moat. It landed flat on the ground, causing a cloud of dust to rise into the air. The bridge was the only access to the castle by land.

Rupert was thrilled at the contrast of the old and the new, traditional and modern, past and future. There was nothing in between, except for his birthday party.

"A drawbridge controlled by remote control? It doesn't get cooler than that," Rupert said to Alan with excitement.

"Did you really believe that your mother was going to live in a medieval building?" Alan laughed.

"You're totally right, but this is different – it's totally awesome," Rupert said.

Rupert and Alan drove across the drawbridge. The car stopped in front of a couple of new horse-drawn carriages – replicas of ones from hundreds of years ago. Mrs Curdy had transformed the battlement into the fairy tale castle. There was still much work to be done before they moved from the guesthouse into the castle.

The security system was being tested so the place was full of technicians. There were sets of controls everywhere. The servants were going mad trying to learn which control activated which door.

"Welcome to the Curdys' castle. Please identify yourself," said a metallic voice. "You are tired, stressed. You smell, you need a shower and a good sleep urgently," announced the speakers at the entrance.

"What's this?" Rupert asked.

"Oh hi, honey, we're still testing the security system," said Mrs Curdy. "This is the very latest system. Once a person stands near the door frame, it only takes five seconds for the system to sense your feelings and intentions, so a thief would be spotted straight away, even if he looked like a saint,"

"Why did it say I needed a shower?" Rupert asked.

"When people are tense, they sweat, so it measures the odour level as well."

"Thieves will soon change their mind once they meet one of these systems," said Rupert.

"So, if I feel thirsty when I arrive at the door, what will happen?" Rupert asked.

"Someone will bring you a drink, of course. It's all been designed primarily for the party so that each guest will be satisfied," Mrs Curdy replied.

"All set and ready for the final test. Repeat, all set and ready for the final test." The person in charge gave the order for the final test.

"A, in position, D, in position, Chameleon, in position." Rupert stared, fascinated with it all.

"I will call this an intelligent castle, icastle, sounds perfect," Rupert said.

"That's exactly what it's called, icastle," replied the leader of the security squad.

Rupert was left open-mouthed when he saw the equipment installed. There were multifunction screen pads for television, Internet, games and music. The floor was a large pad divided into squares by different coloured lines, each line with an individual function. Sports, concerts and interactive games were all three-dimensional using holographs, and one could be part of the team while completely wireless. Rupert concluded that Mrs Curdy had said yes to every new gadget and experiment loving the idea of being the first person to use the latest party ideas.

"Imagine what the party is going to be like, let me walk you through it now that the system is being tested. There are four Great Halls, and I have re-named them for the party, I'll show you. The First Great Hall it's now The Grand Salon," she said.

Rupert saw an enormous area filled with decorated tables, thousands of green helium balloons pushed up against the ceiling, ice statues, imitation trees and flowers. The guests could enter the castle only by The Grand Salon there was no other way in or out on Saturday. It was the most significant room as in this place Rupert would blow out his twelve candles, under a three-metre diameter crystal chandelier, sparkling in the air inviting people to dream and pretend to be whoever they had always wanted to be. The whole atmosphere was designed to help guests free their imaginations and to have unlimited fun. Rupert had never seen a chandelier bigger or shinier than this one.

"The second Great Hall is named The Secrets Room," she said.

This hall was decorated in blue, it was a room in which to tell secrets, and no one could speak out loud as there will be a hidden secret-thief who will steal the secret and broadcast it through the loudspeakers.

"This is crazy… what? A Surprise Room?"

"That's right," Mrs Curdy said.

Rupert could not have imagined one more surprise – this room was purple. It was the room for games and laughter, in the form of a labyrinth, with walls that could move and trap someone for a while, until someone else on the other side touch the wall instantly opening the locking mechanism. There was a mirror that made people ten years older every time they stood in front of it. There were big luxurious sofas that disappeared once you touched them and a jack in the box that would not come out and shouted, "I Don't want to pop out!" – This one was going to be the kids' favourite, trying to convince Jack to come out." Rupert thought.

"This is the Show Room, I have to leave you here honey, I have a few phone calls to make, here, the descriptions are right here." Mrs Curdy said. She handed Rupert a tablet with the descriptions of each room.

Rupert walked alone to the fourth Great Hall, which was now named The Show Room, this hall was in red. A room used for music, artists and magicians, he read. Screens lined up, covering the entire walls to make the guests merge with the musical vibrations, as if it were a live concert. He accidentally went into a room named The Dark Room, he could see next to the sign its real name, Castellan Chambers. No one would want to enter this place. It was jet black inside, but it felt as though there was something in there, moving around, with strange noises too. I won't visit this room, that's for sure. He thought.

Coloured neon lights on the floor were the only guides to the five different entertainment areas. The white wire light was for the employees, stairs and restrooms.

The squad of technicians left one by one, quiet and organised while a machine was counting heads decreasingly as they left.

"Eight, seven, six, five…"

Rupert was curious about his bedroom and decided he would just have a quick look at it. He went over to a wall tablet, typed in the words Rupert's bedroom and pressed the go-button a bright green wire light went on to show the correct floor. Rupert followed it, running up the stairs eager to see his new room.

"Wow," he gasped.

His bedroom was empty but it was located on the mainland side of the castle, with a perfect view from the window to the entrance and the fascinating drawbridge.

"I could stand here forever," he said to himself, looking around to make sure that Miana wasn't spying on him.

"Rupert, are you there?" Alan called from outside the room.

"Come in,"

"How's your bedroom? Do you approve?" asked Alan, who was waiting with Blake tucked under his arm.

"It's perfect. A bed and some curtains is all it needs. The whole idea is amazing, mum has managed to ruin the castle, she killed the interior decoration by disguising it too, all this just for a kids party," Rupert laughed.

"I wish I could sleep here tonight," Rupert said.

"Well, that isn't possible. Your first night in this castle will be tomorrow – birthday eve – and so for everyone else," Alan said.

"Is Blake coming too?" Asked Rupert.

"No, he has to go today. But you two can have five minutes on your own. I'll be back soon," said Alan closing the door behind him.

"Wait a minute, you're not leaving me, are you?" Rupert asked Blake.

"I've accomplished what I came for – now I must be reunited with my master, I'll see you on your birthday," Blake replied.

"What did you accomplish?" Asked Rupert.

"All I was asked to do was to place the frame of the puzzle at a meeting point where the party was going to be held, and so I did," Blake said.

"Where is it?" Asked Rupert.

"The frame can only be traced by my kind, you need to know no more,"

"Just one more question," Rupert said, "why can't I do anything with Alan's Solitaire board?"

"First of all, that board is not Alan's – it belongs to Vincent. He knows that no one can use it as a portal because no one knows about it. The boards are custom made, which means one is the Evil Portal the other one the Good Portal. Now do you understand how irresponsible it was to open the evil portal?" Blake said.

"But nothing happened," Rupert said.

"We couldn't have been luckier," Blake said.

"And who is supposed to know these things?" Rupert asked.

Blake rolled his big black eyes.

"Apparently people who say they know nothing," replied Blake.

"Would you keep the secret? I saved us, come on admit it!" Begged Rupert.

"I have to go now," Blake said.

"Is everyone ready?" Alan called from outside the door.

"Yes, let's go. Wish me luck Blake," Rupert said.

"Good luck, as if you need it," Blake joked then became a ball and got smaller and smaller until he disappeared.

Alan waited outside Rupert's chambers. Cautiously he explained to Rupert that he was under very strict instructions to take him to the Grand Salon for a dance rehearsal. Mrs Curdy had invited her closest friends to help her with Rupert and they had just arrived.

"You've got to be kidding," Rupert said.

"I wish I was," Alan replied.

"I don't dance. I don't like dancing, and no one's going to make me dance," Rupert complained.

"That I know, but most of the guests have been practising a dance. I've been trying my best to convince your mother to leave you out, but she insists that you must join in because today the practice is in the castle,"

Rupert argued all the way down the stairs. When he heard the music he tried to escape, but Alan held his arm until he was in the rehearsal area.

"Rupert, you're finally here. Okay, everybody let's start," said Mrs Curdy, in front of sixty people rehearsing the dance. Rupert was short of words. He looked at Alan, but Alan ignored his gaze and refused to meet Rupert's eyes. There was no way out.

The choreographer came closer with his assistant. Rupert decided to stay calm – he knew he was going to make a clown of himself. The music started, and everyone got in position while Rupert was being helped with some basic steps, which he followed without rhythm. Rupert tripped up almost every single step his feet were completely uncoordinated. He noticed Mrs Curdy staring at him as if she liked him it made Rupert even shyer.

After an hour of rehearsal, Rupert's dancing steps had not improved. He knew that he was never going to get it, no matter how many hours he tried.

"Let's wrap it up," said the choreographer. Those were the best words Rupert had heard that day, and went to join Alan, who watched the rehearsal and did not move from the same place the whole time.

"Wow, you just taught me a lesson about how to be patient," Alan said, "I could see you didn't want to dance, and yet you've worked for an hour practising the worst steps I've ever witness, without any signs of improvement, and all without the slightest complaint, well done!"

"I'll have to agree with you this time – but haven't you noticed how hard mum has tried to make tomorrow the best day of my life, knowing she's not my real mother? She used all these people because she knew I wouldn't defy her in front of them. I may be the most useless dancer in the whole world, but she's the most determined person I've ever known, and, believe it or not, I still had fun," said Rupert, leaving Alan utterly speechless.

Rupert went over to his room in the guesthouse – he looked at his watch and saw that it was only six o'clock. He could barely keep his eyes open. He sat on the bed and started to see that everything was moving then slowly he let his body slide landing on the pillow already asleep.

Chapter Fifteen

ROYAL BLUE

Friday, 20th November

Rupert awoke, uncertain of where he was on the eve of his birthday. He could not remember what happened, but when he felt trapped in his school trousers and shirt it all came back to him. He felt refreshed after a twelve-hours sleep, and for the first time, no dreams to remember. He got changed quickly and soon realised that the guesthouse was deserted. It was an easy guess to know where his family was so he walked over to the castle. Everyone wanted to spend as much time as possible inside the mighty old building. He walked along, in the company of a mixture of feelings, floating on air. As he looked at the building with fresh eyes, he concluded that he preferred the façade of the castle to the interior. Mum did a good job ruining it. He thought.

In a less festive way, Rupert was waiting for the biggest day of his life. In his short life, no other event had been of this magnitude, the exhilarating moments he had experienced over the last ten days had changed him forever, he was eager to turn twelve, but even more so eager to meet his real father and learn as much as possible about his real mother. Rupert did not feel prepared at all to compete against Daltom, Oskar, Elmer, and friends. Would he have to fight, run, answer questions? He had no idea. All he knew was that he must stay alive, as he was the chosen one to put the first point of a star together, but not just any star, The Eight Pointed Star. Why me? He wondered.

Rupert was well aware that he had never achieved anything; Mrs Curdy kept on reminding him of that. He wanted to understand who he really was, and that question was only going to be answered when he turned twelve.

"I wish this was a dream, and I could wake up tomorrow, just being me," he said to himself.

Really? The voice in his head questioned.

"Not really, I didn't like being who I was but I don't like who I am now." He shut his mouth and looked around to see if anyone was listening, he could not believe he was speaking out loud again.

Rupert took his time to contemplate the arena for this mysterious battle. The party preparations had kept the servants busier than ever. Every corner was filled with party decorations. Beside the firecrackers, a big sign with the word Dangerous written in red, it made Rupert raise his eyebrows. The music was carefully selected playing nice and low. Every single detail had been taken care of as per Mrs Curdy's wishes. The venue was full of contrast, inspiring drama and fantasy, all in the same place. A medieval building in which a birthday was going to be celebrated but death was the guest of honour.

Rupert heard Mrs Curdy saying that there had been no cancellations from the guests, already making this, her most successful party, ever, she was expecting two hundred and eighty-five people, of whom forty were children from the ages of six to thirteen. The party would commence with a big fancy dress costume parade, with the arrival of the guests, so she anticipated she was going to have the time of her life.

Rupert had reached the first floor when a delivery arrived.

"Twenty-two," said Eugene as he made his way to the entrance.

This was the twenty-second time he attended the door to receiving a delivery for the party. But this time, the delivery was for

Rupert and was followed a few seconds later by a baker's delivery. Eugene seemed overwhelmed with all the work. Rupert watched from the top of the stairs. He heard when Eugene called Clotilde.

"Please take this parcel for me." Eugene said.

"Of course, is it for Miana?" Clotilde asked.

"No, It's for Rupert from Ms Glitter," Replied Eugene.

"Oh, how exciting," she said.

"Let me help," Miana said.

"No, wait, Miana please don't touch," shouted Rupert. He ran to find his way down. Instead he found himself in a labyrinth full of obstacles stopping him from getting near Miana. He could see her carrying the most important package to be delivered that day.

Jeeves passed by Rupert, barking and running towards Miana, his tail wiggling and his ears up in the air.

"What do you want, Jeeves?" Miana said. Jeeves kept on barking with excitement. He seemed interested in the package Miana was holding in her hands, Jeeves started to jump, trying to reach it.

Rupert stopped dead, his eyes wide open.

"No Jeeves!" his mouth opened letting out a shout that echoed in the ancient castle's walls.

"Stop right there. Naughty dog" Miana also cried, Jeeves had snatched the package from her hands and ran away as fast as he could.

"Come back, bad dog," Jeeves was not going to obey this time. Miana chased Jeeves from room to room, until finally he sprinted out into the garden and disappeared into the bushes.

Rupert went the same way as Jeeves, but there were no traces of the dog. He stayed in the same place waiting for Jeeves to come out and within minutes, Jeeves crashed out of the bushes, yelping as if a gun had shot him, with his tail between his legs and no sign of the package he had dragged in with him. Rupert saw Miana letting Jeeves into the castle – he pushed past her and crawled under a chair, where he lay shaking with his paws covering his eyes. Miana ordered Jeeves to come out, but the dog would not budge. Rupert could see the trembling body of the animal. It was terrified – But... why? Rupert wondered.

Eugene came in and looked under the chair.

"Give him some time. He'll forget why he went under there shortly, you wait and see," he said.

"Right, ten minutes have passed, and now I want you to tell me what happened to the parcel you took out of my hands," Miana growled. She looked from side to side, jumped off the chair, adjusted her pink dress and walked towards the kitchen. Rupert followed her.

"Hello, Pascal," greeted Miana.

"Oh hello Miana, what a lovely surprise. To what do I owe the honour?" he said.

"Can Jeeves have a bone?" Miana asked, "it's a treat for being a good dog." Rupert was intrigued. When did she learn any manners? He wondered. He imagined that she had a plan and waited attentively.

"*Comprendo, comprendo*, here you go," Pascal handed over a big bone that still had some scraps of meat on it. Miana's eyes' widened in disgust when she saw the size of it.

"Come here, doggie. Who's a good doggie, come, come," Jeeves did not seem convinced by Miana's voice – he knew he was in trouble. Rupert laughed. Jeeves started to sniff and sniff. The smell must have been so divine to him that he began to wag his tail and in a few seconds, he was by Miana's side. Once Jeeves was standing on the doorframe, Miana rang the bell, and the entry system began to analyse the dog's senses. Miana's plan had worked perfectly.

"Ingenious," said Rupert.

"Scared, has been attacked and robbed, not hurt but too smelly. Needs a lot of rest. Not harmful to humans," said the robotic voice.

Miana had found out what she wanted to know. Jeeves sniffed the bone and walked back to his hiding place, beneath the chair.

"What did you see out there? Who scared you like that, only my stupid brother can do that," said Miana softly, but Jeeves just whimpered.

Rupert went back to the bushes where Jeeves came from. He could not see any trace or clue to help him find the package, but the stench of a dead animal identified the thief. Rupert imagined that Begnon had confused the costume with the skin of an animal, he could not think of any other reason.

"There it goes, the best costume anyone could wish for, I guess I have no choice but to stay disguised as I always have been," Rupert said to himself as he walked back from the bushes, coming across Alan.

"Who are you talking to? We need to get going, you'll have the afternoon free to explore the castle," Alan said.

"I'm not exploring, but I'm ready, let's go," Rupert said.

No one knew how unique his costume was or what it meant to Rupert, all he knew was that it was gone. He resigned himself to the fact that there was no way back and in silence he went to school. Seated beside Alan, turning the pages of his notebook, he pretended to be revising but he was simply avoiding any type of conversation at all.

When Rupert arrived at school, the first person that he saw was Oskar. He decided not to look at him in the eye.

"Good morning, children, I imagine you all must be nervous, and that's understandable," said Mrs Stevens. "Do remember to keep calm and stay focused. You are already winners in the eyes of our school. We've never had such a number of participants before."

Rupert knew that there will be hundreds of students competing in this test but there was only one Royal Blue badge to conquer.

Oskar stood next to Rupert, only millimetres away from him. Rupert felt his skin with goose bumps.

"Hello bro," Oskar said.

Rupert moved slightly away from Oskar. It was disturbing after discovering that he was Daltom's son.

Mrs Stevens gave each student a school badge with their names printed on it for identification.

"Usually all our hopes are on only one student, I am delighted to see that this time around our chances are greater than ever. We'll leave in fifteen minutes," she said.

Rupert felt that the kindness of Mrs Stevens was just a cover to make him believe she was good.

Mrs Stevens arrived with the children at a building called Royal Blue, a place no one had heard of or seen before now. There was a small group of people checking identities at the entrance. That was as far as Mrs Stevens could accompany her students. Rupert turned towards her before he went in, but she gave him a long, hard stare.

After two hours the exam was over, the students walked out to meet their parents, over two hundred students sat the exam but only one was going to be the victor.

From the room Rupert was in, he could see that Alan had arrive, Rupert had finished and was waiting to be allowed to leave the premises.

Rupert was walking towards Alan when a man dressed in black walked by. He wore a black cowboy hat and in his right hand he had a black sack with something wriggling about inside it. Rupert stared at the bag. The man came close and stared at Rupert with gloating eyes.

Rupert had never met the man before but nevertheless, he immediately knew who it was.

The students came rushing out as a herd, running, looking for their parents.

Rupert saw Oskar and Daltom sauntering towards him. He could tell that unless Alan ran, Daltom was going to get to him first. Alan seemed unaware of the situation, and Rupert could not move his legs, somehow they felt like stumps. Rupert felt Daltom's intimidating presence as he stood in front of him. Daltom looked down at Rupert. Rupert held his stare.

"Don't be scared, little boy. I'll have a lot of fun before I kill you, unfortunately that day is not today, tomorrow," hissed Daltom. Daltom then ripped the badge from Rupert's blazer and looked at it closely.

"I knew it," Daltom said.

"Hey! Give that back, it isn't yours," Rupert said.

Daltom squeezed the badge in his hand Rupert saw blood coming out from between his fingers.

"You'll have it back tomorrow, on your last day alive, birthday boy,"

Alan rushed in and moved into a defensive position. The sack that Daltom was carrying wriggled and the stench coming from within left no doubt that Begnon was inside.

"I only wish that I was the one who'll defeat you tomorrow," Alan said.

"It will be as easy as killing a fly," replied Daltom, holding the sack tightly, as Begnon would not be able to resist the opportunity to use his deadly claws.

Daltom left, the sack in his hand wriggling madly, Oskar came close to Rupert.

"So you are Daltom's son, except you seemed more like his slave." Rupert said.

"Just for you to know that I will be the one who gets the first-star point, I will put the whole Star together, and then I will control humankind. Daltom has been too patient, he could have killed you before, but he is blind with his hate towards Vincent – Tomorrow," Oskar said.

"I'll be there," Rupert replied.

"Is he?" Alan pointed at Oskar as he followed Daltom keeping eye contact with Rupert.

"Father and son," Rupert replied.

"But… your were at his place… Vincent should know this, when did you find out?"

"Yesterday, I'll explain later, just one more day to go," Replied Rupert.

"Since when has Daltom had a son, Vincent never mentioned that," Alan said.

Alan stood staring in the distance. Rupert looked in the direction Alan was gazing, but he saw nothing suspicious.

"Alan, are you alright?" Rupert was shaking Alan to get him out of his stunned gaze.

"What, I, I'm all right, let's go," he replied. Alan did not look all right at all to Rupert. Alan would die if he knew as much as I do, Rupert thought.

"Rupert, do you know that lady standing right there, by the entrance?" Alan asked.

"Oh, that's Mrs Stevens, my science teacher. How come you don't know her, she has been my form teacher for the last five years," said Rupert. "I'm sure she's also part of Daltom's team, she was on our street when I saw Daltom and Begnon for the first time in the dark, I've been watching her,"

"Why didn't you tell me?" Alan said.

"I tried, but you didn't let me talk, but how do you know her?" Asked Rupert.

"No, I was wrong, she reminds me of someone I knew but not it's not her, come on, let's go," Alan said.

"What's next?" asked Rupert.

"If you don't mind I will be out for the afternoon, but will be back before six," said Alan.

"Can I go with you, everybody is running around with the party preparations, and I'll just get dragged into it, I want to go with you. Where are you going?" Rupert asked.

"I'm going to Engelberg and believe me it's going to be a miserable trip for you, please stay,"

"No as miserable as staying at home, I don't mind, I want to come, that's the village where I was born, it means Angel Mountain, doesn't it? – and I don't know what it looks like. I want to see this place before I turn twelve come on."

"I'm not going as tourist and it is miles away, you're better off staying here,"

"I know it's miles away but I still want to come." Rupert said.

"You are not different than Miana," Alan said.

When Rupert and Alan arrived at Engelberg, the view of a wide mountain valley made him rub his eyes, it all looked magical to Rupert, it was the most beautiful place he had ever seen. Welcome to Engelberg said a wooden sign and Angel Mountain was written in English underneath. Rupert was surprised that Alan had not made a comment on the way about the beauty of such a charming village. Alan seemed too preoccupied on his mission. He had explained to Rupert that he needed to find a lady who would help him with a job, but Rupert knew that the story was made up while they were travelling, and nothing Alan could say was making any sense. Whatever he was hiding must be personal and delicate, Rupert thought.

Their first stop was at the Commune Office. Alan went in alone and came out with a paper containing the address of the next place for them to visit. This place was on the slope of the mountain. They finally found the house they were looking for. Rupert waited outside the small wooden gate and saw Alan getting instructions from an old man. They went back to the village and in a narrow street, where all the little shops were located one beside the other, Alan started to look for something, Rupert did not ask any questions. He thought that Alan was perhaps looking for someone who had bad news for him, but Alan never talked about any relatives. Rupert did not mind he loved everything in Engelberg.

Rupert noticed that Alan fixed his eyes on a water fountain by the shops, as though he was daydreaming.

"Alan, are you all right?" Rupert asked.

"Yes, yes, I'm fine, I just found the place I'm looking for, would you mind going to the patisserie to get yourself a hot drink while I have my meeting. I'll be opposite you in the flower shop." Alan pointed at the shop. He gave Rupert some coins for his drink.

"That sounds great," said Rupert. But he was helping Alan with whatever he was lying about. He watched Alan cross the street slowly. Poor Alan, I've never see him that worried before, Rupert said to himself.

Rupert entered the shop and a cowbell rung above his head. The place was full of customers. Rupert walked in timidly, looking at the variety of chocolates displayed in the glass cabinet. The shop assistant came and took his order Rupert chose a chocolate croissant and a hot chocolate. He took his tray and looked around, there were no empty tables, except, for the one in the corner with only one chair, so Rupert sat there. He had a clear view of the flower shop and could see Alan when he finished his meeting. Next to Rupert sat a couple of ladies in their fifties, he guessed. Rupert sipped his chocolate keeping his eyes fixed outside. Alan stood beside the flower shop looking up and down the street with his hands on his waist. What is going on with you today? Rupert asked mentally. Alan seemed in hesitation to enter the store.

"Ursula, isn't that the man that came earlier on to see you?" Said one of the ladies at the table next to Rupert.

Rupert slowly turned towards the street and the only person there was Alan.

"What is he coming back for, I told him everything I know, I am sorry, I am staying here until he leaves, I am not seeing him again," said the lady called Ursula.

"Is he a private detective, with that look I would be scared to keep any secrets from him," joked the lady.

Rupert looked again. He was intrigued now. Those women seemed to be talking about Alan, but Alan was not there earlier. There was no other person on the street but Alan.

"Do you mind if I ask what he wanted, I was here with Elaine when he came, you know, but you made us worry when you put the Closed sign on the door – is he from the Caribbean?" said the lady.

Rupert closed his eyes, he felt short of air, no doubt they had seen Alan, but it was not Alan, It was someone using the costume stolen from Jeeves. Daltom has used the costume to do whatever Alan is supposed to be doing now. Rupert thought.

"It's too delicate Zoe. I can't talk about it," said Ursula.

"Ah no, you can't leave me like this, I swear on my mother's grave that I won't tell anyone," Zoe said.

Rupert saw the lady called Zoe made the sign of the cross on her lips.

Rupert kept his head down. By the silence of the lady who had seen Alan, he could tell that she was going to reveal her secret. Rupert realised that he could not be in a better place to get the information that was supposed to be for Alan and which Daltom has just stolen.

Alan will be very proud when I give him the information he is looking for, Rupert thought.

"Err, well, that giant of a man is suffering."

"Suffering? How can he be suffering, he looks in perfect condition to me,"

"Twelve years ago, at dawn, he gave me a baby, a child he thought was dead, came to life in my arms minutes after he left," said Ursula. Rupert was gutted. He became weak and felt sick.

"*Mon Dieu!*" Zoe said, "what did you do, but if he thought the baby was dead, why is he coming back now?"

"He told me he wants to tell the baby's parents about it, he was the one who delivered the babies, apparently there were two. The parents used to live in the little chalet at the top of the hill," said Ursula, as she sipped from her drink.

Rupert started to sweat. His mind went blank he turned to the street and saw Alan finally entering the flower shop.

"But what did you do with the baby?" Zoe asked, consumed in the tale.

"When the baby miraculously came alive, I took him to the orphanage straight away and rang the doorbell. I had to leave him there, I didn't want to get involved, but I saw someone picking him up and taking him inside. It was early in the morning and was still dark," she said.

Rupert was stunned. He could not believe what he had just heard. He has a twin sibling somewhere. Why would Daltom be asking? How does he know, he must be reading Alan's mind, that's why he's been so close to us all this time but how could Alan have kept this secret, how many more secrets have been kept from me. He thought.

"There is nothing that you can do, this is a big problem," Zoe said.

"What surprised me is that if he was the one who delivered the babies, he should know the gender, and he came to ask me about the gender," said Ursula.

"And did you know?"

"Of course not, I took the baby wrapped in a blanket the way he gave it to me, I kept him no more than fifteen minutes,"

"But you just said he," Zoe said.

"Well he or she wasn't wrapped in pink or blue, I would have taken him or her regardless of the gender, that wasn't a problem then."

Rupert stopped breathing as he had a terrifying thought, can Oskar be my brother? Is that why Daltom wanted to know the gender of my twin sibling? He saw his hands trembling and quickly put his cup on the saucer.

"Oh he is coming out, and he is walking towards us," Zoe warned.

"Let's go to the ladies," Ursula said.

The two ladies stumbled out of their table and rushed to hide in the bathroom. Rupert knew that Alan was coming to get him. He now knew of Alan's secret, how was he going to react, what was he going to say?

The cowbell rang again Alan bent his head down to enter the patisserie.

"We can go now," Alan said, "sorry, you haven't finished, I can wait."

"No, I'm not hungry," Replied Rupert and left while Alan held the door open for him. Rupert has adopted the same mood that Alan was in when they came in. The charm and unique architecture of the village lost its appeal over a cup of chocolate for Rupert. His family had expanded in a single visit to his birth town he now had a brother or a sister, a sibling who was going to share his Twelfth birthday, the same day as him but he was the one getting all the attention. These have been the worse twelve days of my entire life, he thought. *And it isn't over yet*. The voice in his head said.

Rupert did not dare to question Alan he did not know where to start.

"We'll get back home around six, perhaps we can go for a run, what do you think?" Alan asked.

Rupert thought that this could be the opportunity to find out about his sibling. He knew too much now, and it seemed that Alan was the only person who knew of the existence of this phantom child. But Vincent trusted him with my life, he thought.

"I guess I should have an early night, I am a bit tired," replied Rupert.

"Fine, let me know if you change your mind," Alan said.

When Rupert retired to his chambers, the double doors were somehow welcoming him. He expected to open them wide and find a magical room with a floating bed under an open roof, so he could see the stars whilst lying on his bed. The cracking noise of the doors hinges voided the idea instantly. He stepped inside and saw a four-poster bed in the centre of a spacious room all neat and tidy. It felt cold and damp. Rupert hugged himself tight. A high ceiling stood between him and the sky, blocking his view into space. Long curtains touching the floor, made the window almost disappear. He anticipated that the figures in the dark were going to have long legs and arms. He also noticed that there wasn't an en suite bathroom. Rupert looked around, hoping to see Marci somewhere, but Marci was not there, he checked a couple of drawers, and the toy was not there either. He sat on the bed felling minuscule. He knew that the minute he closed his eyes, the figures camouflaged on the walls, window and ceiling were going to come out to haunt him.

It is what it is, said the voice in his mind, clear and firm this time.

"Yes, I know," he replied. Rupert concluded that the only way to keep the shadows away was to keep the brass floor lamps on each side of his bed on. The feeling of uncertainty made him fidget, he tossed and turned in his bed, and did not want to fall sleep. Nothing was going to stop tomorrow from coming. It was inevitable, he was scared and he was not ashamed to admit it. Instead of inhibiting his mind from going wild, Rupert welcomed all the weird moments, people and feelings he experienced over the last twelve days. Once he gave freedom to his mind, he knew that there was no way back. Knowing that he may only have one day to live, he wished he could go back and do things differently. He thought of pleasing Mr and Mrs Curdy by learning another language and playing various musical instruments, but then, he did not want to be like Esteban Lambert. He wished he had been out more frequently and made more friends, but he may have come across people like Elmer and friends, that ended up betraying him sooner or later. He wished for Miana to speak less and stop spying on him but then she would have been a boring sister. Then he realised that no matter which way he looked at his past, he would not have wanted it to be any different.

"This is my fate, to be here, right now, awake, thinking about the past unable to stop the future but with every chance to save it."

You should go to sleep now. Said the voice inside his head.

There was no reply.

Chapter Sixteen

FIRST TWELVE HOURS

Saturday, 21st November

"Happy Birthday to you, you,

Happy birthday to you, happy birthday,

Happy birthday, dear Rupert, dear Rupert,

Happy birthday to you, you."

With the most uncoordinated chorus, Rupert's family woke him up on his Twelfth Birthday. The entire household was in his chambers. They kept on singing while he covered his ears with his pillow. Rupert could also hear Jeeves howling along beside his bed.

"Fine, thank you. Now leave, I want to sleep," he shouted and buried his head again under his pillow. The day has come – I can't believe it's happening, when did I fall sleep? I am twelve, and I will die today. He said to himself. His hands held the blanket tightly waiting for everyone to leave.

Everybody left except for Mr and Mrs Curdy. Rupert saw that Miana seemed to be looking for something.

"Marci is gone," he said sharply. Miana turned her face gave Rupert a stern gaze.

"Birthdays only last one day," Miana said on her way out. Jeeves followed her.

"We know it's your birthday, but it's already eleven o'clock you're wasting your day in bed," said Mr Curdy.

"Rupert, I wish you all the best today and for your entire life," said Mr Curdy, his words were touching, but Rupert knew that it was his dad's way of saying goodbye. Mr Curdy leant over and kissed Rupert on his head.

"Thank you, Dad."

Mr Curdy made a gesture as if he had much more to say but only let out a retiring smile.

"Wait until the party starts - you're going to love it," said Mrs Curdy.

"I'm sure I will, Mum – thank you," that was his goodbye.

Rupert stayed in his bed and watched his adoptive parents leave his chambers. He felt no anger or resentment towards them. He understood that he would not want them any different than what they were, this way, it was easier for all of them to let go of one another, so he could take on his mission.

Alan came in straightaway, bouncing along full of energy, holding a tray with breakfast for Rupert and with the biggest smile on his face.

"Happy birthday young man. I see you're all ready to go, but I'm afraid we can't go out today," said Alan placing the tray at the bottom of Rupert's bed.

"Why is that?" Rupert asked.

"Today you're officially the most wanted boy on earth, by both, good and evil. Look out of your window and you'll see that the battle has already started."

Rupert jumped from his bed and ran to the window. He opened the curtains with both hands. In the distance, behind the castle gates he saw two human figures standing in front of each other, both wearing long robes. One was in black and the other in white.

"Who are they, and why are they dressed like that? Is this part of the party theme?" Rupert was anxious to confirm what he was thinking.

"You were born at five o'clock in the morning and from that time on, both Vincent and Daltom are allowed, by their own rules, to intervene with you, Daltom to try to kill you, and Vincent to protect you. They are as powerful as one another, except that Vincent has the advantage of having you on his side."

... and Daltom, everyone else, said Rupert to himself. Alan's words reminded Rupert about his sibling. I am not his only child, he thought.

"I've been watching them, and they both arrived in perfect time. A second of difference between the two could have changed things, but at present, they have equal powers over the two strongest forces of good and evil."

"Why are they in front of the gate? Everyone will see them." Rupert said.

"They have twenty-four hours to complete the task, which was divided between the two of them. Vincent has the First Twelve Hours. He demanded that no one in Daltom's team should come near you

308

during this time. Daltom has the remaining twelve, and he has demanded that you don't run away."

"I have no intention of running away," Rupert said.

"Who's around them? I can't tell. Why are they all wearing robes?"

"Some of them are quite familiar to you, Rupert. You will need binoculars to identify who is who, here borrow mine. Behind Daltom, you can see Begnon, Sonia and the boys."

"Are you sure that I'm the only masterpiece. How about if they have their own masterpiece and after all, they don't need to kill me." Explained Rupert.

"Impossible," Alan said.

Rupert kept looking through the binoculars.

"So that one is Vincent, my real dad." He adjusted the focus on the binoculars trying to get a clearer look at Vincent's face, but his hood was covering half of his face so he could not get a good view. He saw Gaelle, Lesha, Marion, and Blake.

"You and I will join later," said Alan.

"Marion is walking perfectly? But still that only makes seven. We're one person short," Rupert said.

"Vincent was told that Sonia has no skills at all, and Elmer never had bad intentions so that makes us seven-all, and hopefully, Elmer will join us."

"Hopefully? – Elmer is a traitor. We can't count on him, he won't do anything without his brother." Rupert retorted.

"Anything can happen today, Rupert."

"This is completely crazy," he said.

"By the way, there is a disguise waiting for you outside. Your mother never saw the one Ms Glitter sent you, so she ordered one of her own choice, I think you'll like it," Alan said.

"But I don't want a disguise, I hate them,"

"Then why were you so desperate to find the disguise Ms Glitter sent you?" Rupert could see himself in the coffee shop at Engelberg, watching Daltom dress as Alan using his disguise.

"I was only worried about Jeeves being frightened,"

A knock on the door saved Rupert from any further interrogation from Alan.

"Come in," Rupert said.

"Alan, could I please have a word with you." Mrs Curdy held the door handle waiting for Alan.

"Sure, Mrs Curdy," Alan stepped outside. Rupert ran to put his ear on the keyhole of the door. He could hear their conversation perfectly.

"What are we supposed to do? Are his parents going to come to talk to us? Are we finally going to meet them? Will he know straight away the truth about us?" The questions poured out of Mrs Curdy's mouth. She sounded worried and nervous to Rupert.

"Alan, it may be too late to say, but I wish I had been a better parent for Rupert, I wish I held him more when he was a baby," she whimpered.

"Rupert will understand one day, don't worry, by the way, the whole castle looks fantastic – congratulations, you've done a magnificent job as always, and the dance rehearsal was terrific," said Alan.

"Oh, thank you, you're always so kind and polite. But, you haven't seen anything yet, wait until the party starts it's going to be fab."

"I can't wait to see it all," said Alan.

"Well, I'll let you entertain Rupert while there's still time to get everyone ready. See you later."

Rupert ran back to the window impressed with Alan's cunning way to bewilder his Mum. He heard the door opening and Alan steps approaching.

"It's incredible to see them facing each other, both with the same goal, but with opposite intentions. It was hard to believe they had once been best friends." Rupert said.

"That happens all the time don't worry, those two aren't going anywhere," said Alan, "they know what they're doing. All will begin when the party starts. Not a second before and not a second later, so don't waste your precious time standing there watching them, eat your breakfast."

On the way out, Rupert saw the dolly left outside his chambers, on the top shelf there was a brown disguise inside a plastic bag, a black, velvet cloak with a red border and a gold crown each in separate bags. On the floor a pair of knee leather boots. Rupert shook his head and left. I don't think so.

After lunch, he decided to go for a walk around the castle to see the final details of his party extravaganza and to familiarise himself with the area. Nothing impressed him anymore, only the mighty building made him feel special.

At four o'clock, Rupert saw Miana already dressed in her costume practising her butterfly swings. Half an hour later, Rupert's mother called out.

"Honey, the guests will be arriving in thirty minutes – You'd better get ready."

"I will Mum, don't worry,"

Rupert wheeled the dolly in to his chambers, closed the door and slid the iron latch to bolt the door. He sat in front of the window so he could witness the beginning of his end. But it was dark already, and the garden lights were not bright enough for him to see clearly, even with Alan's binoculars.

Four fifty-five – the clock sounded louder to Rupert's ears, and he could feel in his heart the second hand ticking – tick, tick, tick.

"What will happen next?" he said.

The tick, tick, tick noise was taken over by his heart pounding in his chest, beating quickly; Lub dub, lub dub. The clock finally marked five o'clock and a burst of noise made him jump, then he saw several rockets shoot up into the sky, before exploding in the air and floating in a glittering silver shower, making a magnificent cracking noise to his ears. A bigger explosion with colourful, sparkling lights flew higher into the sky in all directions making the shape of a willow tree, the sparks stayed visible until they almost hit the ground.

Hundreds of chrysanthemums were clearly displayed leaving long trailers in the sky. There was a pause and small stars started to appear in the air, outlining giant letters.

Chapter Seventeen

UNIVERSAL PARTY

Happy Birthday Rupert was written in the sky.

"Now, that is cool," he said.

The dazzling letters vanished into the dark sky and the smoke temporarily blocked his view of the gates.

Rupert watched the drawbridge descend for the arrival of the guests. Within seconds, the queue outside the gate was so long that it went back as far as Rupert could see, an array of colourful hats and wigs were marching enthusiastically towards the castle. Rupert spotted two suits of armour by each side of the gate, he knew they were only for decoration, but decided to put them to use. He looked at the dolly, grabbed the body suit and boots and put them on – this will do, he said and tucked the cloak and crown under his arm. He ran out of his chamber and within minutes, he was by the pillars fitting himself inside one of the suit of armour with a perfect view of the guests as they came in.

The guests started to walk towards the castle, impersonating the characters they had chosen to be on that day. Rupert was amazed by the effort each person had put into dressing up. Everyone seemed eager to be part of the party, confident that they were going to have a fantastic time, He knew that with all the preparation involved, this was a forgone conclusion. He thought.

A man dressed as a Swiss Guard was welcoming the guests. The bright-red and yellow-blue stripes of the costume attracted everyone's attention. He was the person the guests had to go to, to enter the battlement. A second guard was taking the coats, and a third was checking invitations. Each invitation card was coded so that no names were displayed to avoid any identification leak.

Rupert could only see with one eye as the helmet visor had fallen sideways and covered his right eye. He could not make out anyone. He saw the superheroes entering in a flock as if they were on a mission. Then the mythical gods, cartoon characters, politicians, animals and aliens followed.

"My birthday party is an Universal Party," Rupert said out loud.

In the distance, he could see that the punching bag was already getting a hard time.

He turned his head when the helmet touched his shoulder making a clinking noise. He scanned the crowd wondering if he would recognise Vincent when he walked in front of him, then he heard Lesha and Gaelle talking to each other. They were getting closer to his only viewpoint. They were wearing white robes. A third figure walked behind them. Rupert guessed it was Marion. Then, one by one, Elmer and friends walked by wearing their black hoodie robes, Rupert recognised their voices, but could not tell who was who. He waited to see Vincent and Daltom, but they did not show.

A pirate walked towards him, turned around and stood right in front like a pillar, blocking Rupert's only good eye. By the time the pirate moved away, all the guests had crossed the gate and were gathering in the courtyard. Rupert inched his way slowly behind the battlement, freed himself from the suit of armour and went back the same way he had come out, to join his family and welcome the guests into the party.

The Curdys were waiting at the entrance. Rupert was standing by their side wearing the cloak and crown. The crown had a veil attached to it, which covered his entire face. Rupert was grateful his mother had remembered that he did not want people to see his face. The guests' coats had been removed and put away, and now they were coming to be welcomed by the family to start the party. He saw his Mother looking at him and smiling. She put her chin up and started to greet everyone just like a real countess. Even though the corset on her renaissance dress was a bit too tight, she had no problems breathing, but it looked incredibly painful to Rupert. He knew that nothing was going to ruin her moment, she was more than happy to bear the pain.

Rupert smiled and thanked everyone as they passed on their birthday wishes. He spotted the only guests he invited, and immediately regretted ever done so. Elmer and Marlow were wearing black and white striped prisoners' costumes the other three wore bright orange ones. Sonia wore her gothic outfit and Oskar was disguised as a court jester wearing a black and purple harlequin suit. Perfect choice, Rupert thought. Daltom kept his hoodie on and Begnon walked on his back legs, pretending to be a child in a filthy hairy costume.

Rupert felt his heart stop when he saw a man in a white robe getting closer. His overgrown beard seemed real he wore glasses, his eyes staring at him. He was holding and orange ball in his hands.

Rupert had seen that face before – it was his own aged reflexion. Mr and Mrs Curdy did not seem to notice Vincent's resemblance to Rupert. Vincent walked straight at him. Rupert's legs felt week – he lost control of his world when he felt Vincent's presence before him.

"Happy Birthday Rupert," Vincent said.

"Thank you," Rupert replied with a trembling voice, while shaking his real father's hand for the first time. Vincent's voice echoed in Rupert's ears, the sound deep in his heart. They paused for a moment, staring into each other's eyes, and reconnecting as father and son.

"You may want to hold onto this for a while." Vincent passed Rupert the bright orange ball he was carrying. Instantly, the ball morphed into Blake.

"Thanks," Rupert said. He had never been more lost for words. He saw Vincent walking away, disappearing amongst the rest of the guests.

Rupert spotted Lesha and Gaelle they wore silver cosmic costumes with matching shiny makeup. Marion stood tall in front of him dressed as a zombie, waving at Rupert. She kept her hair as usual in two plait tails.

One by one, the members of his family joined their guests, all anxious and full of energy, their bodies swaying to the rhythm of the music. Rupert stood there on his own, thinking what to do next, when a glimpse of a shadow caught his attention, as if a person was hiding behind a column, "hello?" Rupert called out. A white female figure walked slowly from the hiding place in Rupert's direction. She seemed to be floating on air. Rupert could not move the last guest to enter the battlement was familiar to him. He was in front of the witch, but she looked more like a goddess, in a white, almost transparent gown, with hundreds of layers, making it look angelically puffy. Her face was white and the makeup, including lipstick, lashes and nails, shone in a royal blue colour. She held a bundle in her left arm and a crystal Venetian mask in her right hand covering her eyes.

She came in front of Rupert, looked at him for two seconds and walked away, as though he was of no importance to her. Rupert was convinced she was the same lady he saw at the park with Lesha and Gaelle – but who would have invited her? No way, this woman must be one of Mum's friends, Rupert concluded. He admired the way she wore the costume as though it was her everyday look.

"Did you see that?" Rupert asked Blake.

"Did you feel that?" Blake said, "I can tell you now that there is a superior being here, stronger than me, and Begnon together and that will be chaos. I must warn Vincent."

"I want to talk to Vincent," Rupert said.

"He is waiting for you, in the Grand Salon," Blake said.

In a mixture of colourful lights, music, artificial smoke and two hundred and eighty-five guests in disguises, Rupert moved around, he was pushed, bumped and squeezed between superheroes, animals, and cartoon characters, but all he wanted was to meet Vincent.

"Stop, he will meet you here," Blake said, once inside the Grand Salon.

"Rupert," Rupert heard Vincent's voice calling him. He looked to his right. His words were still not there. He felt a strong current running through his body and his legs began to tremble, quickly, he removed the crown and veil and then he ran into Vincent's arms.

"I'm happy to be part of this," he finally said, "I promise I won't let you down. You are... my dad…"

"I am, and I couldn't be more proud," Vincent said.

"I know that Daltom killed my mother, and I'll make him pay for it."

"What – your mother is not dead. She'll meet us tomorrow in the same mountain shed where we saw you last. Our only mission today, is to put the First Point of the Star together," Vincent said.

Rupert felt his soul back in place.

"How do you know that she is alive?"

"We have the light of life, see," Vincent said as he showed Rupert a small pendant with a little light in the centre, "This means that Serena is alive."

"The castle is Daltom's idea, Begnon has put all the ideas into my head, and I asked for it. I'm sorry," Rupert said.

"Daltom is very predictable, he can't live without the dark and cold walls of an old building, but your godparents have done a good job changing the inside, this will gives us a small advantage," Vincent said.

Godparents – Rupert repeated in his head.

"There are too many people here. Daltom will kill all of them if he doesn't get his way. The best thing to do is to avoid him, I can't run away, but they still have to find me, and with everyone in disguise, it won't be easy,"

"It's best if we don't see each other until after our team is complete, keep your veil on son,"

"When will that be, where do we meet?" Rupert asked.

"Only Blake knows that information and he is not allowed to share it, not even with me," Vincent replied.

Rupert decided to explore the rooms. He followed the blue light to enter the Surprise Room. He wasn't sure what he could do, and he was starting to walk away when a gigantic yeti covered his mouth with a big hairy paw. The Yeti pulled Rupert through a secret door into a side room. The Yeti took the mask off, and there was Alan.

"Why am I not surprised," Rupert said.

Soon after Rupert saw Elmer and Marlow entering the room.

"Prisoners' disguises, that really suits you two," Rupert said.

"Happy last birthday," Marlow said.

"Rupert, can I…" Elmer tried to speak.

"Save your words it's too late," Rupert turned away.

Rupert saw Elmer and Marlow arguing. He could not hear a word they were saying, when suddenly, he saw Oskar walking towards him.

"What's up Bro?" he said mockingly.

The word Bro kept repeating in Rupert's head.

"What a coincidence, to have a birthday on the same day as death, we'll have fun with you before it all ends, don't you worry, after all, it's your party," Oskar laughed.

"When is your birthday?" Rupert asked.

"Why, are you going to give me a present? I'll tell you if I knew it, but who knows, it may be today," Oskar said.

Rupert moved away disturbed by Oskar's words. He found himself in the middle of a group of people and from there Rupert was able to see Vincent and Daltom arguing with each other in the corner of the room.

"…I didn't sit still for twelve years. I can assure you now, that you've lost this battle before we even start. Prepare to lose more than a son today. You betrayed me, and everyone will betray you today," Daltom said.

Daltom had Vincent pinned against the wall and as he tried to punch him in his stomach, Vincent pushed Daltom with his hands open as if giving him an electric shock. Daltom was thrown a couple of meters away landing on his back.

"I never betrayed you. All my work has been, is, and will be for the benefit of humankind, and all you want is to destroy everything around you."

"Humankind gives you attention only when you harm them. That's how they've been taught, and today will only be a reminder of that. Your time is over. Your son's death is what I want today, to put the puzzle together. Soon the whole star will be mine and I will be invincible." Daltom laughed.

Daltom turned and mixed in with the crowd. Rupert followed him with a fair distance then he saw Daltom having another dispute, this time with a robust guest. Rupert could not get closer to hear their words but he knew it was Ms Glitter. He joined a group of people and stood facing Daltom to be able to read his lips.

"You're still obviously too slow – the costume has been used already and it gave me some precious information, now, stay away from me." Ms Glitter argued back, throwing her arms in the air and left.

"Stop right there, Daltom," said the Yeti.

No Alan, what are you doing. Rupert said to himself, you are going to get yourself kill.

"Ah…I see, and what can you do, Vincent's failure will have no one to blame but you, useless giant." Daltom let out a high pitched squeaking sound, Alan dropped to the ground covering his ears with his hands.

Lesha, Gaelle and Marion arrived to help Alan and managed to roll his body into a corner. Rupert stayed hidden where he was listening to the girls. They can take care of Alan. He thought.

Rupert walked away, he could hear the acts being called one by one in the Show Room. The performances were keeping everyone entertained and asking for more. Rupert could hear the guests singing and clapping.

Two hours passed and there was no sign of anyone trying to complete the puzzle.

"Rupert, there you are, honey. It's time for the dance come and join us."

"Not now, Mum, please."

Mrs Curdy took Rupert by the hand and stood with him in the middle of the dance area. The rest of the guests gathered, and those participating in the special dance took their respective positions.

The music started and Rupert began to move along with everyone else. Every female member of the party had the opportunity to dance with Rupert.

"I thought you could dance." Lesha teased.

"Don't start," Rupert replied and then, he saw the goddess-looking lady standing close to them as if waiting for her turn. Rupert felt intimidated by her strong presence. Lesha let go of Rupert and he danced with the lady, "awesome costume," Rupert said. The goddess said nothing. Rupert shut his mouth it felt awkward.

The music changed, saving Rupert from the embarrassing moment, everyone moved quickly in different directions, including the goddess. He felt dizzy, dancing was not for him, he thought. He went back to continue his mission and entered the secret room. Lesha held a finger to her lips, gesturing to Rupert to be quiet.

"We must check that our team is complete before we get to the triangle frame, are we missing anyone?" he whispered to Lesha.

Alan, inside his Yeti costume, joined with Blake, followed by Marion, who came out of nowhere.

"We're missing one member of our team we must split up to find him," Vincent whispered.

"You're missing two members." Marion said out loud. As if she wanted everyone to hear her news. Then her words echoed. Different voices were repeating what Marion just said laughing at the same time. Rupert understood that Marion had planned how to break her news there were no accidents judging by the way she said it.

"I knew it, why did no one believe me?" Lesha said.

"It was you who tried to kill me by sabotaging my swing," Lesha shouted. The voices in the secret room where louder and it seemed to be more of them echoing every word. Rupert saw Lesha's level of anger was already off the scale, but Marion kept on provoking her.

"I saw you going to that stupid place, every single day, swinging on that stupid swing, I knew you were part of the this mission and definitely not part of my team, I wanted you out, sac of bones. – Besides, you have no idea how powerful I can be."

"You're so going to regret this," Lesha shouted, but Marion had already run out of the room.

"If you are so powerful, then why do you run, coward," Lesha shouted.

"We must get out of this room or else we are going to end up losing our minds." Vincent whispered to Rupert to pass the message along.

"There isn't going to be a fight after all," whispered Rupert.

"I wouldn't speak too soon," Vincent said.

"We have a few traitors," a voice echoed in the room.

"Who said that, it wasn't me," Rupert whispered.

"Me neither," Gaelle said.

"Then who? Someone else is here." Rupert whispered.

"Who are they?" Oskar's voice was clearly heard.

"The brothers, get them," Daltom's voice was heard. The voices from the secret room were passing the message in Rupert's direction.

"I knew it," Alan mumbled, his hands holding both ears.

Rupert was confused; he wanted Elmer and friends on his team, but how could he trust them knowing they have been with Daltom? He wished Elmer had not betrayed him so they could still be friends.

"Rupert help us to find Elmer and Marlow, they're in our team," Gaelle said.

Just then, Rupert felt a massive net fall on his head. The shocked expression from Lesha and Gaelle were mixed with a loud scream, as the three of them fell to the floor, trapped under a net that tied with a fluorescent cord, making them look as if they were part of the décor. Marion had prepared for them in the Surprise Room.

"There you are, stuck with each other, as always. Someone will pay you a visit soon, seeya…"

Lesha managed to get half her arm through the net and tapped people as they walked by but they assumed it was another trick of the party. The music blocked their shouts for help and being high up no one could see their facial expressions. Rupert saw Elmer and Marlow getting close so he shook the net but he knew it was not going to work.

"This may help," said Gaelle, holding a small bottle of water in her hand.

Rupert snatched the bottle and waited until Elmer and Marlow were right under the net to pour the water. Elmer looked up and wiped the water off his body and carried on walking. When the music was about to chance, Gaelle called Elmer to the top of her voice. Elmer run back and within minutes he set them free.

"Gaelle, please trust me," Elmer begged.

"I do," said Gaelle, getting out of the net.

"I don't," Rupert said.

"Are you alright? Elmer asked Gaelle as he helped her up.

"Excuse me, am I missing something here, you two know each other, for how long. And, how come I don't know anything about it, you're supposed to be my best friend." Lesha said.

"It's a long story, but yes, we did art together at the hostel. I wanted to tell you, but I knew you wouldn't like it"

"Only two days," Elmer said.

"Oh, you sound in love, that's gross," said Lesha.

Rupert laughed admiring Elmer's bravery showing his feeling for Gaelle.

"We don't have time for lovebirds – let's go," Lesha said.

"Let's help the others. I think we should stay together and avoid falling into more traps. We need to put the puzzle together as soon as possible," Rupert said.

"It stinks in here." Gaelle said.

"Castles always stink," Lesha replied.

"Oh, no," Gaelle shouted. Rupert turned and saw Begnon staring at Gaelle. Begnon's eyes seemed on fire, his smell had never been so strong.

"He's going to eat us," shouted Marlow.

"He'll have to eat me first." Blake dropped down in front of Begnon.

"You can't fight me. You'd be in my belly before you could blink," said Begnon, as he pulled a hair from his head to feel pain.

"But you've forgotten that I don't blink," retorted Blake.

Blake stood still and grew as big as Begnon. Begnon's claws grew twice their size. Begnon attacked jumping towards Blake and in mid air Blake defended himself. They stretched and changed sizes many times, but Begnon was much stronger than Blake. Rupert feared for Blake, he had never anticipated anything like it.

"Begnon must have more beings inside him to be that strong," Lesha said.

"Blake doesn't stand a chance," Gaelle said.

"He can't die. He'll disappear when Vincent dies, not before, but he'll lose his powers," Lesha said.

Begnon threw Blake up to the ceiling and for a second Blake seemed glued to it, slowly, he began to fall. Begnon stood with his body wriggling from side to side. His broken tail was slowly wagging with the excitement of capturing Blake with his mouth. Rupert knew Blake had little energy left, and he could not call on Vincent for help.

"Do something Blake," Rupert shouted. But Rupert's pain seemed to make Begnon stronger, and Blake began to fall. He was suspended from the ceiling only by a tiny piece of his gooey skin. He closed his big, deep, black eyes and down he went.

Rupert noticed something moving on top of a table, like a teddy next to a flower arrangement, which seemed to be watching the fight.

"Nooo!" Lesha, Gaelle and Elmer screamed at the same time. Hands over their eyes but Rupert stared at Blake as he fall. The Teddy came out from where it had been standing, sprang into the air and joined with Blake, creating a big spark the moment the two beings joined, blinding everyone in the castle for a second. Blake held himself in the air and stretched his legs – he grabbed Begnon's mouth, closed it and quickly used his legs as if they were a rope, tying Begnon's mouth shut. He spun Begnon around and smashed him into the wall. Begnon lay down like a deflated balloon.

"You should go now. Begnon won't cause any more damage for a while," said Blake in a strange voice that sounded as if it was both feminine and masculine at the same time. Everyone left, except for Rupert, he felt curious about Blake's new look. With another spark, the

Teddy separated from Blake's body. Blake seemed confused, the Teddy was as tall as Blake, wearing white with a royal blue tutu.

"I know you, are you…" said Rupert with confusion as the being disappeared through the wall.

Rupert saw Alan coming his way he seemed recovered from his ear.

"We are complete now so we should get details of the place to put the first puzzle together," Rupert said.

Alan nodded.

"You seemed to have recovered really fast," Rupert asked.

Alan remained silent.

"What happened to your Yeti disguise? Rupert asked. Alan put his hand around Rupert and with the other one he twisted Rupert's arm up behind his back.

"Shut your mouth," Alan said.

Rupert saw a malicious smile in Alan, which did not belong to him. And that voice, Rupert thought. Oskar stood casually beside Alan.

"What are you doing?" Rupert then realised that the man holding him was not Alan. Daltom was using the costume one more time.

"Take him to the dark room, Begnon will come and take care of him." Daltom said. A sharp object pressing in Rupert's back made him remained still. Along the way Rupert felt a switch of hands and now a pair of soft aged hands were holding his arm. He heard the voice of Mr Zhong – the librarian.

Cuffed and gagged Rupert was pushed between his own guests he felt an extra set of hands grabbing his harm.

"I'll take it from here," Rupert heard Oskar's voice.

"Don't mess this up boy, my boss will not be happy." Warned Mr Zhong.

"This will create suspicious," said Oskar removing the gag from Rupert's mouth. Where are you taking me, the dark room is not that way." A narrow door at the end of the corridor was half-open and a dimmed light outside the door illuminated part of the corridor.

"You must get my birthday present before you die," Oskar said.

Rupert stopped as he felt the sharp object pressing in his back again. He saw Oskar digging out a flashlight from his pockets to see the way down the narrow stairs to the dungeon.

"This is how I have lived my whole life, while you roll over in silk blankets. Breathe the stuffy air and feel the damp and cold walls, your only companion will be those two columns, pick one, be my choice, but before you get too comfortable, you must show me that you've done your homework." Oskar sounded as if he was acting in a school play. His voice was nervously excited, and his eyes bulged.

On the wall at the bottom of the stairs, there were twelve picture frames in two groups of six, Rupert came close and read the title: The Voice in the Dungeon.

"I bet you didn't learn the poem as I did, I bet you don't even know that it existed. But before you die you'll recite the poem to me," Oskar said.

"Everybody knows about that poem, but no one knows it by heart," Rupert said.

"Choose one of the twelve stanzas and recite it to me. That will be my present from you – you must know it by heart." Oskar said.

"I only know the first three stanzas. I didn't have to learn it all," Replied Rupert.

"You're in luck today. I want you to recite my favourite one, recite the second one, now," Oskar raised his voice.

Rupert started to recite the second stanza of the poem: The Voice in the Dungeon.

II

Day and night are both the same,

They are as rare as my Christian name.

Between four walls

Not lamp nor torch will light my way,

There are not halls,

Only the voice hid in the walls,

Inside this dungeon looking for brawls.

My mind does not recall what have I done,

It only feels the hard, cold stone.

Today I was called a name I've never heard,

Although, that name is full of shame,

But I must pay I heard it say,

Tears and pain for every day

For all mistakes and all the sins.

So many names, none my own,

My brother's words cut my skin and bones,

Making scars so deep and dark.

The voice awaits and tries to leave,

It must remain today with me

It calls me fright, it calls me night,

I wait to see the light most bright.

Bravo, bravo! Oskar clapped.

Nooo, It can't be. By now, Rupert was convinced that Oskar was his twin brother. Oskar removed the cuffs and attached Rupert to one of the columns with a thick rope.

"I am the masterpiece, you can't do anything without me," Rupert said.

"No, while you're alive, but once you're dead, the first puzzle will be mine."

"Start praying my little bro. There's an Eyeless Komodo lizard in here with you and it will find you and drink your blood before you can say a word. Rupert saw Oskar walking towards a corner and picking up a cage with an animal that looked like a Komodo dragon, it was only a foot in length. He went to the opposite corner and opened another cage, which had two rats inside it. Oskar let the rats run free.

"The lizard will be able to hear their scratches on the floor. The sharpness of its hearing will direct him in their direction within seconds. But loud noises will make him bite anything in front of him. It will double in size each time it kills and drinks the blood of its prey, so by the time it finds you it will be big enough to drink all your blood. The heat of the candle will keep him away from you until it goes out, so you can wait and suffer. As soon as the candle burns out, the lizard will attack you instantly.

Oskar put a lit candle steps away from Rupert and walked up the stairs carrying the cage with the lizard in it. Rupert heard the door being shut. He looked at the candle in front of him and hoped that it would stay lit, but at the same time, to never melt. But that was an impossible ask, from a standard waxed candle. He heard the lizard's nails scratching as it came down the stairs. He then heard a shuffle of claws on the stone floor and a high-pitched squeak came from one of the corners of the room and scratches running away from the same corner. Rupert guessed that one of the rats had been killed, and the other one had made its escape.

Shortly after he heard more scratching on the floor, and a second high-pitched squeal. The second rat was dead now too. The candle was melting rapidly and there was only a quarter left. Rupert was covered in sweat, his muscles tensed and his pulse raced faster than ever before when he saw the lizard roaming around the candle. It had quadrupled in size so that it was as big as a medium size dog, its forked tongue flicking in the air. The candle would burn out in a few minutes, and he was going to be killed by this creature standing in front of him. The lizard seemed to know that he could attack Rupert from another angle and walked around. Rupert wanted to shout for help but he knew the lizard would become more aggressive, and no one was going to hear his shouts above the sound of the music. In this moment of pressure and terror, Rupert had an idea that might just save his life or get him kill instantly. He lowered himself very slowly until his hands touched the floor, he could feel the lizard's tongue touching his hand. Rupert gave a loud shout and the lizard lunged at Rupert, but instead of biting his hands, it cut the rope around his wrist. His hands were instantly freed but the rope burned his wrists badly. He rushed to grab the candle and backed away with jerky steps to the top of the stairs stabbing at the lizard with the candle. The lizard walked close to the candle and followed Rupert. The candle was about to die out just as Rupert opened the door and slipped through closing the door just in time. Rupert ran as fast as he could, noticing that his right hand had a glowing triangle printed on his palm, he stopped to double-check.

"We are complete," he said, "they are waiting for me."

The Higher Tower Rupert, a voice whispered in his ear.

"Who is this? Go away," Rupert found the whisper disturbing.

Blake had placed the triangle frame in the Higher Tower. The voice was soft like that of a child. Rupert understood that that was the way to know where the First Point of the Star was going to be put together. He arrived at the higher tower, but before he entered, he noticed that on one side of the oval balcony Lesha was standing calling Gaelle's name – on the other side Oskar called Marion's name.

Oskar turned around and saw Rupert.

"I – hate – you so much, Rupert." Oskar shouted.

"Run Marion you're the best," shouted Oskar.

"Run Gaelle, I promise you the best trophy ever," shouted Lesha.

"Trophy?" repeated Gaelle and started to run like a hare – within seconds, Gaelle had joined the rest of the team.

One by one, everyone gathered inside the highest tower of the Castle.

Rupert saw Daltom's team had also entered with their triangle glowing on their hands. Both teams were missing their masters and Celestial Beings. Rupert knew that he was not the only masterpiece and whoever arrived first, was going to be able to put the First Point of the Star together. He saw Lesha staring at Marion. He would not want

Lesha ever to look at him like that. He knew that Marion was going to pay big time for what she had done.

The door behind him slowly closed until the noise coming from the music and the guests vanished. Blake had placed the triangular frame on top of a table, under the window over a table covered with many lit candles for everyone to see it.

For a moment, the fighting between the two teams was suspended. Rupert was looking at each teams' members as they faced each other. He saw that the two front positions for each team were missing. He stood facing Oskar, observing his eyes full of venom and he was breathing heavily, like a bull in the middle of a bullfighting arena. You cannot be my twin brother, and if you are you must also be a masterpiece, so why would you want to kill me? Rupert asked himself.

Lesha was staring at Marion, her body fidgeting constantly. Rupert knew that Lesha was going to start the fight at any time. Gaelle looked calm even thought Sonia had tried to intimidate her by staring at her. Elmer stood beside her and next to Marlow, facing Justin and Matias. Rupert still could not believe that Marlow was on the good side. Alan stood like a tower, young and strong but he seemed at a disadvantage with the evil knowledge of the librarian, Mr Zhong. Rupert saw Begnon entering dragging himself forward and landing flat on the floor like an empty stuffed toy.

He knew that whichever of Vincent and Blake or Daltom entered the room first would be the winner, and it would all be over.

There was a knock on the door and everyone turned in anticipation. They stayed quiet, the door opened slowly, and the goddess came in.

"I am terribly sorry, but I'm lost," she said, with the weirdest voice Rupert had ever heard, she sounded old, the lady looked at the two teams in surprise, then stared at Marion.

"Why are you staring at me?" Marion asked.

The lady did not answer and turned around to leave. Daltom rushed into the room, pushing her aside.

A strong wind blew inside the tower, and the candles flames went out, leaving the room in complete darkness. The lights held by each team member consecutively got brighter, one by one.

The evil team's lights were purple, and Rupert's team's lights were bright orange. Rupert saw two orange lights joining his team. The two new orange lights had started to move closer and closer. He knew it was Vincent and Blake.

"I knew that you could make it, Vincent, I knew it," said Rupert emotionally.

The room was pitch black but he could not see who was who. Beside Daltom one of his lights began to lose its brightness and finally it went off.

"Impossible, he couldn't be here," Daltom complained.

Rupert saw the triangular frame floating in mid-air. One by one, the lights from each member of his team formed a triangle smaller than the frame and flew towards the frame reassembling the first puzzle. The triangle frame lit up, illuminating the tower, its brilliance almost blinding everyone. Rupert reached out and held it in his hand. The object was reflecting all colours. It was a small prism. The first point of the Eight Pointed Star had been restored.

Someone knocked heavily on the door again. The triangle dropped and Rupert caught it on the air.

"I'm looking for Rupert. Oops excuse me, it's time to cut the cake master Rupert," Eugene said turning the light on by the switch outside and apologising as if he had bumped into someone.

344

"I'll be there in a moment," Rupert shouted.

Rupert turned around and saw Daltom's team escaping.

"No so fast," Lesha said. She run after Marion, Rupert went after her he knew that Lesha would not be able to control her anger this time. Lesha got hold of her at the bottom of the stairs, grabbing Marion by her plaits, pulled her down and with a knife she snatched out of Marion's belt, Lesha cut off both Marion's plaits.

"Your plaits remind me of the ropes you cut from my swing. Now we are even," Lesha said.

"Stop Lesha, let her go," Rupert heard a female's voice, his heart raced one more time when he recognised Mrs Steven's voice. He stayed back hiding from the teacher.

"I must go now," Mrs Stevens said, "can I have them please." Rupert had a quick peak and could only see Mrs Stevens' hand holding Marion's plaits.

"Sure, but why did you save her, she is evil," Lesha said.

Rupert suspected Mrs Stevens was on the evil side but not that she knew Marion.

Rupert came out to see Lesha.

"How long have you been there? Lesha asked.

"I just arrived, is everything ok? You didn't catch Marion." Rupert lied.

"Oh never mind, let's go," she replied.

"We did it," Rupert said.

"Did we?" Gaelle asked.

"Look at it," Rupert said, pointing at the sparkling prism in his hand.

"Where are Vincent and Blake? They can't chase Daltom we've beaten them." Rupert said.

The guests had been gathered together in The Grand Salon waiting to sing Happy Birthday and to cut the cake. Mr and Mrs Curdy were by Rupert's side, with discretion Rupert bended towards Mrs Curdy him.

"Please tell all your friends I went boarding, that way they won't ask you questions, I will be in touch" he whispered.

Mrs Curdy nodded her head and smiled at him saying thank you.

Rupert saw Blake helping Vincent, who was hanging from the top of the gigantic chandelier. A thick cloud was forming around them and the next time Rupert saw Vincent and Blake, they were on the ground.

"How did Vincent come down so fast as to get stuck in the chandelier?" Gaelle asked.

"That is beyond my imagination," Alan replied.

Everyone started to sing, Happy Birthday to Rupert, but this time it sounded right to Rupert. He blew out his twelve candles, made his wish and said thank you to Mr and Mrs Curdy, although, it felt as if he was saying goodbye. There were lots of photographs taken and discreetly, he made his way out to meet his team again.

"What is happening Mum, where is Rupert going?" Miana asked.

"He's grounded, big time sweetheart," Mrs Curdy replied.

"Finally," Replied Miana with Joy. Rupert turned around and winked at Miana.

"Who put the puzzle together?" Blake asked.

"We did it…" Rupert realised that Vincent and Blake were not involved in the assembling of the first point of the star. But who did it. He wondered.

"You know we didn't do it but soon you will find out," Blake said. Rupert seemed intrigued but he kept quiet.

"We must go now," Vincent said.

"Sure, let's go," Alan replied.

"No, Alan, you have done enough, I'm taking Rupert with me to meet someone who's been waiting long enough," Vincent throw a key in the air, "here this belongs to you."

"Thanks, I understand," Alan looked at the key clenched it in his fist and brought it up to his chest. He left in the company of Elmer, Marlow, Gaelle and Lesha.

Vincent and Rupert walked out of the castle. Rupert wanted to walk over the drawbridge, having conquered the most precious object of all – The First Star Point.

"I'm twelve now, and I'm alive," he said.

"You are indeed." Replied Vincent.

Chapter Eighteen

BEING IN LOVE

Sunday, 22nd November

Rupert and Vincent stood at the bottom of the mountain before dawn.

"Splendid," said Vincent contemplating the irreverent mountain before him. The snow looked immaculately white. Rupert noticed hundreds of trees at the base of the mountain and stared at the gentle movements from the birds in the trees' branches. The moon was refusing to fade away and welcomed them by lighting their way back into the shed. The sun was in a hurry to put its magical sparks back on the ground as they walked up the mountain.

Rupert saw a set of footprints in the snow and decided to follow them. He noticed that nearby, was another set of footprints too, and about a metre away, a group of footprints heading up the hill. They were in different shoe sizes, and they seemed fresh, but he could not see anyone in front of him.

"I guess you're ready to learn a great deal about yourself at this moment," Vincent said, putting his arm around Rupert as he started to answer the hundred of questions Rupert had prepared since he found out about his parents and any other questions coming to his mind right there and then. The journey to the shed became a journey full of discoveries, knowledge and surprises for him. He was learning more in one day than in his entire life.

Rupert felt Vincent's hand squeezing his shoulder. He knew he had made Vincent proud. He knew that his only mission was to enjoy the moment, nothing more.

Blake made his appearance, landing flat beside Rupert's feet.

"Geez, you scared me, where did you come from?" Rupert asked.

"My master does it," Blake said, looking at Vincent. "I don't know how, but I come and go as he pleases."

"Don't complain, you love it," Vincent teased.

"One plus one is three," Blake said.

"Are you learning maths, one plus one is two, Blake," Rupert corrected.

"Ah, but one plus one is three," Blake repeated.

"Blake, is there another being around? Tell me." Vincent asked.

"I told you, one plus one is three."

"Who is it?" Asked Vincent.

"You don't want to know."

"I'm your master. You have to tell me, Oh, I see, you like this being, don't you? Don't tell me… is it…?"

"Correct," Blake replied.

"But how?"

"I told you, one plus one is three," said Blake yet again.

"Oh Blake, you're in love,' Rupert teased.

"Am I?"

As Rupert came closer to the shed, he could tell by the smoke that was wafting out from the chimney that someone was already there, keeping the place warm. Rupert's senses were tingling with excitement. He wanted to memorise every tree, every stone on the ground and the track leading to the place where he had spent the first three months of his life.

He had decided that the past was going to be just that, and he was going to spend the rest of his life with his real parents, creating new memories. He stood in front of the shed and, just as he lifted his hand to knock on the wooden door, someone opened it from inside, leaving Rupert with his hand in the air and his heart exposed and about to jump out of his chest.

"Hi, Rupert you made it," Gaelle said.

"Gaelle, what are you doing here,"

"Waiting," she said.

"What for, I..." Rupert was confused he could not wait one more minute longer to meet his mother, the waiting was agonising for him. Gaelle let the door wide open, inviting Rupert and Vincent inside. Rupert looked around and found himself surrounded by the whole team, except for Marlow.

"Serena organised it all," Lesha said. Her hands were held together and her feet fidgeting as if she would have rather run and hugged someone, but she stayed there in the same spot staring at Rupert timidly.

"But how did you all get here before us? Rupert asked.

"We came after the party finished. In my old mini, which I've not seen for almost twelve years." Alan waved the key in front of everybody.

"Good to see you again, Rupert." Elmer said.

"Thanks, Elmer, it's good to see you, too." Rupert hugged Elmer.

"We promise we won't be mean to you again," Lesha said.

"I was silly, you girls are amazing, please forgive me," replied Rupert. Gaelle giggled, her hands covering her mouth. Lesha looked down at the floor as she placed one foot over the other, staying still.

"I can't wait to see you all together. I mean, Serena, Vincent and you. Sorry but I'll have to see it to believe it," Lesha said.

Rupert looked at Alan and noticed that he still had a piece of cotton wool inside his right ear. Rupert decided to keep to himself the secret about his sibling for the time being. Talking to Vincent, he figured out that he did not know anything about it. He guessed that the secret was mortifying to Alan, and rightly so, a secret of that magnitude would have had huge consequences. He was not going to condemn Alan who had after all, dedicated twelve years of his life to being his nanny. It was only fair to show a bit of mercy, but Rupert could not lie to himself. He would not ask Alan, as the answer he may get was going to be the confirmations of his most terrifying suspicions and he was not ready to deal with it now.

"How are your ears today?" Rupert asked.

"Fine, the cotton wool is just to keep the eardrops inside. I thought I was perfect, but I'm not quite perfect yet," Alan joked looking at Rupert with beaming eyes.

"Thanks Alan, for all your time," Rupert said. His arms wrapped around the colossal man, and it felt as if he was hugging a giant, walking tree.

Elmer stood next to Alan. His hands thrust inside his pockets revealing a shy smile. Rupert could tell that Elmer's mind was somewhere else, perhaps, wondering about his brother's decision to follow Daltom.

"I heard about Marlow, it isn't your fault you know. Marlow will come back one day, he must have good inside to be part of our team." Rupert said.

"He'll never come back. Daltom will change him forever." Elmer said.

Rupert was there only a few minutes, but it felt like an eternity. His priority was to meet his mother, and there was no sign of her.

"Where's she?" He asked in a low voice, to no one in particular, but to everyone.

"Serena will make a big entrance, you wait and see," Lesha said.

Blake started to bump into the furniture and everyone. He waddled from side to side, banging into the walls, twisting his eyes, becoming a ball, then popping his extremities and head. Hundreds of daisies started to rise from the floor inside and outside the shed. Blake's imagination was out of control. Blake pulled out petals off from the daisies and stuffed them in his mouth. Then he started to make weird noises with his lips. Everyone laughed.

"Someone's coming, it's Serena," Lesha said full of excitement while Rupert swiftly crossed to the window to see with his own eyes, and it wasn't a trick.

"Wait a minute. I saw that lady, last night, is she... no way, I even danced with her, why is she wearing that mask? I want to see her face." Rupert was surprised to see the Goddess looking lady coming in the shed. She stood in front of Rupert then pulled a soft toy and placed it in Rupert's hands. The soft toy had a little birthday note with the number twelve on it.

"Marci, you...but–"

"Hello, Rupert." A very sophisticated voice came from Marci's mouth. Rupert could not believe what he just heard. Very slowly

Serena lowered her mask. Rupert could see her hand shaking. But no one could see his trembling heart.

"You…but," Rupert was struck dumb. He experienced a shock reaction when her face was unveiled. A clean face free of makeup and with a glossy natural look. Rupert had never felt this way before. His emotions were proof that he was in front of the most surreal, powerful and magical woman.

Tears of joy immediately appeared in his eyes. He felt that the heavens had just opened above him as he realised that the woman standing in front of him was the woman he had secretly wanted to be his real mother. Rupert was standing before Mrs Stevens, his science teacher.

A moment of silence followed, keeping eye contact, and then within seconds, the promise made eleven years, eight months and a day ago was kept. Tears and laughter were once more mixed with each other. Vincent walked over and embraced them both. It was the best hug Rupert had ever felt in his entire life.

Alan joined in and then Lesha, Gaelle and finally Elmer. Blake stood in front of a wall banging his head without stopping.

"Marci, you've been with me all this time, why didn't you ever talk before?"

"I wasn't allowed, but I've grown," Marci said.

"I know you've grown, that's why Miana was so scared of you, and—"

"Well, I did more than just grow to her but nothing she couldn't take."

"I can't believe I never noticed," Rupert said.

Rupert placed the crystal prism representing the First-Point of the Star on top a wooden cabinet beneath the window. He noticed that it had started to glow as if alive. His eyes brightened up when he saw the rainbow reflections. He held the prism crystal in his hand mesmerised by its amazing brilliance as it caught the sun's rays.

"It's not a triangle. It's a prism. It will be a challenging job to put eight of these together." He said then turned to Serena and Marci.

"Speaking of which, you two were the ones entering the tower in the dark, weren't you?"

Vincent looked at Serena and back at Rupert.

"We couldn't let Daltom win the first point," Serena said, "I can explain it all."

"I can't wait to be enlightened," Vincent said.

"Yes, enlighten us please," Rupert said.

"It was inevitable that Daltom was going to come for Rupert, so I used you to distract him," said Serena, "Daltom then kill an imaginary me in the woods, that trick cost me seven years of captivity. Once free, I became your teacher but I was banned from relieving to you who I was.

"Who put you in captivity." Rupert asked.

"Are you a Celestial–" Vincent said.

"A Celestial Master of the Universe living on earth." Serena Said.

"And all this time, my working on the projects, was all your doing?"

"Definitely not, your genius was the only chance for this mission to begin,"

Rupert could see Blake outside, lying on the floor making snow angels – he seemed out of control. Rupert knew that Marci was responsible.

"He is an idiot. This is the first time I am allowed out in public, and he is ruining it all. Suddenly a big pile of snow slid down from a tree and covered Blake from everyone's view.

"You deserved that," Marci said.

Everyone laughed.

"Well, we have the First-Star Point, the legend is finished," Vincent said.

"And the story has only just begun," Rupert replied.

25428707R00211

Printed in Great Britain
by Amazon